THE BURNING ASH

ASH

RICHARD KISH

First edition April 2019

Book design by Richard Kish

ISBN 978-1-7932-9846-1 (paperback)

www.richardkish.co.uk

For my wonderful family

CONTENTS

Prologue
Treasured Memories

A single cherry blossom fluttered in the breeze beneath the great pale moon; dancing through the air as its siblings began to join it, drawing closer before moving off on a different path. It came to rest on the courtyard ground where a huge crowd waited excitedly for the beginning of the Dragons' Festival. Every year the people of the kingdom gathered beneath the Great Sakura Tree to celebrate the founding of Ryushima. All eyes were glued to the palace doors as they awaited the arrival of their beloved queen.

The distant clock tower struck midnight and the great doors opened, revealing a solitary figure who stepped out into the moonlight tightly gripping her staff. She moved towards the spiralling stairs and began to ascend, drawing a sparkling trail behind her while her sapphire dress glittered in the starlight, seeming to reflect the night's sky. She reached the balcony above and gently positioned herself at the railing. A dragon was emblazoned on the dress and wove its way up her body, glistening with a multitude of colours; her long brown hair cascaded down her back in flowing curls; three covered braids held together by two tanzanite chopsticks in a small bun at the back of her head swung gently behind her; and her crystal

1

crown glowed as she looked out at her people. She tried to smile at them as her retinue made their way up to join her.

With a firm tap of her staff, an iridescent blue flame sprang up in front of her. It split in two, circling both ways around the balcony before climbing up the walls of the palace to reach a giant ornate mirror. When the flames made contact, the mirror burst into life, a gently shifting image appeared on its face; a dancing figure manipulating the flames around her before she was consumed. A small light flickered before sprouting, growing, and blooming into a mighty tree. From the tree sprang an egg which hatched into two fiery dragons which grew and began to fight. In the end, they paused, glimmered, and then the flames died out leaving a halo of light around the mirror.

The woman took a deep breath, looking to her retinue for support. Then she began her speech, "*CHRISTEOS MOZ.* People of Ryushima, today marks the anniversary of the founding of our kingdom." A rapturous applause broke out amongst the crowd. "From the very beginning, we have held true to our tenets of family and trust. We have fought and struggled to get to where we are today and the bonds between us will not be broken." More applause erupted, but the queen shifted uncomfortably on her heels. "As your queen, it is my duty to serve you and I hope that I have done you all proud. I love every single one of you. You have inspired me all my life and I sincerely wish to repay that kindness. Together, we are a family. We stand firm against the world like the Great Sakura Tree and we never forget where we have come from." This was received with a hearty cheer. "The past few years have been difficult. We lost my father and mother last year and we've lost so many other good people…" Her hands shook as she tried to reach the end of her speech. She looked back at her retinue to seek support again before taking a deep breath. "We've lost so many good people but we have persevered and we are stronger now than ever before. We will never forget their sacrifice. I ask that you all join me in a moment of silence to honour those who gave their lives to protect Ryushima."

The crowd dipped their heads and silence swept through the courtyard. Some thought about their husbands, some their wives, some their fathers and mothers, some their grandparents and children. The queen closed her eyes in an attempt to hide her tears. Every year it was the same thing, the pomp of the ceremony leading to a short speech and then that silence. It broke her heart every single time because she knew that there was one person nobody remembered at all. As the years passed it became more and more difficult to bear. With a deep breath she opened her eyes and looked out at the crowd in front of her. Thousands of people stood beneath, bowing their heads in respect to the departed as the wind whipped the cherry blossoms from the tree, scattering them at their feet. As the moment of silence drew to a close, something within the queen snapped. The tears she had been holding back fell. She couldn't keep quiet any longer.

"At this point in the ceremony, I should thank you all for everything you do and we should begin the Dragons' Festival Ball but I can't." Gasps and murmurings spread through the people.

One of the retinue stepped forward to the queen, "Rosalina, what do you mean?" It was the question on everyone's lips. The Festival never changed, it went as planned every year and the people enjoyed themselves. They waited with baited breath for her response.

"Before the Festival continues, I would like to tell you all a story. My story." There was a wave of confusion as thoughts swung from scandal to unknown tragedies, but the queen continued in spite of the crowd's noise. "My grandmother always used to say that life and love was just like that of a cherry blossom. As the petals fall, you never truly know where they're going to end up. They collide with many other petals on their journey, but the unpredictable nature of life means they often must part. What's important is that no matter what happens, it's always beautiful. Ultimately, the only way to stop those we love fading from our lives once they are gone is to remember them; to never leave them behind. That's what I've been doing these past five years: remembering. I've been holding tightly on to those treasured memories so I don't lose him again. It's taken me so long to come to terms with it all, but now I need to move on for all of you. Now that I am your queen, I need to be there and be strong so we can move forward together. The only way I can do that is tell you all the story of how I lost him forever."

"Him?" "Who's this him?" "What is she saying?" "She's never mentioned anything about a man before!" She could hear the crowd muttering to each other, their eyes boring into her, judging her. Her mournful eyes darted to the sky. *Are you out there, watching over me?* she thought, searching for a sign of hope in the darkness. No. He was gone forever and she knew it, she always had. Her retinue tried to stop her from continuing but with a firm tap of her staff on the ground they withdrew. Nothing was going to stop her anymore.

"Five years ago, Ryushima was changed forever. You all remember that. In the past our fate and future as a kingdom was decided by the battles of our then gods, the Almighty Dragons, Fai and Yami. The war between the two dragons raged for centuries, with the two fighting in our presence every year at this very festival after the conclusion of the tournament. If Fai won we were blessed with prosperity, crops flourished, trade was bountiful, and everyone was happy; if Yami won we suffered great torment, natural disasters swept the land, our crops would fail, and many people would die. Every year we celebrated the founding of the kingdom but we always feared for our future. On that night five years ago, that cycle ended and we were saved. You all know that, but you've forgotten

5

something important: the person who stood up for us and saved us."

There was uproar from the people as they protested remembering that night perfectly but then upon trying to replay it in their heads they realised something was missing. A haze fogged their minds the moment they tried to come upon the identity of this person, they could picture the vicious battle between Fai and Yami, the flames that scorched the original Great Tree, Yggdrasil, and the destruction of the courtyard but no trace of a hero remained. They struggled to find something, trusting that their queen would never lie to them but every attempt ended in failure.

"Not only did he free us from what we saw as the inevitable cycle of our lives, he also fought to protect everyone in the universe, those living and those long-since departed, and yet no one even remembers his name." She paused, trying to push his name through her gritted teeth as tears welled in her eyes again. As she pulled herself together and continued, her words gathered strength and force, building in relief as her burden was lifted. "Before he came to us, death was a mystery. It seems odd to think of it like that now, I know, and perhaps some of you don't even think about that time of not knowing anymore. We had our suspicions of what happened after we died back then but we didn't know, after all, how could we? It's impossible. The dead don't come back to life. They leave this world never to return and while it hurts to see them go, we know that that is the way of life. But he came to us. He lived in the afterlife, in Helheim, he was born there and then he came to us. After his time in Ryushima, he took a few of us on a journey, he showed us Helheim, then he was gone and everyone forgot him. It wasn't anybody's fault… That you forgot about him, I mean… Something just happened and the memory of him was gone from everyone except me and I have lived with that ever since."

There was a stunned silence. Nobody knew what to do, what to say. They all thought they remembered what had happened and when they had learned about the existence of Helheim but the fervour with which the queen spoke had them convinced that they had missed something. Those who had felt anger and frustration before began to blame themselves as did the queen's retinue who were horrified that she had kept this secret locked away for so long.

All eyes fell on Rosalina as she quickly wiped the tears from her eyes and spoke clearly and confidently to her people for the first time in what felt like forever. "Hideki. That was his name. Hideki." The queen looked again towards the sky as a smile graced her lips. "He was the only one I've ever loved and I'm pretty sure he felt the same towards me. He arrived in the dead of night not long after the Dragons' Festival about six years ago and in spite of how bizarre everything was, when I saw him something just clicked. Mother always used to say that when you find your soulmate it is like finding your missing half, you just fit together. That's what I felt when I met him. He was sweet and so kind; he was almost too kind really. He truly cared about people and would do anything to make them happy. He was my knight in shining armour, but without the shining armour." The queen grinned a little and there were a few laughs from the crowd as the atmosphere warmed from cold solemnity to a nostalgic glow. This was the woman they remembered as a girl, the one they would protect with their lives. They all settled down on the ground to hear the rest of the queen's tale, desperate to know about this Hideki and what they had apparently forgotten.

"I jest, of course, and I guess my love for him has raised him up in my eyes to be perfect like the mythical heroes of old. Maybe he was, after all he managed to achieve some amazing things. But in reality, he was probably just like any of us. He was merely human, but he saw the beauty in this world and wished to fight for it no matter the cost. From the moment he arrived we went through everything together and after that fateful night five years ago he took us on that journey to Helheim where I lost him forever." She paused, forcing back the sob that was rising in her chest as the images of that day flashed in front of her eyes. "It may take some time but would you all be willing to listen to my story from beginning to end?"

Much to her surprise a roar of affirmations followed. The warm smile returned, lighting up her face. "Thank you all so much. I've told you the outline of what happened so I suppose I should start at the beginning – the night Hideki came to Ryushima. It was the night after the fight between Fai and Yami, Fai had won and everyone in the palace was a little worse for wear from the celebrations but we were happy and at peace. Then out of nowhere, he arrived…"

CHAPTER 1
NASCENCE

Bruised, bloody, and beaten, Hideki's body crashed to the cold hard stone. Through the haze he could see torches burning brightly in the distance. He rolled onto his back to look up at the sky and smiled at the dark blue hue intermixed with piercing white lights. He could just make out a shimmering crystal-like structure above him but couldn't identify it before his exhaustion overtook him and he passed out. The last thing he remembered before losing consciousness was the sound of voices.

One of those voices was that of a young woman, rushing out of the palace doors into the courtyard to see what the commotion was about. She nudged one of the guards who stood at the entrance, "Tom, what's happening? I thought everyone had already left?"

"Oh! Princess Rosalina!" The guard panicked for a moment before saluting the princess.

He received an exasperated sigh in response. "Do you really need to do that every single time you see me? And just call me Rosalina, please! I know I'm the princess but I'd like some degree of normality thank you. Anyway, what's happening? Is there any way I can help?"

"Yes, Princess Rosalina, quite right, um –" He paused for a moment as he noted her look of frustration. "A young man has just appeared out of nowhere in the middle of the courtyard. Nobody knows where he came from but he seems badly injured, your highness. But, everything is under control; some of the knights are beginning to move him to the infirmary."

With a quick nod and a "thank you", Rosalina strode towards the small group of people beneath the Great Tree, Yggdrasil. She'd always loved that tree, ever since she was young. It stood proudly in the centre of the courtyard, a crystalline behemoth unlike anything else in the world. From what she'd been told as a child, the tree was the only one of its kind, created by the founder of Ryushima to signify the spot where the kingdom began. She didn't know whether that was true or not, after all, stories about the past were always filled with holes and were often completely fictional. Still, she enjoyed it whenever her grandmother spoke of the tree and was quite happy to forgive any historical inaccuracies surrounding it.

As she neared the group she caught a glimpse of the blood dripping from the young man's arm. "Quick, let me see if I can help." The knights looked from the princess to the body and back again, unsure of whether to salute or not. "I might be able to do something. Let me see to him, please!"

One of the knights finally plucked up the courage to speak, "But your highness, there's no need for you to get yourself involved in this. It isn't safe, the security of the palace has been compromised, and it's far too messy for a young girl like yourself to be dealing with."

"I will pretend I didn't hear that last bit and I am perfectly capable of defending myself, thank you very much. None of you are trained in healing spells, correct?" Torn between following the orders of the king to protect the princess or those of the princess herself, they were all utterly confused. Eventually the knights all nodded hesitantly, none of them had any magical abilities and since they knew of the princess's proficiency in magic they decided that the best option was to listen to her, while keeping their guards up in case they needed to defend her. "Well then, please put him down for a moment. Now, normally I'd use my staff to help me but that's clearly not going to happen at the moment." She knelt down next to the young man and placed her hands on his chest. She quickly looked at his face, noting the grimace that contorted his features. "Right, let's hope this works as well as it needs to. *Light, shine down upon this soul and heal the wounds that curse him. Cure!*" As Rosalina closed her eyes a green glow emanated from her hands, she gently pushed in the centre of his chest and slowly but surely the glow moved into the young man's body. A few of the cuts on his arms stitched themselves back together and the grimace vanished somewhat. "Well that certainly could have gone a bit better, but that should give him some peace for the time being. Now, if you gentlemen would be so kind as to take him to the infirmary, that would be much appreciated. I'll take responsibility of him."

With a swift movement, Rosalina was off the floor and wiping her hands on a cloth she'd pulled from a pocket hidden in her dress. As the knights began carrying the young man towards the infirmary, Rosalina stared at the ground where he had been lying and was struck by how puzzling the situation was. He'd appeared in the centre of a fortified courtyard, not entering through the great gates or falling from the sky; he was seriously injured but his attackers were nowhere to be seen. Had it been magic? She thought about all the spells she'd learned throughout her training but there were no offensive or defensive spells that enabled anything like teleportation. A cold chill ran down her spine as she turned to face Yggdrasil. Its andalusite trunk remained pure and unmarked as the various gemstone blossoms chimed in the wind, all seemed as it should be but Rosalina wondered whether the tree had had any involvement in this mystery. A long time ago, her grandmother had called Yggdrasil a 'world tree', not that she'd ever explained what that meant. Her glance returned to the spot where the young man had been. Who was he? What was he doing here? Why had he shown up now? There had to be a reason he was here. There is no such thing as coincidence in this world, only inevitability. That's what she'd always believed and this young man's mysterious appearance was convincing her that she was right.

A sword lay a few metres away from where she was standing, it was oddly ornate and unlike anything Rosalina had seen before so she surmised that it must have been forgotten in the commotion. She picked it up and began to examine it. It certainly wasn't owned by any of the knights of Ryushima, their blades had representations of the Almighty Dragons on the cross-guard and specific gemstones in the pommels to signify their ranks. This particular weapon was entirely unique as though it had been purpose-built for its wielder. The hilt featured an elaborate tree-like design; the metallic roots formed a tight knot at the pommel around what looked like an opal, the trunk wound its way along the leather grip before the leafy branches burst out at the cross guard sweeping up before falling back down the hilt like a willow to protect the user's hands. As she unsheathed the sword from its scabbard she noted some elaborate runes working their way down the length of the blade beneath flecks of thick black blood. To Rosalina's surprise, she recognised the runes as the language of the angels, the same language they used in their offensive magical spells. Her eyes traced along the sword as she read out the words: "*BALIT BRANSG EGO DAXZUM LAP ASPAH*, the just guard the holy seed for the infinity within." The phrase meant nothing to her but she assumed the sword must have belonged to the young man and it solidified her suspicions about Yggdrasil's involvement but until he woke up there was very little she could do or learn.

The wind picked up slightly, sounding a beautiful melody from the tree. Rosalina rose from the ground with the blade in hand and made her way back into the palace. As she crossed the courtyard her determination to find out more grew. While her parents would perhaps disapprove of her taking on the young man as her charge, she was sure it was the right thing to do. She hadn't necessarily shown it in front of the knights but when she had gazed at his tortured face she felt a connection with him. He seemed lost, but deep down he was trying to fight through the pain. She had no idea how long it would take to heal him fully or when he would awake, but she decided that she would be there every step of the way. After all, she lived in a world filled with magic; surely it wouldn't take very long.

***

A couple of weeks passed and he still hadn't awoken. After much persuading, Rosalina had managed to get the young man moved to a quiet room with a comfortable bed farther away from the incredibly noisy infirmary. In spite of her father's protestations, Rosalina had stayed by the young man's side. Her visits became her little ritual, coming after breakfast to perform further healing spells then sticking around until late in the evening before heading to bed. Bags were appearing under her eyes and all that encountered her could sense the air of frustration surrounding her.

Mysteries always found a way of getting under her skin and this particular one was driving her insane. The main thing she couldn't get her head around was why the young man had yet to wake up. His wounds had been completely healed, the blood had been washed from his skin and he looked peaceful as he slept soundly in the bed. The sword rested upon the low table in front of her and she stared at it as her foot tapped impatiently on the floor.

She turned slightly to face her staff. From a distance it looked like a mere blue wooden pole, but it had an intricate floral design etched into the bark. Thistles for nobility sprouted up the bottom of the shaft, weaving together to form sprigs of rosemary for remembrance. From these sprigs came lilies for purity and snowdrops for hope. Four trees stood proudly in the blooms; an olive tree for peace, an elderflower tree for compassion, an oak tree for strength, and a cherry blossom for kindness. Coloured gemstones tastefully dotted the design to signal its worth and to imbue it with the natural energies of the gems. At the top of the staff was a large blue rose, which held a large protruding crystal sphere within the bloom. Not only did the staff act as the primary conduit for Rosalina's magic, it also worked to symbolise the values she stood for.

Her glance fell back to the young man. *Once more*, she thought, *I will try once more.* She picked up her staff from beside her and moved to the bed. "Right, enough is enough. You are going to wake up this instant, you hear me?" With a firm tap on the ground with the staff a gust of energy surrounded her, flinging her two wrapped braids and her hair up into the air. Both hands were clasped tightly around the top of the staff as she yelled, "*I call upon the power of the guardian angels, lend me your strength and light…*" One hand slowly slid down the staff as she aimed the orb to the ground and began to draw a circle around herself with it. "*Heal this soul of the curses that ail him…*" A bright white light formed within the crystal and emitted a sparkling trail as it moved. "*Healing Circle!*" With this, the circle was complete and Rosalina tapped the ground with the bottom of the staff once more. A green glowing circle surrounded the bed, pulling in energy from outside and drawing it to the young man's body. After a few moments the circle subsided and Rosalina's spell was complete. She leant her staff against a nearby chair and shook him. "Wake up already, will you?" The closed eyes stared back at her and with a deep frustrated sigh she flung herself into the chair. "This is ridiculous. What the hell have you done to cause this? It isn't based on your injuries. It isn't anything like poison or a magical curse. All I'm asking is for you to wake up!" She closed her eyes and slumped down in the chair. Exhausted and frustrated, she fell asleep.

In the blackness of a dream, two huge crimson red eyes opened, the irises glimmering like flame around the thin slit pupils. She felt as if she was floating in an abyss in front of these demonic eyes that seemed to bore into her very soul. She thought she recognised them but couldn't make out where they

17

belonged. After a few moments a deep rumbling voice began to echo around her, "What do you wish of the boy?" A chill ran down her spine, the same chill she'd felt when she'd gazed at Yggdrasil when the young man had first appeared. "What do you wish of the boy?" As the thunderous voice spoke out, the abyss around her seemed to quake in terror.

"I wish for him to wake up."

A menacing laugh broke out as the eyes began to move around her. "That simply cannot happen, young princess. He has committed a sin from which no soul can be rescued."

Rosalina, swallowing her fear, decided to push forward with the exchange. Was this only a dream or would it lead to a way of waking him up? She had to know. "What sin is so serious that none can be rescued from it? He has every right to live and I have every right to know where he has come from. What is stopping him from waking up?"

The voice paused as the eyes filled with a malicious glee. "I am." The words were spoken with utter malevolence and their force was enough to make Rosalina flinch. "He has crossed a boundary which should never be crossed and She commands that he be eternally punished."

"Don't play that game with me, who is 'She'?"

"I could not possibly ruin the surprise for you, little princess."

"Then what would it take to wake him up? Surely you don't have to follow everything She commands?"

"How ironic for a princess to make that argument, but I will make a bargain with you, little princess. I will allow this cursed boy to awaken on one condition: He forgets about the person that meant the most to him. He'll forever be haunted by a gaping hole in his memory and nothing will ever fill that void." The blood red eyes drew up to her face. "Are you willing to make the decision of that sacrifice for him?"

Rosalina's thoughts were racing as she tried to figure out what she should do. Without that sacrifice, the young man would surely die, with it he could be a shell of his former self, whoever he may be. Something deep within her told her that it was a risk she needed to take. "Yes. Wake him up. Set him free."

The thunderous laugh roared around her once more before vanishing into the ether as the eyes closed. With a start, Rosalina awoke to see a sword pointing straight at her throat.

"Who are you and where the hell am I?"

A smile began to form at the edge of her lips as she looked up into the open eyes of the young man. "The person who saved your life and who has spent the last two weeks trying to nurse you back to health. If you lower your sword, I will answer any questions you have as long as you answer some of mine."

The sword clattered to the floor as he began to take in his surroundings. He could see a bright blue sky out of the window, the deep brown of the bed's frame, the kaleidoscopic pigments of the opal in his sword. He stared at the young woman in front of him, noting the majestic white and blue dragon on her dress and the brilliant shift in colours of the chopsticks in her hair as she moved. Tears welled in his eyes. He was experiencing true colour for the first time in his life.

"What's your name?"

The question startled him for a moment. He had ceased paying attention to the sound of her voice and was completely transfixed by the colour that surrounded him. The joy surging through him was indescribable, he felt excited, terrified, and overwhelmed at the brave new world he found himself in, full of such vibrant beauty. He'd never seen anything like it before. This was the place he'd been dreaming of reaching for so long, a world where everywhere he looked seemed to burst with energy. He never had to return to the dying world of his past again and that thought filled him with hope. Slowly but surely, he began to come to his senses and answered her question. "Hideki. My name is Hideki."

Now that the sword was safely away from her, Rosalina stood up and extended her hand to Hideki, "I'm Rosalina, Princess of the Kingdom of Ryushima, it's a pleasure to finally speak to you."

"Princess?" Hideki's eyes widened as he realised that he'd just threatened the daughter of royalty in this place and exactly how much trouble he would have been in had things gone any further. Not only that but she'd been the one to heal him. In a confused babble he tried to apologise, "I'm so sorry. I didn't mean to – I mean I didn't know – I mean – I –"

Rosalina grabbed both of his hands in hers, "It's ok. I get it. It's fine. You were scared, it's not exactly every day that you collapse somewhere then wake up in a bed with a complete stranger sitting nearby, right? There's no need to apologise." She laughed a little at how odd the whole situation was. "Now sit down for a moment and tell me what you can remember from before you passed out, like where you're from, what happened to you, and why you've come here, if you can."

He followed her orders, sitting down on the edge of the bed and she quickly joined him. "I don't know whether you'll believe me…"

"You appeared out of nowhere in the middle of our courtyard covered in blood and then didn't wake up for weeks in spite of a rather obscene amount of mana being used to heal you. Normally a single powerful spell is enough to deal with the type of wounds you'd sustained and most who are rendered unconscious by their wounds wake up within a few days. I've been here trying every spell I can think of for weeks and haven't gotten anywhere until now. I think I'll believe anything at this point."

He frowned slightly as he tried to piece together everything in a way that would make sense. "Where do you think people go when they die?"

A sort of confused sigh left Rosalina's mouth as she attempted to digest the question she'd just been asked. It had come out of nowhere and it was rather more philosophical and theological than she had been expecting. "I... Well... I don't know. People die and then they go to an afterlife of some sort? People have different words for it all over the world, heaven and hell, limbo, purgatory, the underworld, but no one's ever died and then come back to life to tell the tale, so I've never really thought too carefully about it. Why?"

"Well, that's where I've come from. Everyone there calls it Helheim and it is in essence the afterlife. When people die, that's where their souls go." He paused to let that sink in. Rosalina's brow furrowed as Hideki continued, "Somehow I was born there, I don't know how; it shouldn't really have been possible but here I am. It's lifeless. That's the only way I can describe it. There's no vibrancy or life in anything. In the end, it's just an endless expanse of muted misery." Even when he closed his eyes he could see the landscape of his birthplace, the memory of it left him numb. The sooner he could leave it all behind, the better. "Hershel and Claire - the only people who've ever been there for me over the years - always told me that Helheim used to be one of the most beautiful places they had ever seen, it was a heaven to them at the time but then something changed and sapped it of that beauty." A smile touched his lips as he remembered the elderly couple. "Everyone else said I was a cursed child and they all kept their

22

distance, but Hershel and Claire were always there. Nobody ever explained why I was cursed, they just…" His voice caught as he tried to explain what they used to do but he couldn't finish his point. After a gentle nudge from Rosalina, he continued, "In the end, I just needed to escape. So, I left. Hershel and Claire said there was a rumour about a gate that souls came through when they died; they suspected that people could return back through the gate if they were strong enough. But, nobody knew where this gate was or whether it truly existed; it was just mentioned in this one book by a mad man. So, with only that rumour to go on I went in search of the gate and I must have found it and made it through. I know I got attacked on the way but the whole journey is a bit of a blur. Does that make any sense?" He looked to her for reassurance, hoping that she'd understood him.

Rosalina was in a state of awe. In her head she was trying to arrange the paradox of Hideki's existence to get it all to make sense but nothing worked. It was all so unbelievable and yet, it explained the bizarre appearing act. Her thought process eventually led her to that dream, the boundary that should never be crossed, was that beast referring to the movement from death to life?

"You don't believe me do you?" The disappointment in his voice was readily apparent and she couldn't cope with it when she looked into his eyes.

"No, I do believe you. It's just… It's a lot to get your head around, you know?" She stood up and paced around the room a little as she tried to grapple with her thoughts.

Hideki let loose a deep sigh of relief. She believed him, she actually believed him. His whole body relaxed and he fell back onto the bed. "Did you say this place was called Ryushima?"

Rosalina was quite grateful for the change in subject; it allowed her to shift her focus away from the troubling reality of Hideki's origins and cover something she actually understood. "Yes, the Kingdom of Ryushima. You're currently in the Crown City, Ryukyo, and erm… What sort of stuff do you want to know? Stuff like we're on a small island? Or things about my father, the king?" She stopped pacing as she remembered her promise to her father. "I need to take you to see my father immediately. He told me that he'd only let me help if I took you to see him as soon as you woke up. We need to go." In a flash Rosalina was a whir of activity. She rushed to the wardrobe, pulling out some clean clothes before dumping them on the bed beside Hideki. "If you could get dressed into these, that'd help make you look presentable. I'd rather not take you to see him in pyjamas; it wouldn't really leave a good impression. If you play your cards right he might help you get settled here in Ryushima." She paused as a grin played across her face. "That is, if you wanted to stay here while you got your bearings, I mean, you may not but it might help, right?"

Hideki pulled himself up to look at her and couldn't help but smile. "Why are you so intent on helping me?"

"I don't know. It just felt right, you know? I've never believed in coincidences, so something must have led you to us and something must have led me to be walking about the palace when you turned up."

"Thank you." He picked up the clothes and held them close to his chest. "I really appreciate everything you've done for me. It'd be an honour to stay if your father would let me." He couldn't quite say it aloud but he had to agree with her; something about this felt right, not that he could explain why either.

"I'll just be outside the door, so come out when you're ready and then I'll take you to see the King." With a giant grin on her face, she picked up her staff and left the room.

For the first time in such a very long time, Hideki felt happy. Even in this man-made room, this new world was alive and bursting with energy. He had always hoped that one day he would have a future where he could live rather than merely existing. His life had been one of seemingly endless misery, compounded by the bleakness of Helheim. In contrast, here in the bright and beautiful world which Ryushima was part of, he could finally see the semblance of a future for himself. He did harbour some concern that this world was too good to be true, that it'd all turn out to be a dream or that it'd lose its magical beauty but he couldn't allow himself to think like that. Now was his chance to start again and he was going to take it whatever the result.

Chapter 2
Sanctuary

Within a few moments Hideki was ready. Looking at himself in the mirror, it was shocking to see how much he had changed in the few short months since he'd left his home. His hair had grown out leaving him with a sort of messy mop and he looked a lot skinnier than he remembered being. The clothes Rosalina had given him were only a simple linen shirt, a sleeveless green leather jerkin, a pair of trousers and some socks and underwear. He assumed that his old clothes must have been utterly destroyed on his journey and all that could be salvaged was his boots. He didn't exactly look his best and felt rather apprehensive at being introduced to the king of this kingdom in such a state, but he figured he looked a lot more presentable now than when he'd first arrived in Ryushima. He picked up his sword and buckled it to his belt. With a bit of armour he could have looked almost heroic, but he laughed at the thought and left the room to greet Rosalina.

He was met with a joking "Well doesn't that feel a lot better?" Rosalina lifted herself from her perch on a bench near the window opposite the door and gave an approving nod to the ensemble. "We ended up guessing your size for everything, but it seems like it all fits rather well. I picked it out myself as I thought it'd suit you quite nicely."

She'd begun walking and Hideki dutifully followed, feeling at once relaxed in her company, but he remained in a slight state of shock at the world around him and just how well Rosalina was handling this situation. As they passed down the corridor he could see a large beautiful garden enclosed by the circling walls of the palace. Vibrant flowers ran around the border, working their way in spirals to the lines of blossoming fruit trees which directed the eye to a central fountain and a large cherry tree. He couldn't quite make out the design of the fountain from this distance as it was shaded by the tree, but he could see the water spouting into the air. There was so much colour and life in the garden that Hideki struggled to find the words to ask Rosalina about it.

She, completely blind to Hideki's gawping at the garden and unaware that he hadn't been listening to her for the past few minutes, continued rambling on about her parents. "So, while my father and mother are really lovely and happy to help anyone, do just be aware that they weren't hugely impressed with me dedicating weeks of my time trying to heal you, as I kind of had to miss meetings with quite a few important visitors and I put my training on hold so I could focus my time and energy on you, so there may be a few rather pointed questions aimed at why you magically turned up here; then again they may have just resigned themselves to the fact that I won't always listen to them when they tell me not to do something, I mean, if I wasn't a princess I could have left home to get a job at this point if I wanted to, and I suppose sometimes I do wonder what it would be like to not be a princess because I don't feel particularly princessy, and anyway my parents have always said I was stubborn so they know I have a mind of my own so it's not like they could have stopped me even if they wanted to." Rosalina turned her head to check on Hideki and saw him staring at everything, at the benches, the doors, the floor, the ceiling. Anything and everything seemed new and fantastical to him. "You haven't been listening to a word I've just said, have you?" She didn't receive a response, so she prompted him again, "Hideki?"

This snapped his attention back to Rosalina, "Sorry."

"You don't need to apologise, you know. I can understand why you'd get distracted by it all. This place is perhaps a little overly ornate for my tastes but when you have the ability to do almost anything with magic, what craftsman isn't going to want to show off their skills on the royal palace?" They turned a corner and reached two guards standing in front of a gigantic door. "We're here. Just give me a minute, ok?" She rushed up to the guards to ask whether her mother and father were free as they had been performing some ceremonial ritual or another and she didn't want to disturb them if they were still in the middle of it. One of the guards nodded hesitantly that they'd just finished as he looked towards Hideki. Rosalina signalled for him to join her and they walked through the great door into the palace's throne room.

A great space stood before them; the beautiful marble floor had a regal path down the centre which drew the eye to two golden thrones sitting beneath a gigantic stained-glass window. When the sunlight hit the window just right, its colourful images were projected onto the floor in a dazzling display. In the centre of the window was a magnificently intricate coat of arms. Sat between two dragons was a white and gold shield divided into four quadrants. Two charges adorned the shield, the tree and the phoenix, telling an eternal tale of birth and rebirth. A thin banner wrapped its way around the feet of the two dragons to sit neatly beneath the shield and it read, *MANO I AXOL*, 'The Soul of Humanity is the Glory of God's Creation.' Spiralling out from this crest were scenes of growth and unity, the planting of a tree, a festival of joy, a sun rising over a castle; but then as Hideki followed the images round he spotted the fiery combat of two dragons, people suffering as they fought each other, and the moon casting a solemn glow over a castle. All of these vignettes were enclosed in a woven frame of golden glistening leaves. He'd only been awake in this world for a few hours and it just kept on surprising him. Still, he understood why Rosalina was bringing him here so he placed his focus directly on the figures sitting in the thrones in front of them. The king and queen were bedecked in flowing golden robes, appearing like gods as the window cast a halo of glistening light around them. There was a stern look on the king's face; he was evidently uneasy about this situation but Hideki was able to notice a spark of warmth whenever the king looked to his daughter or his wife. The queen was noticeably more pleasant, with a cheery smile that lit up the room.

"Father, Mother," Rosalina announced with a curtsey, "This is Hideki, the young man who appeared in the courtyard a few weeks ago." She turned to Hideki, "Hideki, meet my parents, His Majesty King Lee I and Her Majesty Queen Sakura."

He began to bow and utter, "It is an honour to meet Your Majesties," but he was interrupted by the king.

"Forget the formalities. What are you doing here, why have you come, where are you from, and what do you want?" The king scratched his beard as he spoke but he never once took his eyes off of Hideki.

While he was rather taken aback by the abruptness with which the king spoke, Hideki told them what he'd told Rosalina; his birth and his departure from Helheim, the gate, his arrival or what he remembered of it and his desire to live his life. Every now and again, he looked to Rosalina for support and she gave him encouraging nods throughout. Once Hideki had finished, the king was deep in thought and an awkward silence descended upon the throne room.

The queen looked across at her husband, rolling her eyes at his refusal to speak for the moment, so she decided to break the silence herself. "Perhaps I should be more surprised and concerned by this story than I am, but there are many strange things in this world. Freak disasters strike when they are least expected, and miracles happen every day. I believe him, Lee. You can see it in his eyes. What do you think?" She spotted Rosalina discretely pumping the air with her fist and had a little giggle to herself.

Scratching his beard some more, the king nodded. "There is little reason to lie about such a story, given the situation. You should know, Hideki, that your appearance here has caused quite a stir especially after my daughter here decided to nurse you herself. The guards have been spreading all sorts of rumours, the mages are up in arms about the impossibility of your arrival, and I dare not even think about the gossip that will have gripped the city. So, the question becomes, what exactly are we to do with you? Do you want to stay in Ryushima or will you just be passing through? And if you do want to stay here, what will you do to make up for the commotion you've caused?"

"Well, if it's alright with Your Majesty, I would appreciate it if I was allowed to live here in your kingdom. I know nothing about this world and you have all already done so much for me, I think it'd be incredibly rude of me to just up and leave without doing something to help."

Rosalina decided that now was a good time to jump into the conversation, "He could live in the palace with us, Father! That way you get to keep an eye on him and he can serve you in return."

The king glanced towards his wife as she said, "You know exactly what I think we should do, Lee."

He nodded and scratched his beard as he looked carefully at Hideki. "How long have you had that sword?"

"For a few years now."

The king stood up. "Can you use it?"

Hideki nodded cautiously.

The king removed his robe and unsheathed a broadsword from the arm of the throne. "Hideki, if you are able, I challenge you to a duel."

Rosalina and her mother let out audible gasps at this pronouncement before Queen Sakura raised an unimpressed eyebrow and said, "Lee, that wasn't what I meant and you know it."

The king ignored her and continued speaking to Hideki. "I wish to see if you are worthy of the duty I intend to bestow upon you." He walked down towards Hideki while signalling for Rosalina to join her mother. "Do you accept?"

Rosalina interjected with a furious, "What the hell are you doing, father? He's only just woken up after being unconscious for weeks, he's hardly in a position to –"

The king gave her a harsh look and although she was still fuming, she didn't push the issue any further. He returned his gaze to Hideki and waited for a response.

After some thought, Hideki answered in the affirmative. "I do."

The two then moved to the centre of the throne room, each now wielding their swords. They began to circle each other, following the path of the projection from the window. The king was the first to make a move, lunging straight for Hideki although this was quickly blocked. As the two blades struck, the king pushed forward, attempting to force Hideki to his knees. With a quick swerve, Hideki managed to escape, swinging his sword around in the hope of catching the king in his back. The king's sword caught Hideki's before it could do any damage, closely followed by a roundhouse kick. Hideki was caught off guard and flung to the floor. His blade clattered away from him, but he managed to scramble quickly enough to pick it up before the king made any other moves.

"Surely you can do better than that. You do your weapon an injustice." The king charged towards Hideki, swinging his broadsword through the air at Hideki's chest. Their blades met once more sending a metallic clang echoing throughout the throne room. Hideki managed to hold his ground and went in for a few lunges at the king but these were all blocked and parried away. They fought like this for a few minutes, clashing, retreating, lunging and dodging. The sternness of the king was slowly but surely giving way to a jolly but determined expression that Hideki couldn't quite understand.

They drew apart and the king thrust his sword to the ground, yelling, "*AVAVAGO VPAAH!*" Rosalina was looking at her mother in shock at the lengths to which her father was going in this fight. She kept trying to shout out to stop the fight but her mother kept stopping her. Queen Sakura agreed with her daughter that her husband's methods were a little extreme, but she trusted the king enough to let the combat continue for a while longer. She wasn't sure what he intended to achieve from this fight, but she believed he was doing what he thought was right and she knew that he wouldn't hurt the young man beyond what was easy to heal. Electricity crackled along the king's blade to its hilt before surging through his body and sprouting out of his back into two mighty wings of lightning. Leaping into the air, the king aimed his sword at Hideki and bursts of lightning shot forth from the blade with a thunderous boom.

Without thinking, Hideki shouted, "*CAOSG!*" His sword grew a dark brown before shooting a torrent of mud globs from its tip into the air. They met with the lightning strikes, nullifying their progress towards him before exploding over the floor. The king laughed before diving towards Hideki, thrusting his blade in front of him. The force of the wings pushed him even more quickly through the air and he was about to launch another surge of lightning when Hideki yelled, "*OZONGON!*" His sword shifted from brown to a light turquoise blue before a mighty gust of wind erupted from it. The wind swirled tornado-like at the king; it struck him, dispersing his wings and preventing his charge from ever reaching Hideki.

The king managed to land on his feet but was noticeably out of breath from the attack. "That's more like it. Show me what you can do, Hideki!"

He readied his sword and rushed towards Hideki once more but just as he was about to strike the great doors were flung open and a loud unimpressed scolding bellow cut the combat short. "What the hell do you think you are playing at Lee? Stop this immediately." The voice came from a shrunken elderly woman hobbling into the room with the aid of a sturdy wooden staff. Ten braids swung from her long grey hair as she walked towards them, almost mumbling her disappointment to herself as she progressed. When she reached them she gave the king a thwack over his head with her staff. "You're meant to be the noble ruler of the kingdom, why in the name of all that is good are you fighting a child in the middle of the throne room? I swear, sometimes I wonder if you're really my son."

The king's entire persona crumbled as he looked sheepishly at the old woman, "Sorry Mother."

"I should think so too." She surveyed the mess around her, spotted Rosalina and the Queen heading towards them and tutted. "And Sakura, you let him get into this?"

"Well, you know how he is, just as stubborn as his mother."

Hideki glanced from the king, to the old woman, to the queen, to Rosalina, and back to the old woman with confusion. They were all so relaxed around each other; he'd never seen anything like it.

Rosalina spotted his wide eyes of terror and decided to cut in before anyone else noticed, "Oh! Hideki, this is my grandmother, Her Royal Highness Queen Beatrice. Granny Bea, this is Hideki!"

Hideki bowed his head respectfully, but just as he was about to greet Rosalina's grandmother, she was right next to him looking intently into his eyes. She stayed there for a few moments without her stare wavering. Hideki quickly realised that she was judging him, trying to appraise his character, and he suspected that her wise piercing eyes would succeed. "You've got a good heart," was her initial proclamation before she continued on, "Don't let the world destroy that. Kindness and courage are two of the most powerful forces in the universe but it's so easy to lose hope in their abilities. Just relax. Have faith in yourself, be decisive, and you'll do fine." She moved away slightly before swiftly whacking him over the head with her staff. "But don't you ever think about getting into a fight with my son again, even if he does try to put it upon you. It just won't do for the king to be getting into scraps. Isn't that right, Lee?"

"Yes, Mother."

"So, can Hideki stay here in the palace, Father?"

There was a small pause as the king composed himself before he responded. "Hideki, I am willing to offer you a life here in Ryushima on one condition. You must swear to protect the life of my daughter and fight for the prosperity of our kingdom. I understand that this is a big ask of you, to swear to protect someone you barely know and fight for a kingdom you've only just entered, but you have shown yourself to be reasonably adept at combat and my mother, my wife, and my daughter appear to trust you. If you make this oath, I too will trust you and do everything in my power to let you live the life you wish to."

Much to his own surprise, Hideki answered after only a small pause, "I will." Part of him wondered whether this was a poor decision, he was scared about the commitment, he was scared about how well he would fit in here, but something compelled him to say yes. The only way he would ever be able to describe it was that it felt right. In the end, that was all he could go on. He'd had a trial by fire, but these people respected him. They looked at him with warm smiles, and in spite of their rather peculiar greeting, they gave him hope.

"Then, if you would kneel, I will make this official." The king gently tapped Hideki's shoulders with his sword one after the other, "I, King Lee I do hereby dub you, Hideki, a Rider of the Light, protector and guardian of the heir to the throne, Princess Rosalina." He repeated the motion with his sword. "As long as you live, you must do everything in your power to ensure that the Kingdom of Ryushima prospers, and follow the Knights' Code of Chivalry. You must be loyal, you must be honourable, but above all, you must do what you think is right and just and protect my daughter with your life." He signalled for Hideki to rise and placed his hand firmly on Hideki's shoulder as his professional royal demeanour settled into a relaxed jollity. "Don't let me down, ok?" Hideki nodded fervently and was about to speak but the king cut in before he could say anything. "Now, you'll join the other Riders of the Light in about a week. First you need to rest up, acclimatise yourself to the way of life here in Ryushima and settle in as best you can. I'm sure Rosalina will happily show you around and help with that, and it's probably best that you get to know each other now because you will be spending a lot of time together once you join the team. I will have the captain train you to ensure that you're at the top of your game and for your service you can keep your room in the palace and join everyone in the Great Hall for your meals. Does that all sound ok to you?"

"That sounds amazing. Thank you so much, Your Majesty!" The gratitude he felt practically lit up his face with a beaming grin.

The Queen had been quiet ever since Granny Bea arrived, but she came in to give Hideki a light hug as she whispered, "I believe you could be destined to do great things, Hideki. I can see it in you, and I know Granny Bea can too. Just have courage and believe in yourself." She moved away and with a look of distaste at the room noted to everyone, "I think we're going to need to get someone in to clean up this mess. I blame you entirely, Lee. We only just got it clean after the festival and now you've gone and gotten it coated in grime and scorch marks."

The King couldn't help but laugh. "We'll get it sorted, Sakura, don't worry, we always do."

And with that, Hideki's journey had begun.

CHAPTER 3
SORROW WITHOUT SOLACE

The wretched plains of Helheim stretched out as far as the eye could see. Sparse bits of greying vegetation speckled the ground around the small stone huts. This small village had earned the name of Wonder's End, and was perhaps the most sought after location in Helheim. It was a place of peace and prosperity in the afterlife, stories had spread across the endless planet of how beautiful it had once been before the veil of darkness had been flung over Helheim. This was where Hideki was born.

His parents had died in an horrific accident, but their love for one another kept them together when their souls arrived in Helheim. They had journeyed for months before finally settling down in Wonder's End. As souls, the physical body was a pure manifestation of humanity and so no longer needed sustenance in the form of food or water, but in order to retain a sense of normality most continued to farm and eat. The primary function that was also lost was the ability to reproduce and yet by some miracle, Hideki was conceived and born, a live, healthy baby boy. Hideki's parents became the envy of all those around them and were increasingly ostracised from the people they had thought were their friends. However, not long after Hideki's birth, his parents vanished without a trace.

The elderly couple, Hershel and Claire, who lived next door heard him crying and came to his rescue and began to raise the young child as best they could. After a couple of years a young woman called Lara arrived in the village and quickly befriended them. Given Hershel and Claire's advanced age, she took it upon herself to care for Hideki. She didn't care for the vicious rumours that were being spread about the boy and so felt it was her duty to disprove them however she could. She gave Hideki an almost blissful childhood until the day of his seventh birthday when she too disappeared. It was at this point that he became known as a cursed child. Any who grew close to him vanished and nobody could figure out why despite their best efforts. The only people who seemed impervious to the curse were Hershel and Claire though they continued to care about the young Hideki. He was always very quiet and reserved, struggling to convey how he felt, and from the day of Lara's disappearance he lived in constant fear of losing more people. Even at such a young age, he started to become aware of how the people in the village treated him and began to think of himself as a worthless monster.

Another new arrival in Wonder's End took on the challenge of raising Hideki, a stern woman by the name of Ramona. She cared little for the child's snivelling and was determined to make him a productive member of society.

Through a strict regime of lessons in everything from social etiquette to reading and writing, she gave him the skills he needed to continue to grow. Though she was never particularly loving, Ramona developed a fondness for Hideki. She was impressed by how quickly he learned, how deeply he seemed to think, and how much he cared for others. The people of the village kept their distance because they were scared and so Hideki always tried his best to steer clear so as not to frighten them. By the time he was ten, he was still a fragile young boy but he had the foundations on which he could grow into a fine young gentleman. On his twelfth birthday, Ramona also vanished. Now that he was old enough to understand what was happening, his heart broke and he shrank further and further into his shell. He became almost husk-like for a while, staring blankly out at the empty, grey horizon that surrounded the village, pacing back and forth with little purpose and bursting into tears whenever he thought about the people he had lost. Why did everyone who looked after him leave without even saying goodbye? He couldn't understand it. He felt more alone and isolated than he'd ever felt before in his life and he blamed himself entirely for what happened. He was the cursed child who made the people around him disappear forever.

Hershel and Claire struggled to console the poor boy. He may have been alive, but he seemed dead inside. They made sure he ate and drank but, no matter how much they tried, he remained unresponsive. For a few months he holed himself away in his home, until one day he met… Until he met…

As Hideki described his past to Rosalina and her family he hit a snag in his tale. He remembered the last several years well, the sword training, the lessons in magic and the language of the angels, his growth into the person he was today, but something was missing. *Someone* was missing. Who had he met that day? Who had taught him everything he now knew? His mind sent searching tendrils out into the deepest recesses of his memory in a desperate attempt to figure it out. He stared at Rosalina, tears filling his eyes and his breathing quickening as the panic set in. He remembered how he had felt. He had wanted to disappear as well. But then they came to him. Who? Try as he might, nothing worked. A gaping hole opened up in him as the realisation struck him and he physically shrank into a quivering mess. "I – I – I – Why can't I – Who –"

The next thing he knew, the tender arms of Queen Sakura surrounded him. "Shush, shush, shush now, calm down, everything is going to be ok, everything is going to be ok."

Through the streaming tears he managed to say, "But I can't remember…"

Rosalina was almost statuesque. It dawned on her just what the voice in her dream had done. It had completely erased this person from Hideki's memory, leaving nothing but a void in its wake. She didn't know what to do. Should she admit what she had done? Would Hideki hate her for it? What would her parents say? She knew she was to blame for this but she had no idea how to fix it. With a look of horror, all she could do was stay silent. Whatever it took, she would do everything in her power to make amends to Hideki. Eventually, she would have to tell him but now was not that time.

The queen held Hideki tightly to her. "It's going to be ok, Hideki. You're going to be safe here. You are free now. It doesn't matter what or who you've forgotten at present because I'm sure the memory will return when you least expect it." Hideki's sobs lessened a little though he remained firmly hunched over. "If you had truly forgotten this person, how would you even remember that you've forgotten them? And if they were the person who made you the person you are today and you had forgotten them, then surely you wouldn't be you. Have hope, Hideki."

Granny Bea chose this moment to interject. "The mind may forget, but the body remembers. Just give it time."

It took a few more minutes for Hideki to calm down, but when he did he immediately apologised for his outburst. "I'm sorry… I didn't mean to –"

"Not another word. There is no need to apologise, young man," said the king.

Hideki looked up at him. The concern on his face was palpable and Hideki struggled to comprehend how these people managed to care so deeply for someone they hardly knew. He was about to apologise for apologising but the king interrupted him.

"Don't even think about it. You have done nothing wrong bar being the cause of Rosalina failing to work on a number of her important duties." He cast a wry glance at his daughter who had by now relaxed somewhat. "You seem like a good person Hideki. However much you've lost, whatever you've forgotten, you have become a courteous and respectful young man. We'll look after you here; don't you worry about that."

All Hideki could say in response, looking at each and every one of them, was "Thank you."

CHAPTER 4
RIDERS OF THE LIGHT

A few days had passed since Hideki had awoken. He'd spent them alone after he'd broken down in front of everyone. Rosalina had tried to show him around the castle but he felt that he needed some time to himself to come to terms with it all. He was still rather shaken by the gaping hole in his memory. Whenever he was alone for a moment he would close his eyes and rummage through his thoughts in the vain hope of finding something, anything, that would fill that void. Every single time he was left disappointed and heartbroken. He was lying on his bed in his room and he still couldn't quite believe what was happening. Just as he was about to be lost in thought once more, a knock came at the door.

"Oi! Mate! You're late for training with the Riders! If you don't hurry up Di is going to eat you alive."

Hideki quickly shot up and buckled his sword to his belt before opening the door to see someone he didn't recognise. The young man, possibly only a year or two younger than Hideki himself, was leaning on a halberd with an amused look on his face. He was rather small and slight, but he held himself with a swaggering air as if to compensate for his lack in stature. For someone in such a hurry he seemed oddly relaxed, sweeping his long black hair away from his sharp amber eyes. The two stood, judging each other, before Hideki finally broke the silence, "Hi, I'm… erm… Hideki."

"Hello, erm-Hideki, I'm Arthur, Arthur Miles Redgrave." He extended his hand towards Hideki, which Hideki hesitantly shook. "You been settling in alright in here? The princess told us about the nut who magically turned up in Ryushima, have to say though, you're not exactly how I'd imagined you to be. You're a bit fresh-faced and nervous for someone who turned up beaten to a bloody pulp, I was expecting you to be as big as an ox or something, with loads of scars or the like, but, eh, it doesn't really matter."

Hideki wasn't quite sure how to take this so he chose the response he thought would cause the least offense. "Erm… Thank you, I think?" He was rather taken aback by Arthur and how different his demeanour was to the people he'd met so far, but he supposed it was something he would have to get used to. "So, erm… shouldn't we be going to that training if I'm, you know, late?" King Lee had been kind enough to let him stay in the palace as long as he completed his duties with the Riders of the Light, so no matter how awful or how confused he felt right now, he knew he needed to pull himself together and move onwards.

With a laugh, Arthur nodded. "Well, yeah. I was mostly pulling your leg about the being late stuff, though Di would definitely kick your arse if you ever *did* turn up late. We probably should get going though, otherwise we *will* be late and I'd definitely get the blame for it. Can't be having that now, can we?" He lifted his halberd off the ground and set off, with Hideki close behind. "You looking forward to meeting the other Riders of the Light, Hideki?"

"Well, yes, I suppose. Though I don't think the king ever explained exactly what you did or who you are or why you're called Riders, so…"

"As I've always said to David, my brother, who's also one of the Riders, as much as King Lee tries to hide it, he's a bit of a fool. According to Di, our Captain, there's meant to be some deep meaning behind the name, like the 'Light' symbolising the princess, and the 'Riders' meaning the cavalry as we're supposed to be the big force that can come in at the last minute and rescue everyone despite the fact we only ever fight on foot. I think he just thought the name sounded good and then tried to come up with some explanation afterwards in an attempt to dig himself out of a hole."

Hideki gave Arthur a slightly quizzical look at this as he wasn't sure whether to laugh or debate with him, and ultimately chose to remain silent in response.

They finally exited the palace and began crossing a large lawn. It appeared to stretch as far as the eye could see with different pathways leading off into the horizon. Straight ahead of them stood a gated fort-like hedge, from a distance it looked like a swaying green castle with high spires soaring towards the sky. If there was one thing Hideki had realised during his time in Ryushima so far, it was that these people liked to show off. If they had the ability to create something, they would. Limits didn't seem to exist to them and they constantly sought perfection in their work. Not a single leaf on the hedge was out of place, not a single wall was crooked, not a single spire was bent. He was about to ask Arthur about this but they had reached the gates of the leafy fort.

"This, Hideki, is where the magic happens. The training grounds. A feat of masterful magical construction, completely encased by a protective barrier so that nothing can get in or out. We can train at full power without hesitation here, pretty cool, eh?" Arthur turned and grinned expectantly at Hideki. "Yeah, my mum's the one who designed it and my dad helped to build it. What do you think of it?"

"It's amazing."

Arthur stared off wistfully into the distance. "Yeah... If only they were still around to see how much we use it..."

This caught Hideki rather off guard, "Oh, I'm sorry, I didn't know that they'd –"

Raising an eyebrow, Arthur said, "I'm the one who brought them up, no need to apologise." Then with surprising frankness he continued, "They passed away a couple of years ago now. Yami, one of the Almighty Dragons, won and with his victory came many calamities. Mum and Dad went off to help one of the villages up in the mountains with some repairs and there was an earthquake. It caused a landslide and the village was wiped off the face of the planet. David and I have been looking after ourselves ever since."

"How awful… I'm so sorry…"

Arthur clapped Hideki on the back. "Don't be. It's just one of those things. Sure it was horrible at the time, and yeah it's hard, but they would've wanted us to live our lives and so that's what we're doing."

A cool icy voice cut into their conversation and Arthur winced as he realised just what was coming. "Arthur, you're late."

"Sorry, Di!" Arthur sheepishly tried to rush into the training grounds but the tall blonde woman stopped him.

"That's Diana, to you Arthur. Now as punishment, do twenty laps of the training grounds." Arthur was about to interject but she glared at him and he set off on his run. Diana turned her attention to Hideki. Her hard stare softened slightly as she shifted from stern captain to welcoming teacher but she was still very cold. Her piercing blue eyes contrasted greatly with the deep crimson ribbons that hung from her long hair among the three wrapped braids. Her athletic figure was protected by light armour on her chest, shoulders, hips, and legs, a glistening ivory colour rimmed with golden edges. Beneath the armour was a flowing red robe that split off into two long tails of fabric at the back. She was both elegant and practical, making for a very imposing figure. "So, you must be

51

Hideki." In an instant Diana seemed to have judged him worthy of something but retained the steely look in her eyes. "I am Captain Diana Caius of the Riders of the Light. You will now do everything I say until I deem you ready to make your own judgements. Is that clear?"

Hideki nodded.

"Good. Now you've already met Arthur and Princess Rosalina, correct?" Hideki nodded again. "So, the final member of our team is David. He's just over there doing target practice."

She pointed towards a man standing amidst fifteen or so wooden target rings. He quickly glanced at each of the targets before letting forth a thunderous roar of "*PLADPH ORS!*" A murky black substance formed itself into an arrow as he pulled his winged bow taut. There was a moment's pause before he let the arrow fly directly into the bulls-eye on the target in front of him. In a flash he spun around firing more of these dark arrows into the targets. Five more remained and he aimed his bow up to the sky. As he let go the arrow leapt into the sky, breaking up into smaller arrows which shot off in different directions, closing in on their targets to create a bubbling black bear trap in the air. He'd gotten a bulls-eye on every single shot. He grinned proudly as his fist pumped the air.

Before he could do anymore, Diana shouted over to him. "David!" In an instant he came running over. He was only a little bit taller than Diana, but very much the opposite of her in everything bar athleticism. He had the same messy black hair and amber eyes as Arthur, but he had much more chiselled features. An air of confidence emanated from him as he stood proud and tall in his black armour and faded turtle green jacket in front of them.

Despite the seeming cockiness with which he held himself, as soon as he spoke you could feel the relaxed warmth with which he treated life. "Hi Hideki, pleasure to meet you, hopefully my darling sweetheart hasn't scared you off yet." Diana let a wry smile perch on her lips before shaking it off as soon as she noticed Hideki looking at her. "Well, just make sure you do what she says, she's sort of a big deal around here y'know, child prodigy and all that." He winked at Diana before scarpering back to his training before she could say a word.

"You were a child prodigy? What did you do?"

Diana closed her eyes as she tried to figure out how she was going to explain this. In the back of her mind she was thinking about how she was going to kill David later for this, but now was not the time for petty squabbling. "I've been the reigning champion at our annual tournament since I was fifteen. In short, I am not someone you want to mess with, do I make myself clear?"

"Crystal clear." Hideki was now more than a little terrified, but he still needed to know a little more. "So... why did the King choose you all to protect Rosalina?"

With a roll of her eyes, Diana answered rather bluntly, "Because we've all proven ourselves worthy of that honour. Six years ago, a group of bandits attacked my village. I killed every last one of them single-handedly. The year after, David defended the walls of the Crown City from a horrific monster attack, slaying more than even the most highly trained of the real soldiers. Arthur has still yet to prove himself, but he and David are inseparable and the King took them in after their parents died so it made sense to let them work together. We've been working ever since to look after Princess Rosalina, to be her guardians and her friends. And since we are her friends, she knows that we will protect her with our lives. Any questions?"

"No, not at all," Hideki said. He did have questions. He had lots of questions. But now wasn't the time for that. Diana was clearly slightly offended at his questioning her authority to protect the Rosalina and he didn't want to annoy her further.

"Now, as you can see, David's training, Arthur's doing laps, and over there Princess Rosalina is studying up on some magic before she begins her training for the day." She gestured across the great area. Looking around, Hideki's eyes lingered on the princess and he started to relax a little more. Diana noted this but didn't mention it as it wasn't important right now. "As for you, Hideki, you will begin your training with me. Your first challenge will be a quiz to test your knowledge and how you would react in certain situations, and then you will have a quick sparring session to see how you put your knowledge and skills into action. Are you ready?"

With a deep breath, Hideki nodded. "Yes I am."

Chapter 5
Battle Tactics

"Question One: How do you perform magic?"

Diana's first question was incredibly broad and complex, but Hideki tried to answer to the best of his abilities. He spoke of the life force of the world, mana; energy that fuelled everything from humanity to the animals to the plants. Every living being had its own natural supply of mana but they could make use of more through the power of language and a physical conduit. These conduits mostly took the form of weapons; swords, staffs, bows, axes, and so on. The language, whether angelic or not, allowed the caster to form a mental image of the magic they wished to use. The mana then got drawn into the conduit where it took on the properties of the spell being cast before being expelled into action. There was at once a very precise but very loose art to firing off a successful spell, some managed to grasp it immediately while others struggled with it their entire lives. Diana was rather impressed by the depth of Hideki's answer, as she'd expected he would have been one of those lucky few who just had the knack for using magic.

"I had an excellent teacher… not that I can remember anything about them. For some reason the words 'understanding breeds progress' are stuck in my head but I couldn't explain why even if I wanted to." A twinge of sadness flickered in his eyes, but Diana quickly moved forward with her quiz to prevent him focusing too intently on what he'd lost.

"Question Two: What would happen if you used up too much mana?"

This was a rather simple question, though an incredibly important one. While people could draw in more mana and so sustain themselves and their combat for much longer, it was impossible to keep it up forever. Eventually, if they weren't careful, people could completely exhaust themselves of mana at which point they could end up killing themselves. It was possible to save those suffering from an excessive depletion of mana as long as healing spells were administered in time. One of the most important elements of combat was mana conservation, treating it almost like stamina.

Diana nodded. "I believe that's something we will need to focus on specifically. It seems that when you arrived you were very low on mana. I don't know whether that was down to how you managed to turn up here or not, but improving your efficiency with mana should do wonders." Before Hideki had time to breath she continued, "Question Three: Say you were to face an unknown opponent in battle, how would you gain the upper hand?"

Hideki pondered this for a moment, trying to come up with an answer that he thought would most impress Diana.

There was something about her that just commanded attention. She was the type of person you wanted on-side, that you wanted to please. "I would first try to judge what type of fighter they were depending on their weapon, stature, and stance. Then I'd play the fight defensively until I could see a pattern or an opening in which to strike. At that point, I could gain the upper hand."

"What happens if they too tried to act defensively? Not every foe can be goaded into attacking you. How would you react then?"

This caught Hideki by surprise and he began to criticise himself in his head for being so stupid. He tried to respond but all he could get out was a stuttering, "Well... I..."

Looking him square in the eyes, Diana merely said, "Don't falter because you've made a small mistake and don't talk yourself down. I'm here to judge you and I will tell you if you do something wrong or answer incorrectly. So, answer my question. How would you react if your opponent tried to act defensively?"

This snapped Hideki out of his rut and he was able to quickly respond with, "Well, I'd have to go on the offensive. If the offensive is fast enough to catch them off guard then no matter how defensively they try to fight, there should be openings."

"And what if someone tried that on you and you were trying your defensive manoeuvres?"

After some more thought, Hideki had his answer. "Then I would have to go on the offensive too. Match their speed but keep my guard up at the same time."

Diana nodded once more. "Ok, good. All are viable tactics, though I would pull you up on one key issue. You are entirely correct about trying to figure out your opponent's skills, strengths, weaknesses, and so on; and about trying to understand patterns and openings. The issue comes with your tactics. You would want to begin a fight defensively or offensively but there was no mention of shifting tactics depending on the flow of the fight. Not all battles can remain in a single gear. Think of them like waves, they flow in and then retreat regularly but the force behind their movements shifts all the time. It doesn't matter how you think the fight is going to go, you need to be able to react to what's going on in the moment. Do you understand?"

"I do, yes."

"Good." At this point, she looked over towards David, then Arthur, then Rosalina, making sure Hideki followed her gaze. Then she followed with her next question. "Question Four: Your teammate is injured but you think you can finish the fight without them, how do you approach the situation?"

Hideki answered this without hesitation. "I'd help my teammate."

"Why?"

"If they are suffering from a life-threatening injury or a mana deficiency then immediate action is needed. If I tried to finish the fight, then it may be too late to save them and I wouldn't be able to live with myself."

Diana could see the earnestness in his eyes. While all his previous responses had been reasoned and level-headed, this type of situation reached down to the core of who Hideki was. She admired that kind of response but felt the need to push a little harder to get him to believe in himself more. "But what if your attempt to save them resulted in your own injury or death? Then nobody could defeat your opponent. Surely that's a worse outcome?"

"I'd sooner die than lose my allies and friends when I know I can save them."

"Well then, that leads us rather neatly onto our next question. Question Five: You must face a powerful foe by yourself. All of your allies are dead and you have no hope of back-up arriving. What do you do?"

A steely grit entered Hideki's voice as he responded. "I would do everything in my power to defeat the enemy even if it cost me my life. If I've got nothing else to lose then I will fight until there's no more strength left in my body to move."

Diana's questioning of Hideki continued for another hour, each question designed to make him think carefully about his moral compass, his combat techniques, and his relationships with others. By the time they were finished, Hideki was mentally exhausted. He knew what was coming next and he wasn't sure whether he was entirely prepared for it. After so much intense thinking, the prospect of a sparring match against Diana was terrifying since she still seemed so cool and collected.

In a flash, she pulled a dazzling rapier from her belt and readied herself to attack Hideki. The hilt had a crescent moon knuckle bow and loop guard, linking up to an intricate series of rings extending past the cross guard. The moonstone pommel continued the lunar theming of the weapon and seemed to be drawing in the light from around it. Diana's lips moved silently as she drew a lightning bolt in the air with the tip of her rapier. Quickly realising that she was about to attack, Hideki withdrew his sword and prepared himself for the inevitable attack.

The attack did not come immediately as Diana mouthed more words and drew a circle before cutting it in half. Suddenly, Hideki's limbs began to feel sluggish. He tried to run towards Diana but struggled to move his feet at any sort of speed. Before he'd had a chance to comprehend the situation, Diana had cast two spells, one to speed up her own movements and another to slow him down. It took all his strength to try to counteract it. Through gritted teeth he roared, "*Let my feet fly, Haste!*" His sword took on a yellowish glow before the mana flowed through into him and he began to feel normal again.

The edge of a smile danced across Diana's lips before she charged towards him, thrusting the blade rapidly towards his chest. Hideki leapt back and repeated his spell once more. Now he was on equal footing in terms of speed. He thought about some of the lessons Diana had taught him already throughout her quiz and decided that his best course of action at present was to go for the offensive and try to find an opening. He knew that from the length of Diana's rapier he needed to get into close combat in order to lessen her advantage over him, so he leapt at her with a jumping slash.

She saw the move coming and sidestepped the blow effortlessly. Now they were in close quarters, the two were locked in a speedy flurry of blows. The swiftness with which Diana used her rapier was astounding. It was all Hideki could do to keep up with her and no matter how hard he looked he couldn't see any openings to make a decisive blow. The two drew apart for a moment and both took the opportunity to launch offensive spells. A split-second after Hideki's sword glowed red and he yelled "*IALPON*", Diana's rapier glowed blue and she roared "*ZLIDA.*" A ball of flame leapt forth from Hideki's sword but as it flew towards Diana it was dowsed by a steady stream of water coming from her rapier. Steam rose into the air as the two attacks counteracted each other, and both Hideki and Diana chose this moment to resume their close quarters combat.

No matter what Hideki tried to do, from feinting to getting in a counterattack after a parry, seemed to work. Diana blocked each and every single one of his strikes. He had expected her to be a formidable opponent but he had hoped to get at least one strike on her before she called the sparring match to a close.

What he didn't realise was that Diana was hoping for exactly the same thing. Throughout the entire match she had been using sloppier techniques than she would normally use to ease Hideki in more gently. She refused to give him an entirely easy time, but she had wanted him to spot her tendency to lung to the left and make use of that. As it stood, she was impressed at Hideki's fervour but disappointed at his lack of perceptiveness. He thought deeply about things, that much was clear from the way he had answered her questions, but he didn't always see what was right in front of him. It would perhaps take longer than she had originally thought to get him up to the standard she believed he was capable of achieving, but with the right exercises she was certain she could get him there.

After a few fierce exchanges, Diana decided it was time to end the sparring match. Without missing a slash, she got her foot behind Hideki's and pulled back, sending him toppling to the floor. He looked up at her with a face flushed with disappointment and admiration. "Thank you, Captain, it's been an honour to spar with you."

Diana was rather flattered by this but tried to not let it cloud her judgement of Hideki. "You've got guts and a reasonable amount of talent, Hideki. I'll give you that. But you're blind when it comes to your opponent's moves. You spend half your time thinking about where the openings or patterns are and the other half reacting just in the nick of time to prevent yourself being very badly injured. What you're lacking is perceptiveness and a clear head in battle." Hideki was crestfallen until Diana continued, "But that'll come with experience. Good job on your first day."

This cheered Hideki up immensely and he gave her a toothy grin as he thanked her once more.

"It's going to get a whole lot more difficult from here on out. You've got a lot of work in front of you, Hideki. Got it?"

"Got it."

Chapter 6
Cherry Blossom Shower

After a few more days of training, Hideki had begun to settle into his new way of life. The training itself was difficult and exhausting, but already he was beginning to feel more alive than he ever had when he'd lived on Helheim. He still hadn't managed to spend too much time alone with Rosalina but he knew that a lot was expected of her and she didn't have much time to spare. He'd seen her at the training grounds and they'd exchanged some niceties before Diana cracked the whip, but little else.

Then, one morning there was a knock at his door. Much to his surprise, it was Rosalina, as happy and bubbly as ever. "Hideki!" Within a second she was hugging him. He just stood there in shock for a moment before hugging her back. "I've been wanting to talk to you for days but what with training and my duties and all of that, I've not been able to get the chance. But now Granny Bea wants to speak to you about something and she sent me to come and get you! I think she knows I'd been wanting to speak to you otherwise she would've gotten one of the messengers to do it."

"Your grandmother wants to speak to me? What about?"

"I think she said it was something about a prophecy or a vision or something. I swear she does this almost every week or whenever anybody visits the kingdom, but there we go. Do you want to head over there with me now? And then afterwards, maybe I could show you around the city. You've been cooped up in the palace grounds since you got here, it'd be nice for you to see the real Ryushima! Plus, since you're technically one of my 'bodyguards' nobody should have a problem with it. How does that sound?"

"That sounds wonderful, thank you. I think a bit of a break would do me good."

"Well, come on then, let's go!"

And with that, Rosalina grabbed Hideki by the hand and started dragging him to wherever Granny Bea was. As their fingers interlaced, Hideki was overly aware at how sweaty the palm of his hand was becoming and how soft Rosalina's hand was. She didn't seem to notice his clamminess, as all she did was smile at him as they walked through corridor after corridor. As they started heading down one of the palace's many spiral staircases, Hideki realised they hadn't said much on their journey so far, they'd just remained content in each other's company. He liked that. In spite of the beautiful surroundings; the flowers in ornate vases, the intricately detailed paintings, the magnificent tapestries; he only had eyes for her. The slight bounce in her step matched her wonderful smile and lovely eyes. She was like a ray of sunshine, lighting up the world around her.

Rosalina noticed his gaze and decided to tease him a little. "What are you looking at me for, Hideki?"

His cheeks flushed as he tried to come up with an answer that wouldn't embarrass him, but he struggled and the words that came out of his mouth were an incoherent mess. He'd try to start a point only for it to run as far away from him as possible. In the end he had to settle for a sheepish "Sorry."

Rosalina frowned. "What are you apologising for? I was only teasing you."

Shrinking into himself, Hideki could only utter another "Sorry."

Rosalina stopped and looked him dead in the eye, "You don't need to apologise. Please, otherwise you'll start making me feel bad. If anything, I should be apologising to you for –" She cut herself off as she realised what she was about to say. She couldn't say it right now. He'd hate her for what she'd done and she couldn't bear that. She'd spent so much time trying to help him after he'd arrived that she'd grown rather attached to him. Him hating her would break her heart.

"For what?"

"For... not doing enough to help you settle in." Rosalina felt awful for lying to him but she saw no other way out of the situation her big mouth had just landed her in.

Thankfully, Hideki remained in the dark about the reasoning behind his lost memories, though he was ultimately rather confused by Rosalina's apology. "But you definitely don't need to apologise. You've done more than enough to help me settle in. You spent weeks trying to heal me, you got your father to let me stay here and you've been nothing but kind and welcoming to me. I should be saying thank you more. And sorry for apologising so much… I suppose, it's just a natural reflex. After years of being told I was cursed, I'm used to assuming I'm doing something wrong. I'll try and get better at that if I can."

Breathing an internal sigh of relief, Rosalina opened the large glass doors in front of her and took Hideki out into the garden. He recognised it in an instant as the one he'd seen on his first day awake in Ryushima, the one within the walls of the palace with the fountain. Now that he was stood at its edge it was even more beautiful. A rainbow of flowers skirted around the border of the garden, the reds and the pinks and the purples intermingling with the pastel blues and the golden yellows. The multitude of blossoms spiralled out across the flower beds to create a feeling of unity. As with everything Hideki had seen around the palace it was grandiose and yet entirely tasteful, walking just on the right side of that thin line between stunning and gaudy. At the edge of the flower beds stood the lines of great fruit trees which arched over the gravelled pathways leading to the centre of the garden. The light dappled the ground through the leafy shield, creating a slight shimmer wherever it touched the path. As they made their way through the arch, the breeze rustled the trees above them, sending with it a shower of white apple blossoms. Some landed in Rosalina's hair, and Hideki couldn't get over how much they suited her. Rosalina in turn let forth a tremendous inelegant snort as she saw the flowery hood Hideki's head had received. Brushing his hand over his hair, Hideki realised what Rosalina had been laughing about and began to laugh too. As the giggling ended they came out into the centre of the garden.

Beneath a gigantic cherry tree stood a rather peculiar fountain. He hadn't been able to see the sculpture from the windows on that first day but up close it was fascinating. In the middle of the deep pool of water was a lotus flower from which rose the crystalline figure of a beautiful woman. Her dress swirled around her as she thrust a knotted staff towards the sky. The water rose through the figure and erupted out of the tip of the staff creating a waterfall that dove back into the pool. As it fell, the water seemed to hit a force field which prevented it from landing on the sculpture itself. When the light caught the crystalline figure it sent out dozens of glistening rainbows across the pool's surface and through the fine mist in the air. It was unlike anything he had ever seen before. But, what was perhaps the most intriguing was that on the base of the fountain there were markings in the angelic language, in large protruding symbols it read: '*OIT IANA. IXOMAXIP TA FAXIMAL AAO IHEHUDZ.*'

"This is the Daughter of Light. Let her be known as one with the infinite among the children of the light." The amused voice of Granny Bea was unmistakable even if he had only met her once. She stood up from the bench that sat just in front of the cherry tree and walked over to the two of them. "This fountain and the Great Tree, Yggdrasil, in the courtyard are the only things we have from the time of the founding of Ryushima. The lady you see before you Hideki, is the mythical queen that brought this kingdom together, the Infinite Daughter of Light. Does she look familiar to you, Hideki?"

Hideki's heart missed a beat. Did Granny Bea know something about him that he didn't? Did she know something about his parents or his past? "No… Should she?"

Granny Bea laughed before continuing, "Of course not. She's a woman from centuries ago that may not have even existed. I mean, of course, having grown up in the afterlife there's always the possibility of running into mythical people long dead, but really I just like messing around with people. Passes the time rather well, don't you think? After all, nobody can say a bad word against me what with my being the Queen Mother and my age." Her jolly laughter filled the air once more. "I bet you were rather excited or terrified at the prospect of a vision that was the pretence for getting you here today."

Hideki was hit by a wave of relief at this, he didn't want to be at the heart of some mystical ancient prophecy or some prophetic vision of the future, he just wanted to have a happy and peaceful life that he could call his own. But, the lack of a vision did leave the question of why Granny Bea had wanted him to come and speak to her today and why in this garden.

Clearly understanding what he was thinking, Granny Bea answered his queries. "I wanted you to come here today to understand our history. You probably saw the stained glass window in the throne room, all of the dragons in our iconography, the Great Tree Yggdrasil and now this fountain, and were wondering what it's all about. If you are to have any chance of living peacefully within our culture, you need to know where we've come from just as you have told us about yourself. Come, both of you, and sit." She led them over to the bench. "Hideki, let me tell you the story of Ryushima."

Little was actually known about the original founding of Ryushima. All the legends ever passed down were the stories of a mythical queen giving birth to the two Almighty Dragons, Fai and Yami, in a small village on the island. Given her power, she amassed a group of followers who decided to name the island, Dragon Island, or Ryushima as the queen translated it, after the two Almighty Dragons who gave the people hope. A special tree was planted in the spot where the queen's little village had stood, the world tree, the Great Tree Yggdrasil. This island grew in power as news of the queen and her dragons spread throughout the world, attracting the most talented people from across the globe. As they came together the people developed a hybrid culture, borrowing traditions and designs to become a truly inclusive society. The new kingdom prospered for a time, growing and evolving as more and more people brought their ideas with them. But one day the queen vanished. The people searched and searched across the world to find her but to no avail.

With the loss of their mother, the dragons descended into a fit of madness; they began to fight against each other over their contrasting beliefs, causing devastation wherever they went. It took all the strength the people of Ryushima had to contain the violent force, but it ultimately broke them. They entered into a civil war, some siding with Fai, the dragon who embodied wisdom and kindness, and others siding with Yami, the dragon of strength and courage. The war raged for hundreds of years and the kingdom began to crumble under the weight of the destruction. But then, as so often happens in stories, two star-crossed lovers from either side came together and ended the war by doing what always needed doing. They got the two sides to sit down and talk, to negotiate, to compromise. When the weapons had ceased shedding senseless blood, the two lovers allowed each side to see how similar they were and how they could once again be that utopian society once more.

At this point, the hazy legends ceased and the documented history of Ryushima began. Those two lovers became the first official King and Queen of the Kingdom of Ryushima. On the day of their coronation they set down in law the core tenets of how the kingdom would survive and prosper. To end the war, a bargain was struck up. The Almighty Dragons would go their separate ways until one day each year when they were to return to Ryushima and continue their fight. Whichever dragon won the battle that year would mark how the year would be treated. In this way, the people were reunited. A sculpture of the legendary first queen was created as a symbol of their determination to regain the utopia of their early years.

As the centuries passed, the people forged a strong bond, one that would never again be broken by disagreements. But, they achieved this at the cost of their freedom. None were willing to accept this truth, not even Granny Bea as she described to Hideki the kingdom's history, but deep down they all knew it. Through tradition they had been shackled to the whims of two ancient beasts that now seemed only to care about destroying the other. The people were happy, and had been for such a long time, but they yearned for the day they could choose their own path together.

Hideki asked Granny Bea why the people of the kingdom had never fought back against the dragons once peace had been restored but received only looks of shock, fear, and disgust from both her and Rosalina. It was then that he realised that Ryushima was like a swan; graceful, beautiful, and perfect above the surface, but paddling frantically and furiously underneath to keep going. They were a powerful and peaceful people, but they crippled themselves out of fear of change. They wanted better, needed better, but they couldn't see how it was possible. Change would destroy the peace and beauty they had and that wasn't something they could bear to lose.

Chapter 7
Timbre of the City

After a rather hurried goodbye, Rosalina dragged Hideki out of the garden and into the nearest room she could find. Her face was flushed a deep crimson and she was clearly rather flustered. "What the hell was that?"

Hideki wasn't quite sure how to respond. He was desperate to defuse the situation but it was clear he'd struck a nerve and there didn't seem to be a way to make things better. "I was only asking a question, Princess. I'm sorry if I offended you and Granny Bea."

Rosalina's hand slammed down on a nearby table, nearly about to scream but she managed to control herself. She inhaled deeply and slowly moved her hand away. After a few seconds she stared into Hideki's eyes and tried to explain herself as calmly as possible. "The Almighty Dragons are our protectors; they are our gods. Without them, none of us would be alive today and so we respect them. To defy them or even think of fighting back against them is blasphemous. All who have spoken that way about the Almighty Dragons have died a horrible death soon after and so…" Rosalina got lost in the thought. She'd never had to explain something like this before to anyone, it was just the done thing. Would they be better off without the constant changes in direction? Was there really a connection between speaking out against the Almighty Dragons and death? She didn't know.

"So… what?"

"So… we've never questioned the way things are." Rosalina now realised why she'd gotten so angry. It was because she had been scared and she suspected Granny Bea felt the same way. They were scared at having something so fundamental to their world be shaken by a truth they couldn't effectively argue with. A new interpretation of the afterlife they could deal with. Knowledge about the unknown was welcome. But changing something known into the unknown was terrifying. They were scared of change. And Rosalina was scared about what might happen to Hideki. "I'm sorry for snapping like that. It was uncalled for." She hugged him and the brief argument was over.

In order to try and make it up to him, Rosalina knew she had to show him as much of the city as possible. The two left the palace through the front gates, passing the magnificent Yggdrasil on the way. A long road lined with trees, flags and bunting stretched out before them and Rosalina happily skipped down the pathway without a care in the world. There were a few citizens coming and going down some side streets but none came up to disturb them. The citizens saw the princess, smiled and waved at her, an act she reciprocated, and then they got on with their business. Hideki had thought she would get mobbed by hordes of people the second she left the palace but that simply didn't happen.

Once they reached the end of the long road, Hideki could see out over the entire city. The first thing he noticed was the great wall that circled the city. It stretched high enough into the sky to afford the city protection, but not so high that it prevented the sun from getting in. Red lanterns dotted the parapets in between two great pagodas that acted as watchtowers. The rest of the city was filled with a plethora of homes of varying architecture. Seeing the wildly different styles all united was proof enough to Hideki of Ryushima's hybridity. Some would probably have described the Crown City, Ryukyo, as a hodgepodge, but what had clearly happened was people had built the houses of their dreams using techniques from across the globe.

Standing tall over the city was a brilliant white clock tower. A thin rail wound its way from the base to the stained glass clock face where one black and one white dragon united to form the circle. A series of bells hung from the roof, ready to ring at the turn of every hour or for special occasions like the Dragons' Festival. It had the potential of being a rather imposing structure, but it emitted an air of comfort and balance. When Hideki asked about the clock tower, Rosalina spoke fondly of its ability to bring everyone together. It was a symbol of hope and unity for the people, as whenever the bells chimed all looked up at the clock tower and in that moment, they were all one. It was only a small instant, but it was always strong enough to do its job.

As the two walked down the hill where the palace stood, they chatted about everything from the plants to the people. They eventually reached a marketplace filled with the largest assortment of goods Hideki had ever seen in his life. Fruit stands stood next to the most extraordinary fabric stalls, and nearby one merchant created ornate bespoke pieces of jewellery right in front of her customers while another chiselled away to manually sculpt little wooden figures. It was a little overwhelming to begin with, the sights, the smells, the sound, were all just a bit too much for Hideki but when he saw the smiling faces around him he couldn't help but relax. No one here seemed to be judging him and that put him at ease. He caught a few people speaking amongst themselves about the young man strolling about with the princess, but none seemed too concerned to make a fuss.

One by one, Rosalina visited each of the stalls and bought a little something from the merchants. It was a long process; the pleasant greeting, the small talk about what a lovely day it was and that this was one of the new Riders of the Light who'd just arrived in Ryushima, the querying about what new products they'd gotten in over the past few weeks, Rosalina constantly making sure that the merchant wasn't giving her a discount just because she was the princess, the cheerful goodbyes, and so on and so forth. The bags gradually got fuller and fuller and Hideki ended up carrying most of them.

"Do you do this often, Rosalina?" He asked her once they'd covered about half the stalls in the market.

"I try to get down to the market at least once a month, after all, it gets me out of the palace and meeting the people I'm meant to serve. These people work so hard to make a living and it's our duty to make that as easy as possible for them. So, coming into the city and buying a little something means they are that bit better off, and it shows them that I care about each and every single one of Ryushima's citizens. And anyway, they all make and bring such wonderful things, how am I meant to resist coming and learning about their lives and their work? Everyone has something special to bring to the world, and I love finding that sort of stuff out, you know?"

Hideki could tell by the earnest look on her face that Rosalina truly believed she was doing good. When he saw how touched the merchants were when she gave them her undivided attention, laughing and joking about with them, he knew that she was doing the right thing. She made everyone she spoke to feel special. Even just watching the interactions, Hideki felt joy stirring in his heart.

Rosalina glanced back at him as they began to move to another stall. "What's that smile for?"

Hideki hadn't even realised he'd begun to smile and blurted out, "It's because you're wonderful." He then realised what he'd said and quickly tried to make the situation less awkward. "I mean it's wonderful. What you do, I mean." He stared intently at his feet in an attempt to hide his embarrassment.

With a coy smile, she responded, "Why thank you." She paused for a moment, then continued, "on both accounts."

And then they'd visited every stall in the marketplace. The sun was just beginning to set, bathing the city in an orange glow that crept over the walls making the clock tower stand out even more in the skyline. The bells began to chime with a rousing melody that rose and fell like the ocean's tide. The city stood still as all eyes fell on the clock face. Hideki looked around to check if what Rosalina had said was true, and no one he saw, young or old, man or woman, was looking anywhere but at that clock tower, all with a content smile on their faces. Soon enough, the bells went quiet and people returned to the hustle and bustle. The merchants began to pack up their stalls and head home after a hard but satisfying day's work. That was Hideki and Rosalina's cue to return to the palace, and they did so, carrying Rosalina's horde of purchases with them.

Chapter 8
Romance

As Hideki sat down for dinner in the great hall with Arthur, he was surprised at how far he had come. A few weeks had passed and he was already feeling so much more comfortable and confident in himself. He no longer felt the need to shrink away whenever anything happened, he just stood tall and dealt with it as it came. He was just explaining that he'd never felt happier to Arthur when he noticed that Arthur wasn't really paying a whole lot of attention to him, instead choosing to just stare off into the distance as if in thought.

"Arthur? What're you thinking about?"

Immediately, Arthur was focused again and with no hint of tact asked, "When the hell are you going to tell the Princess that you fancy her?"

It seemed to come out of nowhere and Hideki flushed with embarrassment as he spat out the mouthful of food he'd just started to eat. "What? I don't – I mean I – I – Where did you get that idea from?"

Arthur shot him a sardonic smile as the two of them glanced at the chunks of food that now covered the table. "You'd have to be blind to not notice the way you look at her." After that, Arthur's expression softened and he gave Hideki a cajoling elbow to the arm, "Come on, tell me everything! When did you start having feelings for her? Why haven't you said anything yet? When are you going to tell her?"

Hideki had improved at dealing with these sort of awkward situations, but he really didn't know how to deal with this one. He'd known he'd felt something towards Rosalina since the day he met her, he'd known that everything felt right when he was around her, but he'd never faced up to those emotions before. "Nothing can happen between us, Arthur. She's the princess and I'm just a knight of sorts."

"Oh come off it. Don't give me that old cliché. What d'ya think's going to happen? That she's going to politely decline because she's too high class for you? Have you seen the way *she* looks at *you*? She absolutely feels the same way. And if I wasn't telling you this, David definitely would be. He definitely knows what he's talking about when it comes to women and love, after all, he's the one who got the ice queen Diana to fall in love with him."

This made Hideki re-evaluate the situation somewhat, maybe it was worth him saying something. He could see before him an entire life with Rosalina, but he'd been shying away from it because the prospect of rejection or making the situation awkward terrified him. He had grown much more confident but this had been a hurdle he hadn't quite managed to overcome yet. "Yes, I really like her, Arthur, ok?"

"Well then, you need to tell her. Right now." Arthur stood up, grabbed Hideki by the arm and forcibly dragged him to Rosalina's room in spite of Hideki's protestations. While Arthur had a rather diminutive stature, he was surprisingly strong when he wanted to be. The ease with which Arthur got Hideki to move was probably also due to Hideki's unconscious desire to do this right now. Before Hideki had any real time to process what he was going to say, Arthur had knocked on Rosalina's door and there she was, as wonderful as ever. "Princess Rosalina, I believe Hideki has something he wishes to speak to you about."

This piqued Rosalina's curiosity and she ushered them in. Arthur, politely declined and with the cheekiest grin in the world scarpered back to the Great Hall. Rosalina closed the door after him rather confusedly before turning her attention to Hideki. "What did you want to speak with me about?"

"I... erm..." Putting everything he thought about Rosalina into words was more difficult than he could have ever imagined. He glanced around the room, at the books piled high next to a comfortable chair, at the elegant floral dragon tapestry that adorned the wall, the forget-me-nots that sat in a vase on the window sill; everywhere he looked he saw signs of who Rosalina was as a person and he loved every bit of it. "Could we possibly sit down?"

Twigging that something was afoot, Rosalina perched down on her bed and Hideki joined her there. She placed her hands on his and searched for an answer in his eyes. "Come on, spit it out, what did you want to speak to me about?"

"I –" Her big beaming eyes were so warm and endearing, and before he realised it, he was leaning in toward her. To his surprise, she met him half-way and they kissed. It was only for a moment, but in those few precious seconds their hearts and souls were one. Everything felt as though it was right with the world. When they parted they became an awkward muddle of apologies for overstepping the boundary and became silent as neither knew quite what to say. At last, Hideki was able to break the silence, "I really, really like you, Rosalina."

"I really, really like you, Hideki." They both sat there grinning at each other for a while until Rosalina flopped back on the bed. "So, what do we do now? Do we tell everyone?"

Hideki flopped back to join her. "I don't know. Can we? What about your parents? Would they be ok about, you know, us?"

Letting out an exasperated sigh, Rosalina turned over to face Hideki. "I mean, they should be, but then they are always going to be over-protective of me so… I'm not sure. We could always just keep going as we're going. After all, we spend enough time together as it is so it's not like they'd get suspicious. Also, what exactly can they do? They can't change the way I feel about you, just as they can't change the way you feel about me. But then again, they could send you into exile.

That's what people always do in the fairy tales. Then again, it's not like fairy tales are entirely all that realistic…"

They spent a few more minutes in deep thought before finally settling on leaving it between themselves, and Arthur, since he knew anyway. It was a hornet's nest they weren't especially keen on kicking. All was well in their lives right now and being separated would destroy them. In a few months' time, perhaps things would be different and the king and queen would easily accept the relationship.

After another blissful kiss, Hideki left to go and find Arthur to figuratively murder him, but mainly to thank him for what he'd done. Rosalina returned to the book she was reading but she couldn't really concentrate, so she amused herself by humming the melody of a song she'd always loved. Neither could quite believe what had happened, but it filled them with such joy that they didn't care about the world around them, they could only think of each other.

As Hideki almost skipped down the corridor he ignored the knight walking in the opposite direction to him. He had subconsciously noted the odd flecks of red liquid on the chest plate and the fact that the knight's helmet visor was down but he didn't question it. After all, why should he? Everything was good with the world and absolutely nothing could dampen his spirit.

He'd nearly made it back to the Great Hall when suddenly, Arthur came charging around the corner, eyes wide with fright when he saw Hideki. "Where's the princess?" It was the most serious tone of voice Hideki had ever heard Arthur use, and it was then that he realised something was very, very wrong.

"She's in her room." He daren't ask the next question but he knew he had to. "Why?"

"Someone's broken into the palace, the mages think they've come to assassinate Princess Rosalina."

In a split second, Hideki sprang into action back the way he had come. Every curse under the sun ran through his mind and all he could do was pray he was not too late.

CHAPTER 9
RED AND BLACK

There was a harsh knocking at Rosalina's door. It was rather insistent and something about the force with which the fists were hitting the door concerned her. She got up and grabbed her staff before opening the door a little. That was enough for the assassin to force his way into the room, whipping a sword from his belt and brandishing it towards her as he grinned malevolently. "Prepare to die, Princess."

Rosalina's grip tightened on her staff and she started to whisper a spell under her breath. "*BRGDA*." She tapped her staff on the ground and a milky haze grew in the crystal ball. Before the assassin could take another step he slumped to the floor, fast asleep. With a sigh of relief, Rosalina considered her options. If there were any more attackers, they'd surely come here and they may not all be as slow and dull-witted as the man who lay like a steely lump on the floor. She knew she could protect herself but she needed back-up just in case someone caught her off guard. Hideki had headed back to the Great Hall to see Arthur. That's where she needed to go. In the hope of evading any assailants who knew the main pathways of the palace, she decided to take a shortcut down a side passage that few knew about.

The second she turned the corner into the passage, Hideki burst into her room in a panic. Sweat ran down the back of his neck as he saw the sleeping man on the floor but no sign of Rosalina. Close behind him were Arthur and a few of the other knights who'd been alerted to the crisis. The second they saw that the princess wasn't there, they began to fear that she had been kidnapped after defeating one of her attackers but Hideki didn't believe a word they said. He couldn't see her staff anywhere so that meant that she had it with her, and that meant she was safe for now at least. A battle plan was drawn up to search the palace in order to find the princess but once everyone set off in different directions, Hideki had an idea. Where would Rosalina go if she was in danger? She'd try to find one of the Riders. Where had Hideki been going after he'd left? The Great Hall. It was just a thought, but it was all he had. He'd failed in his duty to protect Rosalina, if only he'd stayed with her for a few more minutes none of this would have happened. It was his responsibility to fix this.

As he ran he unsheathed his sword and prepared himself to face whatever danger lay ahead but he wasn't entirely ready for what he saw behind the doors of the Great Hall. In the middle of numerous trashed and upturned tables was Rosalina, surrounded by twenty or so hulking knights wielding an assortment of cruel weapons. Staff held high, Rosalina had created a barrier around herself but she was clearly straining from the pressure of withstanding the vicious blows.

"HEY! Get away from the princess!" Hideki roared as he began to charge towards them.

One of the attackers, a balding man with a scar running down his face, laughed at the challenge and as soon as Hideki got near, he swatted him into a nearby pillar sending Hideki's sword skittering across the stone floor. "Is that the best the knights of Ryushima can do? They're so sure of themselves that they're blind to us sneaking into the palace and then they throw a scrawny brat at us? It's pathetic. C'mon boys, let's show this runt what a terrible mistake he's made." Without a care in the world, the brute sauntered over to Hideki and lifted him up by his throat. "What's your name, brat?"

Doing his best to remain calm, Hideki stared the brute down before swinging his foot forcefully into the man's groin. This was enough to get him to drop Hideki. After quickly grabbing his sword, Hideki turned on the man, "My name is Hideki and you are not going to hurt her." A raucous laughter erupted from the attackers and a few more stopped their onslaught on Rosalina's barrier to make Hideki's defeat as easy as possible. Raising his sword in the air, Hideki began to draw in some mana before roaring, "*AVAVAGO VPAAH!*" The sword glowed yellow and crackled with electricity before rushing to his back and bursting out into the thunderous wings. Using these wings, Hideki leapt into the air and began hurling thunderbolts at the assailants but while it staggered some of them, the lightning blows seemed to fizzle the second they hit

89

the armour. Since that didn't seem to work, Hideki decided to change his tactics and use a different spell. *"CAOSGON!"* His sword glowed brown before forming some large stones at its tip and firing them. This knocked out one or two of the attackers but before Hideki could do anymore he was struck by a table that had been flung towards him. The lightning wings vanished and he fell to the ground. As he landed he heard a loud crunch and the feeling in his left arm vanished.

Three of the men closed in on Hideki but he couldn't move. His head was reeling, his ears were ringing and he could faintly taste the blood that trickled down his face. "Rosalina… I'm sorry."

He closed his eyes. He thought that this was going to be his end. But then, deep down inside him he knew that that wasn't true. He wanted to fight. He needed to fight. When he opened his eyes he saw the men back away in fear. What he didn't realise was that he'd begun to glow and a forceful whirlwind had kicked up around him. The desire to fight grew stronger and stronger until a gleaming orb of pure light burst from his chest. It spiralled into the air, gradually growing in size, morphing into shape. A long spiky tail whipped out followed by four clawed feet, two enormous wings and a long, scaled face. The light crackled before exploding, sending bolts of lightning down to the ground. With a tremendous thud, a powerful golden dragon landed next to Hideki, shielding him with its wing and glowering furiously at the attackers.

A deep gravelly voice rumbled out across the hall, "I am Mjölnir. What is your command, Master Hideki?"

Shock and awe swept through Hideki. "What are you?"

"We have little time, Master Hideki. What is your command?"

Hideki looked towards the attackers and noticed that Rosalina's barrier was nearly destroyed. "Protect Rosalina by defeating them all." He clutched his arm as the pain shot through it again. "Please!"

Mjölnir nodded and set upon the attackers, sending them flying through the air with a flick of his tail. One attempted to stab the mighty dragon in its leg, but Mjölnir didn't feel a thing. He arched his head over the man, jaws gaping wide, and ate him whole with a sickening crunch. Then, he reared up on his hind legs, opening his maw and letting loose a blistering barrage of plasma balls. The plasma collided with the attackers and exploded, destroying some of their armour and making them run for the doors. But before Mjölnir could attack any more his time was up and his body dissipated into the ether with a thunder clap. At the same moment, Rosalina's barrier shattered around her. She desperately tried to launch a spell, "*DOOLAP PIR…*" But she didn't have the energy. She'd wasted too much mana on the barrier.

The attackers knew that now was their chance. Hideki was weakened and no longer had his pet dragon to defend him and Rosalina was a sitting duck. They closed in on the two of them and all hope seemed lost.

The doors to the Great Hall slammed open. "What are you boys doing in here?" The attackers turned to face this new foe. "Are you hiding something from me?" Before they could blink, Diana thrust her rapier through one of the attacker's throats. She withdrew it and immediately planted the blade in another's gut. "Nobody harms those under my protection. Do you understand?" One of the brutes charged at her but she deftly sidestepped him, stabbing the rapier through his leg and sending him crumpling to the ground. She noticed some of the unusual damage around the Great Hall and in the process of kicking one of the attackers in the face she asked, "What the hell has been going on in here?"

Rosalina, now safe for the moment behind one of the tables, answered, "Hideki summoned one of the Vardr!" This was another mistake as some of the brutes who had momentarily forgotten about her decided that they needed to complete their mission before their seemingly inevitable death.

Diana's eyes lit up with a near sadistic glee. "Well, if they were scared of that, they're going to be terrified of what I have in store for them." For all her coolness in training, Diana was a devilish presence in battles with such high stakes. A controlled crimson fury ran through her veins as she cut down another of the attackers. Ten still remained but that was nothing. Diana drew a crescent moon with her rapier as she called upon her guardian, "*PAMPHICA, A GRAA ORS, YOLCAM VANGEM, SELENE!*"

A light shot up from Diana's rapier to the ceiling, circling around until it created a glistening moon within the hall. Some of the attackers tried to charge Diana while the light was still moving but before they could reach her a figure began to descend from the moon, a figure in flowing black slowly drifting downwards. Long black hair swept around her rolling black dress as she opened her milky white eyes. A crescent moon protruded from her head like horns and her pale skin seemed to almost shimmer in the light of the hall.

"Selene, destroy all bar one."

No more needed to be said. The mysterious woman flew through the air towards the men about to reach Rosalina. Her nails extended into razor sharp blades and she cut through their armour as though it were paper. With a wave of her hand small moon-like boulders appeared out the portal overhead and crushed her foes with no mercy. Three down. Six to go. She turned towards the four men surrounding Diana and danced across one of the upturned tables, grabbing a nearby torch and clobbering the closest brute. She flipped over him and impaled another with the torch. A lick of the lips later and the next man was cut down and the next. Seven down. Two to go. One of the brute's swung his mace at the mysterious woman but her nails sliced through the metal chain and then his neck. The other made a valiant attempt at attacking her from behind with a deafening charge but she raised one finger to the sky and another moon boulder silenced him forever.

Only one of the assailants remained and he cowered in front of Diana, pleading for his life. "Please, I'll tell you everything! About the plot! About the mastermind! I'll tell you everything! Just don't kill me!"

Diana nodded at the mysterious woman and she placed her nails gently against his throat. "Why did you attempt to assassinate Princess Rosalina of Ryushima?"

Sweat rolled down the snivelling assassin's face, landing on the mysterious woman's nails and breaking into two the second they made contact. "Because She ordered us to."

Hideki had managed to gather enough strength to stand and as he struggled over he asked, "Don't play that game with us. Who is She?"

One of the nails danced across the assassin's chin and blood began to trickle from it. "The – The – The Mistress. Nobody knows her real name, she just turned up one day and offered to pay us more money than we'd ever need if we killed the princess. She never said why! I swear!" He frantically stared from one stern quizzical face to the next hoping to see some sign of mercy. "I didn't want nothing to do with the job but the rest of the team said we couldn't turn it down, that it didn't matter why! Please you got to believe me!" Another nail nicked the back of his neck. "The Mistress said that killing the princess was the second step in her plan to do… something or other. I don't think she ever said what her plan was but it was definitely the second step. Please don't kill me!"

Rosalina had finally made her way to Diana and looked intently at the man's face. "He's telling the truth, Diana."

The fire vanished from Diana's eyes and her stance softened. "Thank you, Selene."

The mysterious woman nodded and vanished into the ether. The assassin crumpled to the floor in exhaustion. And with that, the battle was over. Eventually, a squad of Ryushima's knights found Diana healing up Hideki and Rosalina and they gawped at the destruction that lay before them. They promptly arrested the assassin and took him to the dungeons; in the meantime, all manner of servants descended on the Great Hall to begin the clean-up and to help out both Rosalina and Hideki. The worst had thankfully not come to pass, but lessons needed to be learned by all.

Chapter 10
Training

The fallout from the attempted assassination of Princess Rosalina was enormous. The King and Queen were left in a state of shock at how easily their defences had been breached. They had always believed that they were safe due to the peaceful relations Ryushima had with the kingdoms across the globe, but evidently that was no longer the case. After a brief investigation, it was found that the group of assailants had snuck in through a secret passageway that led in from the coast. As nobody expected the royal family to be attacked, none of the knights questioned seeing a man they didn't recognise within the castle. Perhaps it was arrogance in their security, perhaps it was naiveté, but in the end all that mattered was that Rosalina was safe and nobody had been fatally wounded in the attack. It was then decided that knights or members of the Riders of the Light would be with the princess at all times. Rosalina wasn't especially happy about this as she felt it hampered her freedom, but she understood that her mother and father only wanted to protect her.

It took Hideki a good while before he was able to come to terms with what had happened. He blamed himself for not staying with her just a few minutes longer, for not finding her fast enough, and for not being strong enough to protect her. If Diana hadn't shown up, they both would've been dead. Rosalina had tried to thank him for doing what he could to help but he shut himself away in shame. However, it wasn't long until Diana forced him to get back to work.

A training session was called and while everyone was a little uncertain after what had happened, there was a firm determination to get stronger so it never happened again. "Hideki, summon your Vardr."

Hideki looked at Diana in confusion, "What's a Varder?"

David decided to answer this one before Diana could get a chance to respond. "Vardr." He wrote it down in the sand as Varðr. David saw Hideki's confusion and said, "It's written with that letter, eth, usually, but it's not really fashionable to use it these days so most people just write Vardr." He put his hand on Hideki's shoulder. "Have you ever heard people talk about their guardian angels?" There was hesitant affirmative nod and so David continued. "Well, the Vardr are the physical forms of those 'guardian angels', they are in essence guardian deities who are there to protect their master. Whenever a mage ends up in a very dangerous situation where their life is at stake, the Vardr come to their aid. For some arbitrary reason you have to call on them to protect you after that first time and it requires a ludicrous amount of mana, but hey, none of us make up the rules for this sort of rubbish."

"So, what happened to you guys for your Vardr to appear?" Hideki looked around at Rosalina, David, Arthur, and Diana, intrigued at what stories they might have to tell.

Rosalina giggled as she recounted her tale. She had been a little girl and she'd been playing hide-and-seek with Granny Bea. She had a brilliant idea for a hiding place, the balcony looking out over the courtyard. Unfortunately, it wasn't her best moment as in attempting to look out over the balcony to see whether her grandmother was coming, she fell over the railing. In that moment she was rescued by her Vardr. "Do you want to see her, Hideki? I tried summoning her after you called forth Mjölnir but I was just too tired." He nodded at her and she raised her staff to the sky, yelling: *"DOOLAP PIR, ODO MADRIAX OD TORZU, NE EXENTASER, AMATERASU!"*

That familiar ball of light flew from Rosalina's staff and glided through the sky, releasing a trail of burning white and red feathers as it went. It appeared to reach out to the sun, soaring higher and higher towards it; then as it reached its zenith two feathery wings shot out of the ball casting a dazzling light upon them all. Taloned feet, a head with a sharp pointed beak, and magnificent peacock-like tail feathers sprung forth next and as the light began to diminish it was clear that the bird was covered in flames. With a pirouette in the air it shook off these flames and descended to perch on the ground next to Rosalina.

It nuzzled her gently with its beak and seemed almost overcome with relief.

A soothing melodic voice rang out from the bird as it spoke to Rosalina. "I'm so glad you're ok, Rosalina, I was so worried."

"Well, it's all thanks to Hideki and Diana."

The bird graciously bowed its neck to Diana before turning to Hideki. "I have not met this child before, who is he?"

"Mother Ammy, this is Hideki, he's one of the Riders of the Light now, he turned up here after escaping from Helheim. Hideki, this is Amaterasu, my Vardr, she's a phoenix."

"Yeah, because our princess is such a special and unique little snowflake." David sarcastically remarked.

Rosalina glowered at him as he burst out laughing. "We don't get to choose who our Vardr are, David. What does Granny Bea always say? They represent your very soul."

"If only that were true…" Arthur muttered under his breath.

"What did you say Arthur?" she asked.

Arthur shrugged and shook his head. "Nothing." Hideki noted something in Arthur's eyes. It clearly was something, but he wasn't going to pry right now.

"Mother Amaterasu is a powerful Vardr indeed. She is a force to be reckoned with in battle, but you really need to master your mana consumption, Rosalina." Diana sighed a little

99

as she recalled her frustrations. "I understand how difficult it is to maintain a barrier from the onslaught of so many people but you should have had enough to call forth Mother Amaterasu, and if not you should have called her sooner." She turned to Hideki, "I'm not going to criticise you for being unable to control yours, but that is something we are going to work on. By the time we're through, you should be able to work with your Vardr as I do with Selene."

"What is she? She was… terrifying."

"Selene is a moon deity. She's known across the world by many names, Kaguya, Luna, Chang'e, and so on; but to me she is Selene. A few years ago a group of mercenaries attacked the city walls and I made a stupid mistake that nearly cost me my life. Selene came down and she saved me. Outside of that you don't need to know anymore. We fight together for the good of those we wish to protect."

"Can we see Hideki's Vardr now?" Arthur asked, trying to avoid anyone asking him about his Vardr.

Diana nodded. "We only have a few hours to train today, so we probably should move on quickly. Hideki, what you need to do is channel mana into your weapon, then call forth your guardian in the language of the angels. Just search inside yourself for the words and you'll find them. Keep calm and ensure a steady flow of mana is maintained. Only you can find what works for you, but once you've got the balance, your

Vardr will be able to fight alongside you for much longer. Got it? Now, go."

Hideki thought deeply as he tried to figure out what he needed to say. He held out his sword and began to pull in the mana from the air. The words seemed to appear from the depths of his mind's eye, drifting into focus like crackling sparks. "*YOLCAM…CORAXO…ARPHE… TELOCVOVIM… MJÖLNIR!*" The blade crackled with small lightning bolts and sure enough, the mighty dragon that had protected him in the great hall stood before him once more. As the others gawped at the creature, Hideki grimaced as it felt as though the wind was being knocked out of him. He began to draw in more and more mana and eventually the sensation faded. He opened his eyes and Mjölnir was still there.

The dragon looked inquisitively around the training ground and was pleasantly surprised to see no danger in the immediate vicinity. "Why have you summoned me, Master Hideki?"

"Because I need to train in order to be able to call you when I need you most, Mjölnir."

The dragon laughed, and the ground seemed to shake as it thundered through the air. "Well then, I will happily oblige, Master Hideki. What do you require me to do?"

"You don't need to do a thing, Mjölnir." Diana said, "Hideki, however, needs to complete the obstacle course while retaining your presence here. You too Rosalina. Let's make it a race, shall we? It'll make things rather interesting." Diana signalled for David and Arthur to grab some chairs so they could watch.

Rosalina bit back a little, "But Diana, it's totally impractical for me to do that obstacle course in a dress. If you'd warned me before I could have prepared myself."

Without missing a beat, Diana laid down the law. "But you may not get the chance to prepare yourself. Did those attackers give you a chance to ensure you were practically prepared? No. You need to be able to take action no matter what you're wearing or how unprepared you are. There's little any of us can do to protect you if you aren't capable of looking after yourself on the battlefield. And I've seen you fight, Rosalina. In time, you shouldn't need us, but we'll be there all the same because that's what family does." It was at this remark that Rosalina gave in and readied herself to tackle the obstacle course. She hated it when people used the argument of family against her because when it came, she knew the other person was right.

So, both Hideki and Rosalina reached the starting point and when Diana gave the cue, they both set off at a sprint. Mjölnir and Amaterasu lay down nearby and chatted between themselves while they watched their masters race. Hideki and Rosalina leapt over hurdles, clambered up rope ladders, scrambled through hoops, slalomed between pillars, tackling every obstacle with as much energy as they could. There was a general air of politeness about the race as neither wanted to actively beat the other; when one slightly overtook the other they'd slow down a bit. In spite of the physical strain, they were both smiling and laughing at each other as they ran. By the time they finished in a tie, they dropped to the floor in exhaustion. It was only then that they bid their Vardr farewell and the creatures vanished.

As they giggled on the floor, Diana strode up to them. "That'll do, you two, that'll do."

CHAPTER 11
WALK OF THE HEART

As the days turned to weeks, peace began to return to Ryushima. The people were still shaken after the attempted assassination of the princess, and the gossips around the city were all too pleased to pick apart the whys and wherefores of the attack. However, the royal family had put on a brave face as the time passed and eventually the people's confidence in them was restored.

In the meantime, Hideki and Rosalina had continued to train harder and more thoroughly than ever before. They were inseparable, each pushing the other to get stronger. Diana was particularly impressed with their newfound work ethic and encouraged them at every turn. She could see what they were capable of. In her heart she knew that one day they would both surpass her and she couldn't wait for it to come. To take the next step, she had a little chat with Granny Bea about how to teach Rosalina one of the most powerful spells known to humanity.

"Granny Bea, I think she's ready to learn Restoration."

The elderly woman tilted her head with an owl-like inquisitiveness. "Restoration, you say?"

"Yes. She's reached a point where she can maintain contact with her Vardr for well over an hour during strenuous conditions. If she's capable of doing that, she's capable of manipulating an incredibly large flow of mana to herself and others. I know that her majesty, Queen Sakura, always struggled with the spell but she said that you'd perfected the technique many years ago." Diana's reverence for Granny Bea was palpable.

There was a coy glance from the old woman before she asked, "And you want me to teach my granddaughter how to use it? Correct?"

Diana felt relieved to hear Granny Bea make that suggestion. "I would be very grateful if you could. I know my way around a battlefield and I've gotten my offensive magic down pat, but I've never been too good at healing spells."

Granny Bea gently embraced Diana as she said, "Of course I'll teach her. It would be an honour."

And with that, Granny Bea took over Rosalina's tutelage. At first Rosalina resisted because she didn't want to be separated from Hideki and the others, but she eventually gave in as she knew it was her duty to become as powerful as possible in order to protect the people. For her first lesson, Granny Bea sat Rosalina down to explain the core principles of the magic they were about to perform.

"When you were a little girl I told you that one day you'd learn incredible spells that could save millions of lives.

Diana thinks you are ready to begin that challenge and I do too. You may have heard of Restoration and Resurrection spoken of among the mages. They are in essence the holy grail of healing spells. Restoration allows you to control vast swathes of mana, drawing it from even the most minute of places and sending it wherever you please. Resurrection on the other hand allows you to bring people back from the brink of death. None have yet managed to successfully use Resurrection, but we have mastered Restoration; or at least I have anyway. That's the main thing I will be teaching you. It may take a while, but we will get you there, without a doubt."

Rosalina listened attentively for hours on end to Granny Bea's explanation; in awe at the intricacy with which mana could be drawn out of even the most unusual things. From the tiniest pebble to the largest beast, mana could be borrowed from anything. It was as difficult as drawing blood from a stone, but so rewarding when achieved. It relied upon being at one with the universe, breathing in sync with the world around you, breaking down the boundaries between the self and nature. Rosalina laughed at how much it sounded like the fairy tales of old.

"You can laugh all you like, Rosalina, but these ideas and expressions become clichés because they're true. They're also useful, because although they may seem trite, people understand what they mean. That's half the battle won right there. Now, let us begin properly."

Months passed and Rosalina seemed no closer to grasping the complexities of the spell. She'd talk it over with Hideki whenever he was placed on guard duty for her. It was frustrating. She was so used to being able to quickly understand and use magic spells but this one had her stumped. In spite of all Granny Bea's help, Rosalina had only managed to draw a miniscule amount of latent mana from the world and it generally fizzled out before it could be of any use. Tensions were running high and so Hideki suggested that she take the night off; visit somewhere like the clock-tower and just take her mind off things.

So, after obtaining permission from her parents, Rosalina and Hideki made their way to the top of the tower and stepped out onto a small balcony just below the clock face. They leant on the railing and just looked out over the city as the sun began to set. A faint breeze danced through the air, whipping the golden clouds in small swirls in the sky. Hideki gently put his arm around Rosalina and she nestled into him for comfort. They didn't need to say a word. As the sun cast its last rays over the city, there was a moment of beautiful calm. Flocks of birds glided serenely back to their nests and the stars began to pepper the intangible canvas of the sky. They kissed briefly and all their worries melted into the ether. All felt right with the world. There may have been struggles, and there may still be difficulties, but they knew they could face anything together.

"Do you know what next month is, Hideki?"

"No, I don't think so?" he responded quizzically.

Rosalina glanced up at the rising moon. "It's the Dragons' Festival, which means you'll have been here for a year." She let loose a nervous giggle as she looked into his warm, glistening eyes. Then, with absolute sincerity she said, "Thank you for coming to Ryushima, Hideki." He wasn't quite sure how to react to this, but it made him feel so happy inside. "You could have gone anywhere, but you turned up here. I remember thinking at the time about how there were no coincidences in this world, and I'm more sure of that now than ever. If it weren't for you, I probably wouldn't even be here right now. Those assassins would've killed me before anyone could come to my aid. And even if not, I don't think I would've been who I am right now were it not for you. So, thank you, from the very bottom of my heart."

"I should be the one thanking you, Rosalina. Without you, I wouldn't have a purpose. I'd have landed here and probably been chased out of every place going. Nobody would've believed me; nobody would've trusted me. But you did." Hideki looked down on the glowing city as the lamps were lit. "I never really had a home or a family before, and now I've got you, Diana and David, Arthur, Granny Bea, your mother and father… So, thank *you*, Rosalina."

The two stood in contented silence for a while longer and then they decided it was time to head back to the palace.

When they returned they were met with a few annoyed grumblings about how late it was but these were batted away with a sincere apology and a gentle smile. Most of the members of the royal household had noticed that something was going on between Rosalina and Hideki but they all kept their mouths shut out of politeness. The kids would let everyone know eventually, but only when they were ready.

Chapter 12
A Thousand Words

All too soon, it was nearly time for the Dragons' Festival. Preparations for the event had been running for weeks as the palace readied itself to entertain the people of Ryushima. Bunting was strung from the branches of Yggdrasil to the surrounding walls and giant baskets of hanging flowers were carefully hung up. The normally quiet courtyard was awash with festive activity and colour and everyone seemed to be in a particularly good mood. As everything was put in its traditional place, the servants laughed and joked to each other about any and all gossip they'd heard. One particular rumour suggested that David was going to propose to Diana at some point over the course of the festival but no one had quite managed to locate a trustworthy source just yet. Perhaps it was just wishful thinking on their part as they were always quite fond of a wedding, but where there's smoke, there's usually a fire. They'd also heard that the King was set to make an important speech about the future of the kingdom, but the contents of that message were a mystery.

The joy was keenly felt by Rosalina who was practically leaping off the walls with excitement. As the start of the festival drew closer, she constantly rambled to Hideki about how amazing it was going to be. She spoke fondly of her father's previous speeches and couldn't contain her glee when it came to the evening's ball beneath the stars. It was quite clearly the highlight of her year, and that was infectious. Hideki had frequently seen Diana smiling as of late, particularly whenever she was off-duty. David was as witty as ever but Hideki had spent so little time with him that he really couldn't figure out what the guy was thinking about half the time. Arthur, however, had become less and less of a show-off as Hideki had gotten to know him. He still had his tendencies, especially in front of his older brother and Diana, but he didn't come across nearly obnoxious as he had when Hideki had first met him.

When the first night of the Dragons' Festival came, the atmosphere was electric. The royal family and their retinue waited behind the palace's great doors as the citizens of Ryushima flooded into the courtyard. The king, bedecked in a flowing purple cloak, gave a cheeky grin to the queen as he righted the crown on his head. Hideki and the other Riders of the Light were stood just behind Rosalina who, in Hideki's mind, looked more beautiful than ever. There'd been some brief instructions of what they were to do: The king would make his way up to the balcony, they would follow shortly afterwards and stand near the windows, then after the mirror's display and the speech, the real party would begin. Before Hideki had really had the chance to comprehend what was about to happen, the doors opened and the Festival began to run like the well-oiled machine it was.

The crowd covered seemingly every inch of the courtyard and the hearty cheers boomed across the courtyard. Men and women of all ages smiled at the king as he made his way up the spiralling stairs to the balcony. They whooped and hollered as Queen Sakura, Granny Bea, Rosalina and the others soon followed. It was a sensation unlike anything Hideki had experienced before. The pure unadulterated collective elation shone throughout the people like a burning torch in the night.

As the cheering slowly died down, the king raised his sword and brought it down on the balcony's railing. An iridescent blue flame sparked into life, splitting in two before skittering up the walls to the great mirror's face. The two flames reunited and created a magical moving picture on the mirror. Dragons fought, figures danced, trees bloomed, and when the tale was done, the flames died out leaving only a halo of light as their legacy.

With a none too subtle thumbs up to the retinue, King Lee confidently began the traditional speech of the festival. "*CHRISTEOS MOZ*. People of Ryushima, today marks the anniversary of the founding of our kingdom. From the very beginning, we have held true to our tenets of family and trust. We have fought and struggled to get to where we are today and the bonds between us will not be broken." Applause erupted and the king nodded acknowledgement. "As your king, it is my

112

duty to serve you and I hope that my family and I have done you all proud. We love every single one of you, and without your hard work, this mighty kingdom would lay in ruins. Together, we are a family. We stand firm against the world like the great Yggdrasil and we never forget where we have come from." As usual, this was received with a particularly enthusiastic cheer. "This past year has been an unusual one. For starters, we gained a new member in our household who I'm sure you've all seen about the city at some point with my daughter." At this point he gestured towards Hideki who flushed slightly when he realised all eyes were on him. "Since then we've learned about the reality of the afterlife, and I've noticed a general air of hope amongst you all. It's been wonderful to see. But then we nearly lost my beloved daughter to those assassins. If it weren't for the Rosalina's skill with magic, the bravery of young Hideki, and the strength of Captain Diana, I cannot bear to think about what may have happened. In our time of peace and prosperity, perhaps we have gotten too comfortable with the status quo. We were so certain of our protection that we nearly lost one of the people most important to us. That will never happen again. We won't actively seek war, but we won't sit by and let those who seek to destroy us have their way. We are a kingdom of freedom, a kingdom of unity, a kingdom of hope. We may make mistakes, but we learn from them and we will use those lessons to strive towards a brighter

113

future for our children and our children's children. Are you with me?"

The people had been quiet while the king reached the end of his speech. He'd been oddly serious, but this turn towards the patriotic stoked the flames of their passion and they cheered their affirmation.

"Before we continue, can I ask for a moment of silence and reflection to honour those who have given their lives to protect this wonderful kingdom?"

The silence quickly fell, and the huge crowd dipped their heads. Out of the corner of his eye, Hideki caught David's hand slide reassuringly into Diana's and he saw Queen Sakura place her arms around Granny Bea. As the silence continued, Hideki thought of the parents he'd never known, the people who had tried to bring him up, the kindly old couple, and… He paused as he remembered that hole in his memory. He'd managed to cope without it but it still gnawed away at him whenever he couldn't get to sleep at night. Who was that person he'd forgotten? How had they simply vanished from his mind? He looked up and his eyes darted from the king to the queen and Granny Bea to the other Riders of the Light and finally to Rosalina. This was his family now and he wouldn't change it for the world.

"Thank you everyone, for all that you do." King Lee bowed and his speech was done. He removed his cloak and draped it over the balcony before yelling at the top of his lungs,

"Now let's begin the Dragons' Festival Ball!" He thrust his finger towards the sky and a series of magic-based fireworks soared into the air from atop the parapets. A band of musicians sitting around the mighty Yggdrasil began to play and the people cheered with jubilation. They all drew together and began to dance in organised chaos. The king swept towards the queen and the two launched into a musical whirlwind which descended the stairs and joined the crowd at large. The retinue followed and soon they were all lost among the people. No longer were they royalty and subjects, they were merely the people of Ryushima.

As the music swelled, more fireworks leapt into the sky and exploded in a plethora of colours. Red rings skittered across the stars; cerulean chrysanthemums gained form as they reached their zenith before vanishing in a sparkle; and jasmine palms jitterbugged to the beat as the purple peonies fox-trotted against the black night. It was a visual spectacle like no other and really encapsulated the joy they all felt. It was almost like a dream.

Hideki and Rosalina stayed close to one another as the jig progressed. Eventually the strings slowed to a beautiful ballad and all the couples in the crowd joined together for a wonderfully romantic slow dance. There was an awkward moment of should we, shouldn't we before the two drew their bodies together and began to sway. In that instant, they finally realised how right everything felt in each other's arms. As they moved they felt as one, like a star returning home to its rightful place in the sky. They stared longingly into each other's eyes to the point where the people around them seemed to vanish into the ether. For all they knew or cared, they were the only ones dancing that night beneath the starry firmament.

"I love you."

"I love you too."

As the embers of the dancing fireworks rained down around them, they kissed.

CHAPTER 13
BELIEF

One minute there was music, the next silence. All eyes fell on Hideki and Rosalina. There was a ripple of sound as a path between them and the king and queen appeared. Hideki and Rosalina froze as they realised what they'd just done and winced at what they expected the reception to be. Rosalina looked sheepishly at her father and mother but was surprised to be greeted by warm smiles and a brief nod of acceptance. A cheer swelled through the crowd and the music kicked up again. Everyone returned to their dancing as if nothing had happened, leaving Hideki and Rosalina stunned but elated. The level of acceptance throughout the people should not have been a surprise when all was considered, but it did catch the two of them rather off-guard. Rosalina thought of all the love stories she'd ever read and none were ever this simple. Something always went wrong; there was supposed to be drama to bring the lovers closer together. If it was not her parents' disapproval, then what was it? The prospect terrified her. For Hideki there was just the relief at people finally seeing him as a decent human being worthy of love. As the two thought deeply about the situation, they remained close and spent the rest of the night dancing in each other's arms.

The next morning all the people talked about was the princess and her sweetheart, seemingly forgetting the King's speech as they got swept up in an infinitely more enjoyable subject. Some got carried away with talks of marriage and more heirs to the throne while others couldn't hide a twinge of jealousy; but ultimately most were just happy to see their princess in love. It gave them a symbol of hope which was always particularly welcome. In the meantime, Queen Sakura had a few words with Rosalina while King Lee spoke to Hideki. It was mostly to get affirmations of their feelings and their commitment to one another. While they were apprehensive about their daughter's future with Hideki, they trusted her judgement and both could see quite clearly how sincerely the two loved one another.

Once they were finished the focus shifted to the tournament that was due to take place. It was to be a thirty-two-man knockout tournament, any warrior was fine to enter no matter their weapon and the only rule was that under no circumstances were lethal blows allowed to be used. This was a tournament of honour. The purpose was for the warriors to display their skill and see who was the strongest in the kingdom. While healing spells could do a lot, near murder was both distasteful and excessive considering the tournament was to be seen by people of all ages. It was as much a performance as a competition.

All of the Riders of the Light were entered and Diana was giving them a pep talk before the tournament. "You'll all be fine. You're among the best fighters in the kingdom. There are only ever a few seasoned warriors in these tournaments who are likely to give you trouble. There could be the odd surprise but as long as you stay on the ball you should do well in this tournament. Obviously, we're eventually going to have to face one another but when that time comes you cannot hold back. We are all friends and will remain friends after this, so you must give it everything you've got. This is a showcase for us and should prove that Rosalina is under the best possible protection." She winked at Hideki. "And since she's going to be watching, we can't disappoint her now, can we?" Hideki giggled nervously before nodding determinedly. "And remember, I've won this tournament for the past five years… So good luck."

It didn't really inspire the greatest confidence in Hideki or Arthur, but David just took it in his stride and gave Diana a cheeky peck on the lips. "You're going down this year, Di."

"Oh really now. You and what magical luck fairy?"

David looked to Arthur, "Well, surely Arthur could hook me up with Gloriana and then you wouldn't stand a chance."

Arthur flushed with embarrassment and walked out of the tent where they were standing.

Hideki stood up to follow him, briefly asking, "What was that about?"

David stopped him. "It's fine, I'll go. Arthur's always been a bit self-conscious about his Vardr. I joke about it with him to show that he shouldn't care about it, but every time he freaks out about it. I shouldn't have said anything... I'll go sort him out. See you at the tournament." And with that he was gone.

Diana sat herself down next to Hideki. "You know that everyone was waiting for you and Rosalina to let them know you wanted to be with each other, right?"

"Really?"

"You really are naïve, aren't you Hideki?" She sighed and placed her hand gently on his shoulder. Hideki had seen glimpses of this side to Diana before but he'd never felt her let her guard down like this before. "I was just the same when I was younger. I tried to keep my relationship with David a secret from my parents for years. Easily the worst decision I ever made. I spent so much time worrying what other people would think that I didn't consider how that secrecy affected me. I should have told you both to be open about things months ago but you needed to figure it out yourselves. That's always the way with these things." As she spoke her foot started to draw circles before she stopped it and look at Hideki's eyes intently. "You both deserve to be happy, so be open and honest with everyone, ok? And don't let the others know this, but I expect you to win this thing, got it? Win it for Rosalina."

"I will."

"Good. See you in the finals, Hideki."

They laughed as they stood up and began to make their way to the opening ceremony. Hideki was really appreciative of Diana's vote of confidence and while it did put the pressure on, it gave him a goal. He knew that ultimately nobody would care about the result. Nobody would see him as weak or a failure if he didn't win, but he badly wanted to win. It would prove to himself how much he'd grown and improved since he'd arrived in Ryushima. There was also the thought in the back of his mind that suggested a victory would mean the people would see him as worthy of the love of their princess. It was a matter of pride and he believed he could win.

At the brief opening ceremony, Hideki could see the other sixty-three warriors that were to participate. There were some hulking brutes and there were some skinny folk, there were maces and clubs and broadswords and claymores and glaives and scythes and chakrams and more, it was truly going to be a diverse competition. Five matches. That's all he needed to get through. Five people stood between him and that victory. He grinned at Rosalina who was sitting in one of the stands and she grinned back. He was going to do this and nothing was going to stop him.

Chapter 14
You Will Know Our Names

Looking at the way the tournament that was set up, Hideki realised that should both Arthur and David win their matches he would have to face them both in order to reach the finals where he would in all probability face Diana. He had understood the possibility but he had hoped for Arthur and David to be in the other half of the tournament so he only needed to face one of his friends. Clearly, he was going to have to face all of them. The only positives he could really find were that at least this tournament would definitely be a true test of his abilities and he wouldn't have to face Rosalina in battle.

The first match of the day was Diana versus a knight who went by the name of Jason. Despite the heat he was dressed entirely in black and wielded an odd-looking sabre. Diana surveyed the man as best she could in the moments before the battle began and noticed a weakness in his stance. He seemed to shift on his feet with an intense nervous energy that would have unnerved most, but Diana was more curious than anything. When the signal was given, he sprang towards her. Diana only had seconds to deflect the sabre before the knight was upon her. He gripped her wrist and attempted to fling her over his shoulder. Thankfully, she'd dug her heels into the dirt and so she didn't budge when he pulled. With a cloud of dust, her foot collided with his back and he let go of her wrist. He frantically spun around and began slashing at her with the sabre but his frustration allowed Diana to dodge the blows effortlessly and respond with her own vicious flurry. In only a few moments she had gained the upper hand and so she to toy with her prey. A quick evasion from her led to an even quicker slash at his heels to send him stumbling. Then with military precision, Diana kicked him hard in the back and sent him flying across the arena.

"I'd heard about men falling head over heels for me, but I never knew it would be quite so literal." She winked at David who was on the side-lines before running towards her opponent. As he struggled to pick himself up, he glared at her furiously. Diana bent down to his level with a sardonic smile. "Now stay down." She brought the hilt of her rapier down on his head and he was knocked out. Righting herself, Diana dusted her hands off and strode over to David as her victory was announced. There were cheers from the crowd and it was quite evident that it came from a place of pride and awe. Her opponent was carried off and quickly healed before the tournament could continue.

Hideki's first battle went by with little upset as his foe caved under the pressure of the occasion. It only took a few firm slashes to the chest and his opponent gave up as he couldn't match Hideki's skills and was painfully aware of it.

David's battle flew by just as quickly. Hideki had never really seen David battle before and wanted to get a better grasp of his combat style, so it didn't help that David's fight ended up being so short. Before he had too much time to dwell on what lay ahead, it was time for Arthur's first fight.

Arthur stood tentatively in the arena, shuffling nervously on his feet. His opponent loomed large in front of him; a great hulking giant covered head to toe in vermillion armour. Arthur gripped his halberd tightly in preparation for the challenge that awaited. Why did he always end up getting screwed over by life? He tried to put on his show of bravery but in the face of this hulking behemoth his courage had all but vanished. He could see the look of worry on David's face and the firm encouragement on Diana's but neither did much to allay his fears. How was someone so small meant to defeat someone so large, even if they did have magic on their side?

The signal was given and the match began. Before Arthur had time to move, the brute swatted him to the ground. The wind was thoroughly knocked out of him and Arthur struggled to pick himself back up. Under his breath he muttered a healing spell and immediately felt a bit stronger. The giant charged towards him again and though Arthur tried to side-step out of the way, he was grabbed by the giant and flung into the air. Before he landed, Arthur stabbed his halberd into the ground, spinning around the pole, and used the momentum to kick the giant in the face. He silently swore in his head as the brute wrapped his arms around Arthur's legs and brought him down hard on the ground. It was a miracle Arthur's neck wasn't broken but he managed to scramble away and make some distance between them.

Frustration was the flavour of the day as Arthur tried to get a few pot-shots at the giant. "*MALPRG!*" Fiery darts leapt forth from his halberd and bombarded the brute, but he merely shook them off. "*CORAXO!*" A thunderbolt struck the giant in his chest, but he laughed and cracked his knuckles. "*GIXYAX!*" The ground beneath them shook violently. There were cries from the stands as they felt the repercussions of the attack. Safety precautions had been taken with the arena, setting up a similar barrier that surrounded the training grounds, but even it could not prevent the effects of an earthquake. The giant seemed to lose his balance for a second and Arthur chose this as his moment to attack. He lunged forwards and viciously swung his halberd towards the brute's side. This ultimately failed too, as the giant caught the halberd and used it to slam Arthur once more to the ground.

This time, instead of allowing Arthur to escape, the giant caught him and pinned him to the floor. An evil glint shot through his eyes as he began to pummel Arthur's face. The pain was immense and Arthur could feel the blood gushing from his head as each punch came. He tried to get the brute off of him but wasn't strong enough.

"ARTHUR!" The panicked roar of David cut through the pain and Arthur became aware of a commotion on the sidelines. The normally cool David was frantically trying to break his way into the battlefield to come to Arthur's rescue but was being restrained by some officiants. "Call off the fight! CALL OFF THE FIGHT!" Arthur could hear something from the king that sounded like an order to stop the match. The brute paused ominously. Then he lifted Arthur up by the scruff of his neck and flung him once more to the ground. The memory of his Vardr entered his head. She could save him. But then the embarrassment set in. He didn't need her to rescue him. He had to be a man and do it himself. He needed to prove that he was strong enough to live up to his brother, to live up to Diana, to live up to what Hideki had managed to achieve in the past year. He couldn't cope with the embarrassment of everyone seeing his Vardr. He would sooner die than let that happen.

As he struggled to his knees he could just about hear the voice of Diana cutting through the ringing in his ears. "Call forth Gloriana, you idiot! You are not any less of a man because she's your Vardr!" He clutched his head and recoiled at the mottled sticky mess he could feel. He looked up and saw the giant menacingly coming over to him. Guards had now entered the arena and were rushing to protect him.

The giant kicked Arthur over and placed his foot on his head. "Nobody move or the kid gets it." The guards stopped in their place and cries of horror surged through the audience.

She really was his only hope. He silently swore, biting his lip as he exhaled deeply. He had no other choice. He gripped his halberd with what little strength he had and clawed deep inside himself to find the mana he needed. Then, he shouted as loudly as he could, "*CACACOM OD FIFALZ QTING, EXENTASER TOHCOTH, GLORIANA!*"

One of the guards took one step forward and the giant raised his foot in preparation of crushing Arthur's skull. He was too busy focusing on the guard to notice Arthur's halberd glowing with an emerald hue. He failed to see the tiny ball of light that leapt forth, leaving a cascading flow of sparkling petals in its wake. As the sparks touched the ground, flowers sprouted forth and began to bloom. The giant in a fit of rage brutally brought his foot down. To his surprise he did not hear the exploding squelch of a human skull. Looking down the giant was baffled at the sight of large peony blocking his foot.

"No one is allowed to harm young Master Arthur!" The giant tried to force the peony down but it exploded and knocked him over onto his back. A small silhouette appeared above him and flew in close to his face. "You will pay for what you've done to young Master Arthur!" A tiny winged woman hovered mere inches from his eyes. Large intricately patterned golden wings held her aloft, buffeting her flowery dress. Her fiery red hair seemed to glisten under the sun and matched the brightness of the daisies, dandelions, and daffodils of which her dress was composed. The giant was about to burst out laughing when the faerie queen, Gloriana, summoned forth a large rue flower and aimed it squarely at his skull. A fantastical beam of energy burst forth from the flower and the brute's expression changed from madness to terror. Gloriana started circling the brute before raising her hands to the sky. The ground rumbled before a mighty oak thrust upwards through the earth into the brute and launched him into the air. With a quick gesture vines sprouted forth from the oak and began to wrap their way around the giant until only his head was visible. A rapid pirouette summoned a lotus flower and with a furious jab, the giant was flung into it. The lotus flower closed up and a muffled scream could be heard. Gloriana gently floated down and tapped the flower. It opened and the giant was presented to the guards, restrained and unconscious.

In her fury, Gloriana had almost forgotten about Arthur's injuries and she quickly returned to his side. David, Diana, Hideki, and Rosalina had already forced their way to him and Rosalina was in the middle of using a healing circle on him. The faerie queen sighed with relief now that Arthur was safe and she perched gently on a floating elderflower that she had called forth.

Arthur looked at his Vardr and tears welled up in his eyes. "Th-" He tried to push the words out but he struggled due to the shock of what had just happened.

"I believe the term you're looking for, young Master Arthur, is thank you."

As the wound on his head began to stitch itself back together thanks to Rosalina's magic, Arthur finally managed to say it. "Thank you, Gloriana."

David hugged him tightly. "Don't you ever do that to me again, d'ya hear?" Arthur nodded slightly. David loosened his hold a little before punching Arthur in the arm.

"Oi, what the hell was that for?"

"For being a massive idiot."

"You should've called on Gloriana sooner. You knew you were in danger and yet you staunchly refused to use your trump card." Diana tutted her displeasure, but it was clear that even she was hugely relieved that Arthur's wounds hadn't been fatal. "Gloriana is your Vardr. She is the most suitable guardian for you. She's every bit of your kind heart personified. So what if she's a faerie? That doesn't make you any less of a man, Arthur."

The tears that had been welling up burst and Arthur began to weep. "But Hideki gets a huge dragon, Rosalina gets a phoenix, you get Selene, and David has Ziz. They're all so awesome and I've got —" He looked at Gloriana and his sobs grew louder. "I'm sorry..."

"And damn right you should be," Rosalina butted in. "You do realise that you can understand the true essence of a person by their Vardr? Gloriana is small, yes, but she's brave and compassionate; capable of overcoming any hardship in the face of uncertainty. You may not like to think it, but in your

129

heart of hearts, that's you, Arthur. You put on your attempt at confident machismo, but that's not you and never has been. You don't have to be a stereotypical warrior to be respected, you've just got to be you. Isn't that right, Hideki?"

Arthur looked up at Hideki and saw his friend's smiling face. "She's right, you know. I for one have always thought more of you when you're just being yourself. If Gloriana here is any indication of what you're capable of, then you should certainly have more faith in being you."

Through the blubbery snot, Arthur managed a laugh and another thank you. Gloriana left her floating elderflower and gently kissed him on the forehead. "You're in good hands, young Master Arthur. Listen to them. And next time, don't wait so long to call me. You know how much I love to get in on the action." With a delicate giggle she waved goodbye and vanished.

Chapter 15
Reach Out To The Truth

Arthur's battle saw the first day of the tournament come to a close. As the people returned home for the evening there was a general sense of unease. Where had this blood-thirsty individual come from and why was he so dead-set on causing grievous harm to his opponent? A large number questioned whether he had come from the same source as Rosalina's would-be assassins and that thought certainly played upon the minds of King Lee and Queen Sakura as they discussed how to proceed with the tournament.

The king furiously scratched at his beard as he tried to think. The queen looked on him with concern and placed a gentle hand on his shoulder. Thick lines of guilt furrowed King Lee's brow and he seemed almost defeated. "We're cursed, Sakura, we have to be. How else can you explain it all? Ever since the last festival these monsters have sought to destroy us whenever our guard is slightly down. And poor Arthur, he was almost..."

"You shouldn't blame yourself, Lee. Don't you remember the tournament the year before Rosalina was born? Your father let far worse than what we just witnessed slide. The poor man had to have his legs amputated because the mages' spells had very little effect. That man was quite literally cursed. Yes, you should have called for the match to end sooner, and you should definitely apologise to Arthur for that. But I suspect it would've had little impact on the outcome. That monster clearly wanted Arthur's head and nothing you could have done would have stopped him." The queen embraced him and pecked him on the cheek. "Perhaps the best solution is to cancel the tournament."

There was a glower of outrage from the king before he settled into quiet contemplation. "We cannot do that Sakura, and you know it. Tradition states that the tournament must go ahead or the Almighty Dragons will be displeased. I cannot be the first king to cause the ire of the dragons." He picked himself up and turned to his wife. "We will continue with the tournament. Show a front of solidarity. We cannot allow ourselves to be scared into submission by these monsters." He puffed up his chest slightly in an attempt at seeming heroic but immediately dropped the act when Queen Sakura began to laugh at him. "None of the other competitors seemed to be of the same mould as that brute, they fought with honour and integrity. If they fought their first battles like that, then there is no reason to believe that would change. But, if we could cast a spell over them all to prevent them launching any killing blows then perhaps we can rescue this tournament yet. Can a spell like that be performed?"

A sharp, shrill voice cut into the room. "I should hope so." Granny Bea followed shortly after and gave a sagely nod to them both. "I don't know why you never thought to introduce something like this sooner. I believe you'll need two spells to pull it off effectively. Fortify should cover the defensive side of things rather nicely. Unfortunately, it's protection will make everyone's weapons as worthless as mere blunt clubs, but it'd ultimately be safer in the long run. Then, if you slightly adjust the wording of Block, you should be able to eradicate any killing instincts. If you cast Fortify, Sakura, I'll handle the Block. We should be sorted in no time."

And so the plan was put into action when the tournament resumed the next morning. After the panic of the previous day it felt like everything was under control. The spells were cast and the remaining warriors were made fully aware of the consequences should they attempt to break the spells.

Despite being advised to drop out of the tournament after the events of the previous day, Arthur stubbornly claimed to be ready to battle. He'd spent most of the evening resting and performing healing spells on himself. He would not dishonour himself by dropping out. He'd already been forced to face the embarrassment of his beating, Gloriana, and sobbing in front of so many people. He was not about to let that be the memory people had of him for the next year. Unfortunately, his next opponent was Hideki. Arthur knew he had a technical advantage thanks to the length of his halberd, but Hideki had greater control over his mana. In this world filled with magic, frequently that extra finesse with mana made the difference. Still, he would face his friend standing proud and strong. If he was going to lose this fight, he was going to give Hideki a damn good one.

The two stood next to each other as some of the other battles took place. There was an awkward gentle banter between them as they waited for their fight but Arthur could tell that Hideki was currently feeling rather uncomfortable. When their turn came, Arthur made a point of saying "Don't hold back" as they walked into the arena. He wasn't sure whether it would make a difference, but he hoped it would.

Hideki was nervously tapping the pommel of his sword as he waited for the signal to be given. He knew this fight was probably going to come eventually but he really wished it hadn't come so soon after the incident the other day. He was already uncomfortable at the prospect of seriously fighting his best friend but he felt even worse when he'd seen the lengths to which Arthur would suffer for his pride. The conflict raged inside him as time ticked on and he willed the moment to never come. He wasn't sure whether he could do this anymore.

And there was the signal. Arthur lunged toward Hideki with the spike of his halberd. Hideki managed to block it by the skin of his teeth. With frightening speed, Arthur swung the halberd around so as to flank Hideki's sword but this too was blocked. Due to the length of the pole Arthur was in very little danger for the time being. As the halberd sliced through the air, Hideki couldn't draw near. Every time he tried to make a move closer, the halberd would come soaring round at which point he had to block.

"Come on Hideki, is that the best you got?" Arthur taunted. He quickly retracted the halberd through his hands and shouted "*MALPRG!*" The fiery darts shot forth from the weapon leaving smoky trails through the air.

"*ZLIDA!*" The burst of water leapt from Hideki's sword and dowsed the fireballs before they could get much further.

Arthur fired spell after spell at Hideki, but rather than attempting to mount a counter-attack, Hideki just blocked them with whatever spell necessary. The frustration of this choice was evident on Arthur's face. "I said 'Don't hold back.'"

As Hideki defused another spell he said, "I don't want to hurt you, Arthur. Not after…"

Arthur flinched. "You'll hurt me more if you don't give it your all." His eyes narrowed as he readied his halberd for an all-out assault. "I refuse to win or lose without a challenge. Now get your arse in gear and let's see which of us is the better warrior. Got it?"

Arthur's eyes lit up with determination and Hideki could see how much this meant to him. "You're on."

"Good."

With that, they charged into close combat. Their weapons clinked and clanged as they collided in the frenzy. Neither would give an inch as they slashed at one another. Arthur was the first to land a decent blow, grazing Hideki's arm as he thrust past Hideki's sword. The slice left a mark but didn't draw any blood. They both glanced at it in amazement before frantically re-engaging. The confidence that the spells the queen and Granny Bea had cast were definitely still working made them fight even more vigorously.

As their fight continued, they both began to loosen up and enjoy themselves. The audience began to cheer as more and more successful blows landed. Arthur and Hideki were roused by the cheering and tried to further pick up the pace. They swung and blocked faster and faster to the point where the weapons looked almost like a blur. It was a pace neither of them could sustain for long but they would never admit that.

Hideki decided to try and break the stalemate to prevent himself from tiring out. With a rapid spin Hideki kicked out Arthur's feet from under him and dropped him to the floor. A roar of applause shot through the audience as they thought the battle was coming to a close. Holding his sword close to Arthur's chest, Hideki, through much huffing and puffing, said, "Are you done yet, Arthur?"

Through his own wheezing, Arthur sputtered out, "Not a chance, mate." He batted the sword away with his halberd and used the pole of it to get himself off the ground. He grandstanded a bit to the audience, largely to hide his tiredness. "It's not over until it's over."

Hideki chuckled at this as they stared each other down. "Thank you, Captain Obvious."

"Oh, ha, ha, very funny."

The two took another few seconds to catch their breath before trying to pull off a finishing blow. They were both clearly exhausted and one decisive blow would almost certainly bring the battle to a close.

Hideki decided to go on the offensive first. He drew back from Arthur as he readied his sword and then began to charge with a roar of "*AVAVAGO!*"

Arthur realised what Hideki was going for and so followed suit. He pointed his halberd in front of him and charged, shouting "*LALPIRGAH!*" as he ran.

Their weapons glowed crimson and a brilliant white before releasing almighty beams of lightning and fire. As they got closer, the beams collided in a magnificent explosion. When the sparks and the smoke had begun to settle, the two beams remained locked in combat. Hideki and Arthur had stopped running and were doing everything in their power to overpower the other's beam. The audience were on the edge of their seats.

As the struggle raged, Arthur could feel his mana getting closer and closer to its limits. He didn't have enough energy to win. He knew that and he suspected Hideki knew that. The only thing that could be done now was to give Hideki some sort of signal that he was done without letting on anything to the audience. Over the thunderous crackle of the warring beams, Arthur yelled, "I guess this makes us rivals, mate! We're so evenly matched and everything!"

Hideki was confused for a moment. "But, how can we be rivals if we're friends?"

"People do it all the time! Now, shall we see who's stronger?" Arthur said with an exasperated wink.

And now Hideki knew what Arthur meant. Drawing on some of his deepest mana reserves, Hideki sent a surge a power rushing through his sword and into the beam. It doubled in size and began to quickly engulf Arthur's. Arthur tried to fight back as best he could, but he really didn't have any mana left to safely use. The beam of lightning zapped about the flames and struck Arthur square in the chest. He landed harshly on the ground and just lay there. Hideki walked up to him and pointed his sword over Arthur. "Are you done, Arthur?"

Arthur opened his eyes and laughed. "Yeah, I'm done. Congrats, mate."

Hideki was announced victorious and he quickly helped Arthur to his feet. As the two left the battlefield, they couldn't help but smile. Before they reached the other contestants, Hideki quietly said to Arthur, "You did yourself proud out there, Arthur."

"Thank you, Hideki. You did yourself proud too."

Chapter 16
The Arrow Was Shot

After a few more fights, the day was done and the tournament had reached the end of its second round. The next day the third round took place but it was largely uneventful. While the audience had begun to grow weary of the combat, they knew it was going to be a particularly interesting final day. In the morning there would be the semi-finals: Hideki vs David and Diana vs one of the other royal knights. In the afternoon, the finals would take place. The result of Diana's battle was a foregone conclusion by this point, but everyone was fascinated at how Hideki and David's battle would go. If Hideki won, it would be a battle between student and teacher; if David won, it would be a battle between lovers. Either result would lead to a truly interesting encounter and that was the thought that allowed them to get excited at the prospect of another day of fighting.

At dinner that night, the Riders of the Light were huddled together in between an almighty throng of knights trying to speak to them. The knights desperately wanted to know how everyone was so powerful. Diana forthrightly pronounced, "Hard work, endless training, and natural talent. Now would everyone leave us alone. Three of us have very important battles tomorrow and we could rather do with the peace and quiet." The knights paid her no attention and continued asking questions and trying to cosy up to them.

The normally unflappable David looked from a frustrated Diana to the knights around the room and angrily rose from his seat. Letting loose a bellow unlike anything Hideki had ever heard before, David yelled out, "Captain Diana told you all to leave us be. Either follow her orders or pay the consequences."

The knights cowered slightly as David's voice sliced through the din. It took only a slight twitch of his eyebrow and they all scarpered as far away as possible. Hideki couldn't help but be impressed. "How did you do that?"

The anger in David's face dissipated faster than it had appeared and his genial amused look returned. "You've just got to know which buttons to press. Plus, everyone runs scared when the calm ones lose their temper. And anyway, nobody ignores my Di."

"'Your' Di, eh David?" came Diana's unimpressed but ultimately thankful jibe.

With a cheeky wink, he said, "You know what I mean, Di."

And with that she smiled and said, "I know."

Arthur cut through their loving gaze by deciding now was the best time to ask who he was supposed to root for tomorrow. "So, what the hell am I meant to do? Obviously I want you to win, David, since you're my brother and all. But then, Hideki's my best friend and he kind of owes me after beating me. But then, if one of you gets into the finals, I should also be rooting for you Diana. You lot really do know how to make things difficult, don't you?"

"Well, why can't you just root for everyone?" Hideki asked.

"Because that would just be boring and you can't sit on the fence when it comes to these things. Where's the fun in that?"

"I'll never forgive you if you don't root for me, little brother." David said rather sarcastically.

"Well, if you're going to be like that, I'm rooting for Hideki."

David laughed. "Oh really now. Well I'm just going to have to pull out all the stops now, won't I?"

And so they continued on until they went to bed. When they finally awoke and made their way to the arena, the mood was still one of jollity but it was tinged by the tension of what was about to take place. Only two people stood between Hideki and the title of champion, David and what was most likely to be Diana. As David and Hideki walked onto the battlefield, Hideki tried to think of all the times he'd seen David actually fight in the hope of finding some weaknesses. He realised this tournament was basically the only time he'd seen David in actual combat, and those matches had all ended before Hideki could really get a feel for David's style. He knew that David's skills with a bow and his mana arrows were unparalleled but very little else. In that respect, Hideki realised that to stand a decent chance at defeating David, he would have to try entering close combat in order to prevent David from using his bow. How successful he could be in achieving that was a different matter altogether.

"How the hell am I meant to fight you when you've got a face on you like that?"

Hideki hadn't realised that his brow had been particularly furrowed in thought and immediately felt somewhat embarrassed. Still, he suspected this was an attempt to put him off and he wasn't having any of it. He shot back with, "Well, can you blame me when I have to fight a face like yours?"

"Ouch, Hideki, that hurts me so deeply." David's voice was dripping with sarcasm as he spoke. "I'll have to make you pay for that one."

The signal was given and David immediately drew his bow, firing a blast of energy at Hideki. It was quickly batted aside, but David followed up with two more in quick succession gradually moving father back as he fired. Even though these were dodged, David had given himself a considerable amount of distance from Hideki. "Good luck getting anywhere close now."

Hideki raced through the options available to him. He could just charge headfirst towards David slicing through any arrow fired, but that was rather risky and pretty foolish. The arena was too open to flank. He could try using magic to distract David. He could spiral around too, getting closer and closer until the gap was finally removed. That was it. Spinning his sword around his head, Hideki yelled, "*MALPRG!*" The flaming balls blasted forth from the blade in every direction before beginning to home in on David. As David began to shoot them all down, Hideki shouted, "*Let my feet fly, Haste!*" His sword glowed yellow before rushing the mana down through his body. Immediately, Hideki felt quicker and began to run towards David. As soon as the fireballs in front of him were obliterated, Hideki changed his angle and began to circle in. Scraping his sword against the ground, Hideki yelled, "*GIXYAX!*"

David felt the rumbling earth beneath his feet and couldn't help from laughing. "You think an earthquake is going to make me lose my footing? Don't be ridiculous." He knew his tactic of keeping Hideki away couldn't last forever. He aimed his bow towards the sky and with a wild grin said, "*ARPHE PERIPSOL, VPAAH ZONG, ZIZ!*" He shot a glistering golden arrow into the sky and jumped as high as he could. The arrow collided with a magic circle which had appeared in the air, shattering it. Through the broken shards came a winged beast that quickly swooped down and plucked David up with its talons. "I never introduced you to my Vardr, did I, Hideki? Let's shift this battle up a gear or two, shall we? Ziz, do your thing!"

Hideki stared in awe as Ziz spread its tremendous wings out. The wings blocked the sun from Hideki's view in such a way that it appeared gilded by a crisp golden band. Its bird-like head twitched this way and that, and it let forth a rousing melodic screech from its beak. Its body was like that of a feathered lion and it gently swayed beneath the massive wings. While Hideki was awestruck, David manoeuvred himself up onto Ziz's back and the mighty Vardr eagerly eyed up Hideki. It beat its wings and sent mini tornadoes towards him.

There was little else that could be done. Hideki faced down the tornadoes and aimed his sword at them. "*YOLCAM CORAXO, ARPHE, TELOCVOVIM MJÖLNIR!*" In a burst of lightning, Mjölnir landed and the force dissipated the oncoming threat.

The dragon spotted Ziz and raised a quizzical eye. "It's been a long time since we last fought, Ziz." Ziz screeched mockingly in response, so Mjölnir quickly nodded his head at Hideki. "Get on, Master Hideki." Hideki did as he was told and made his way to a spot between the spikes on the back of Mjölnir's neck. As soon as he was safely in place, Mjölnir leapt into the air towards Ziz.

In seconds, David was firing arrows imbued with mana by a cry of "*CAOSG*" towards Mjölnir and Hideki. Ziz beat its almighty wings and sent the arrows hurtling with even greater force. A beam of lightning shot forth from Mjölnir's open maw and disintegrated the arrows before they had a chance to get too close. Slicing through the air, the beam clipped one of Ziz's wings. The creature squealed horrifically. Its head twitched angrily and in shaking its body, David dropped from its back. Before David could fall too far, Ziz somersaulted through the air and he landed right back where he started. Now that David was more firmly seated, Ziz charged towards Mjölnir.

The two collided in a flurry of slashes. Mjölnir's claws violently cut through Ziz's feathers while Ziz's talons ripped away Mjölnir's scales. Their wings frantically beat against the air to stay air-born. There was ultimately very little that Hideki or David could do but cling on for dear life. Ziz managed to get its beak close to Mjölnir's ear and screeched so loudly that the dragon began to descend rapidly. Drawing back, Ziz sent forth two enormous tornadoes and squawked victoriously.

"Mjölnir! Pull up! Mjölnir!"

As the ground drew closer and closer, it seemed like a crash was imminent. As the world spiralled around him, Hideki wondered whether this was the end of the match. He couldn't take on Ziz and David by himself. And even if he could, he could be knocked unconscious by the force of the landing. "MJÖLNIR!" This final cry snapped the dragon out of its state of confusion. He righted himself, opening his wings out wide. His feet touched the floor and he used the momentum to run and launch himself back into the air. Batting his wings furiously, he cancelled out the tornadoes before they could reach him.

"Ziz, I'm gonna need you to go all out, bud."

The winged beast nodded and spread its wings out as far as they would go. A shiver ran through its body and razor sharp feathers began to shoot forth from its wings. They positioned themselves in an increasingly large circle around Ziz. When the horde of feathers seemed to pepper the sky, David readied an arrow and yelled, "FIRE!" As his arrow flew, the feathers followed, raining down on the incoming Mjölnir and Hideki.

"Is there anything you can do, Mjölnir?"

"I've got something in mind, Master Hideki." The dragon let loose another beam of lightning but as he flew he began to roll through the air and gently circle his head. The lightning cleared swathes of the feathers but it couldn't prevent at least some of them from slicing across Mjölnir's body. Thankfully, the roll gave him just enough opportunity to share out the damage so he didn't receive any truly serious injuries. Putting more force into the lightning beam, he targeted Ziz.

With a guttural roar the beam doubled in size and struck Ziz in the chest. The winged beast squealed in pain, glared at Mjölnir and vanished in a sprinkling of feathers. David looked at the empty air beneath him and cursed loudly. He quickly began to plummet but Mjölnir grabbed him in his claws.

They all landed and Hideki clambered down to find David laughing his head off on the floor. "What's so funny, David?"

David picked himself up and dusted himself down. "I've not had that much fun in a fight in a very long time. We need to go all out in training more often." He patted Mjölnir's leg, "And thanks for bringing me down gently big guy."

The mighty dragon nodded graciously. "It was a pleasure, Master David."

"I think we can call that game, set, and match, don't you ref?" David said, signalling his surrender. "Try as I might, I'm pooped. I suppose that's what you get for whipping out your trump card a little too early, eh?" He returned his bow to its holder and held out his hand to Hideki. "Well done, mate. Now you just got Di to defeat. I for one, certainly do not envy you one bit."

Chapter 17
In Charm And Allure

The result of the second match of the day was Diana's inevitable victory. Everyone expected it and there were cheers all around when she won. Now the focus shifted to the final battle and the anticipation crackled in the air. They all knew what Diana was capable of and most of them had been in awe of what Hideki had managed to achieve so far. This final was to be one that they would never forget and they couldn't wait.

There was a brief moment of respite while everyone broke for lunch to rest and recuperate. It was in this moment that Rosalina managed to speak to Hideki for what felt like the first time since the tournament began. A rush of pride and love brimmed on her lips. "You're doing so well, Hideki! I mean, I knew you could do it all along but you're really actually doing it! I knew I made the right choice on that night last year. I knew it."

Hideki blushed. He sheepishly started to look away but stopped himself and looked straight into her eyes. "I'm going to win for you. I promise."

She kissed him gently and embraced him. "Thank you, but don't do it for me. Do it for yourself. Prove to my father that he was right to put his faith in you. Prove to David and

Arthur that they lost to the best man. Prove to Diana that all of her teaching has paid off. But most of all, prove to yourself that you deserve everything you've earned. I believe in you and I'll be rooting for you no matter what."

"Thank you, Rose."

Rosalina jumped back and eyed Hideki up curiously. "Rose?" She rolled the name around in her mouth. "Rose… You know, I've never had a nickname before, Hideki." She thought about it a little more deeply. "Rose… You know what? I like it."

Her charming smile made Hideki grin. He always felt so happy when she was around and her coming to see him now gave him even more drive to win this tournament. Nothing was going to stop him now, not even the frightening force that was Diana.

All too soon afterwards, Hideki was stood opposite Diana on the battlefield. The roar of the audience echoed around them as the excitement rose. Banners flew and trumpets sounded to signal this greatest of battles. Before the match could begin, King Lee needed to make an announcement. "People of Ryushima, these two warriors have fought valiantly to reach this final bout. Whatever the outcome, both should be applauded for their skill and courage in the face of many powerful opponents. The victor of this match will be crowned the Champion and will be forever remembered in the annals of history as this year's strongest warrior." From his throne in the stands, he pointed a ceremonial staff at Diana and Hideki. "Captain Diana, Hideki, are you ready?"

They both nodded.

"Then let the battle commence!" He aimed the staff towards the sky and with a quiet utterance of "*LALPON*," he launched a firework into the air.

With the deafening bang of the firework, Diana and Hideki lunged towards each. Their blades glided past each other's bodies as they dodged out of the way. At such close proximity they appeared as a whirl of limbs and metal. Feet whipped around in lightning fast kicks, rapier clashed with sword as each tried to disarm the other, and in the middle of it all, Hideki could only focus on the slightly sadistic gleam in Diana's eye. As she efficiently countered any move he made, he could see an overwhelming sense of pride and excitement lighting up her face. She wasn't going to make this easy.

He thought back to that first sparring match he'd ever had with Diana. She hadn't used any buffing or debuffing spells yet like she had back then. This was his chance to get an early advantage. He leapt away from Diana and uttered, "*Let my feet fly, Haste!*" His movement speed drastically increased and he flung himself back towards Diana with a furious flurry of blows.

As she blocked every single strike, she laughed. "Trying to use my own tactics against me, eh? That's not going to get you very far, is it now, Hideki?" In between blocking one swipe and sliding under the next, Diana quickly drew her lightning bolt and used Haste on herself.

Before Hideki had time to counteract the spell, Diana was upon him with her own vicious assault. He had to use all the athletic prowess he'd attained to defend himself from her attacks and struggled to see how he was meant to overcome his teacher. She knew every move he could possibly make. She'd taught him those moves; she knew exactly how to counter them. His only hope was Mjölnir. Surely even Diana would struggle with a beast of Mjölnir's size? It was worth a shot either way. "*YOLCAM CORAXO, ARPHE, TELOCVOVIM MJÖLNIR!*" With that pounding clap of thunder he'd come to find such comfort in, Hideki summoned forth the mighty dragon. Mjölnir let forth a tremendous roar that shook the ground around him and he eyed up Diana in preparation of an attack.

"Do you really think that is going to intimidate me?" Diana said calmly. In a swift arc, she drew the crescent moon and yelled, "*PAMPHICA, A GRAA ORS, YOLCAM VANGEM, SELENE!*" In seconds, the Amazonian figure of Selene stood proudly in front of Diana. "Selene, if you would, I've got a dragon problem you need to deal with."

Selene nodded. She soared through the air towards Mjölnir, nails extended. As Mjölnir span around to whip her with his tail, she effortlessly glided over the top of it and soundly kicked the dragon in the face. The force of the kick was so strong that Mjölnir was sent rolling across the ground. Licking her lips in excitement, Selene went in for the kill. With a spiky pirouette she began slashing her way around Mjölnir's body, cutting through his scales and drawing blood.

"MJÖLNIR!" Hideki started to run towards his Vardr. He couldn't watch this happen.

"Your fight is with me, Hideki." Diana stopped him from going any further. "Mjölnir's going to have to fight for himself now."

As Diana swung at Hideki, Mjölnir finally managed to land a blow on Selene. In her attempt to cut through one of his legs, he'd managed to bash her away with his tail. Free of her onslaught, he began his own assault. Rapid bolts of lightning burst from his mouth towards Selene, kicking up dust wherever they went. And with that, the fight kicked up a gear. As Diana and Hideki were locked in a furious sword fight, the two Vardr unleashed increasingly stronger attacks on each other. Moonrock boulders came down like meteors, torrents of lightning rained down onto the battlefield, and the previously sunny day grew dark and overcast. The audience could feel the tense power in the atmosphere and it was terrifyingly exciting. These two mighty spirits in their combat were affecting the very weather around them. Neither would budge despite being struck by such forceful blows.

It became impossible to know what to focus on as everything seemed to explode around the battlefield. It was becoming clear to Hideki that he was running out of mana, and he could tell from Diana's grimace that she was nearly at her limits too. He needed a miracle to finish this battle now.

Through the din, he could hear Rosalina yelling, "I believe in you Hideki!"

He could do this. He knew he could. He just needed that extra bit of power. He could feel something stir deep within him. It was the same feeling he'd felt when he first summoned Mjölnir. It was like a comforting swell of encouragement to fight. Words began to form in his mind and he knew what he must do. With every inch of his being he shouted the words, "*YOLCAM GIXYAX, MICAOLI VOVINA DS MACOM CAOSG, JÖRMUNGANDR!*"

Diana jumped back in shock as she heard the spell. "That can't be… That's impossible…"

Hideki's sword glowed a deep muddy brown before a ball of light charged into the earth beneath him. The ground shook violently and started to crack nearby. Then, as a gigantic hole opened up, the light re-appeared, extending in a serpentine spiral. Spikes burst forth down the length of the light's back and a long scaly face began to take shape. The beast opened its huge maw to reveal rows of serrated teeth and a hissing forked tongue. It let forth a deafening roar and the light crumbled from around it to reveal earthy brown scales highlighted by a mossy green underbelly. Four clawed feet hung down as the beast floated in the air.

153

"How can you summon two? That shouldn't be…"
That was the first time Hideki had ever heard Diana's voice
quaver. The shock and awe was evident from her face alone.
Hideki was also particularly surprised as he had thought he was
nearly out of mana, but with the appearance of this new mighty
dragon he could feel a renewed sense of energy coursing
through his veins. This was the miracle he needed to win.

"Jörmungandr?" Hideki asked what he assumed was the
dragon's name. It nodded. "Please help out Mjölnir!" It looked
over at the two Vardrs fighting and nodded once more. It set
off towards Selene, looping through the onslaught of attacks.
When it reached her, though she tried to defend herself,
Jörmungandr tightly wrapped its body around her. It squeezed
tightly and with a silent scream, Selene vanished from the
battlefield. It turned its attention back to Hideki and after a
brief flight, swished its tail around him. One roar later and
Hideki felt a surge of energy.

Jörmungandr's tail flicked away and Hideki launched
himself at Diana. She valiantly blocked the first few blows but
she was quickly disarmed. The shock had caused her
concentration to lapse and she was already quite tired from the
fight so far. She looked into Hideki's eyes and could see how
much this meant to him. She could probably fight for another
minute or so, but she knew that with Selene gone she couldn't
come out of this victorious. She held up her hands and uttered

the words she'd hoped she would never have to say in battle: "I'm done, you win."

There was silence as the dust settled and the audience began to comprehend what had just happened. Captain Diana, the champion of this tournament for years, had lost. Hideki had won. Then, the cheering and applause exploded through the stands.

Hideki just stared between his sword, his two Vardr, and Diana's now smiling face. He couldn't believe it. He'd actually done it. He'd really actually done it.

CHAPTER 18
MIRACLES

The next few moments were a blur. Hideki remembered Rosalina scrambling down through the stands and rushing across the battlefield towards him. She'd flung her arms around him and kept saying how amazing he was. He remembered the look on Diana's face, it had been like that of a mother bursting with pride. He remembered David and Arthur joining in on the congratulations and being swept up in the excited crowd that followed. Everything else, however, just melded together into a jubilant haze. Copious amounts of confetti rained down on the battlefield as the trumpets rang out triumphantly. He was the eye of the storm in this chaotic typhoon of joy. Time seemed to slow around him and he just felt overwhelmed by it all. The love and praise flooding around him was more than he could have ever wished for. His mind wandered back to Helheim. If only everyone there could see him now. Would they finally understand that he wasn't cursed? He wasn't an abomination that shouldn't exist. He was capable of making something of himself. He could achieve whatever he set out to do. He never wanted to forget this feeling.

As the day turned to night, the celebrations continued. A gigantic procession filled with banners wormed its way back to the palace's courtyard where a grand feast had been laid out for all. People sat down wherever they could and tucked into to all manner of wonderful foods. The delightful aroma of slow-roasted meats of all shapes and sizes wafted into the dusky evening sky. Everything was beautifully tender and none wished to leave a single morsel un-eaten. People laughed and cheered and ate and ate and ate. Pageants of desserts followed soon after with humongous decorated cakes designed to look like the Almighty Dragons or the palace or the entire kingdom of Ryushima itself. Even now, Hideki was amazed at the spectacle the people of Ryushima were capable of producing. It was all so fantastical in its extravagance.

When all were done, King Lee rose from his seat, glass in hand. "Ladies and gentlemen, I would like to propose a toast to our new champion, Hideki." He turned to face Hideki who was sat a few seats down with Rosalina and the Riders of the Light. "When Hideki arrived here last year, I was initially rather unsure about him. After all, who magically turns up in the middle of a courtyard covered in all manner of injuries? But my lovely daughter took pity on him and made it her duty to ensure he recovered. Anything could have happened. But when he came to, he proved himself to be a kind and capable soul. When he first met me, I challenged him to a duel and he accepted. Ever since, he has been an asset to our kingdom and a true companion to Rosalina. I couldn't ask for any more in a knight. You have done yourself proud, Hideki. Congratulations." He raised his glass into the air, "To Hideki!"

The people responded with an ecstatic, "To Hideki!"

"And before I bid you all a good night, I believe one of my knights has an announcement he'd like to make."

Eyes darted around the courtyard to see who would make a move. After what seemed like an unbearable pause, David stood up and moved over to Diana.

Diana stared at him with a confusion of emotions plastering her face. Embarrassment, excitement, worry, happiness; they all coursed through her as she waited for him to speak.

In as overblown a manner as possible, David began with, "My darling Diana…"

"David, what are you…?"

With more sincerity, he continued, "Do you remember the day we first met?"

"Yes, you said I had a butterface and ran off laughing like a lunatic," she said with a wry smile.

"And then you chased me down and punched me in the face. And then you immediately apologised and asked me rather calmly why I had been such a meanie."

"Did I really say meanie?"

"Yes, Di, we were seven. Anyway, I said it was because you were really pretty and that my friends had dared me to ask you out but I chickened out at the last minute. And then you laughed too. Strangely enough, we've been friends ever since. Every day you put up with my sarcastic remarks and witty jokes —"

Diana interjected, cocking her eyebrow. "Witty?"

"Oh just let me have that one, Di," he said waving the remark away with his hand. "You put up with me every day and I'd be lying if I said you weren't the love of my life. Just think, if I hadn't been a cheeky little blighter when I was a kid, I would never have had the guts to speak to a girl like you. And if you hadn't punched me in the face, I might have turned out to be a bigger jerk than I am today."

Through a slight giggle, Diana asked, "Are you going to get to the point, David?"

"I'm getting there, geez. I'm trying to be romantic here!"

"By reminding me about the day you called me ugly?"

"You know what I mean, Di." He ran his hand through his hair as he tried to relax a bit. "You made me the person I am today, Di. We just fit, y'know? I make you laugh, you make me smile. We're a damn good partnership, you and I. And that's why I want to spend the rest of my life with you, Di."

"David, are you doing what I think you're doing?"

"What do you think I'm doing?"

"Asking me to marry you?"

With a face of gleeful mockery, David said, "No, I was going to ask you if you wanted to get a cat." He grinned further

159

when he saw Diana's knowingly raised eyebrow. "Of course I'm asking you to marry me you beautiful fool." He went down on one knee and produced a ring from his pocket. Glistening tiny feathers looped round like angel wings to form the band and perched atop the wings was a shining diamond enclosed in an ornate silver crescent moon. He held it out to Diana as he said, "Will you marry me, Diana?"

She stared deeply into those big hazel eyes and smiled. Then she punched him in the arm. "That's for pulling this on me in front of everyone." She punched him again. "That's for being too cheeky for your own good." She punched him a third time. "And that one's to really pay you back for calling me a butterface when we were seven." They both laughed and then she continued. "And on the subject of marrying you, I yield under great persuasion; and partly to save your life, because I know you couldn't survive without me."

"Is that a yes?"

"Of course it's a yes, you idiot!"

The two kissed. David put the ring on Diana's finger and stood up to kiss her once more. Cheers rang out across the courtyard at the news. They all loved a good wedding, and what with Rosalina and Hideki being together too, the people were just over the moon with giddy discussions of romance. If they hadn't already been filled with a unified warmth in their hearts, they certainly were now. Beneath the now rising moon, everything felt right with the world. Lovers were coming together and hope for the future was in the air. If only everything could stay like this for all eternity, they'd all live happily ever after like the fairy tales of old. But, as they continued their celebrations, they were unaware that all too soon their lives would be changed forever and there was nothing anyone could do to stop it.

CHAPTER 19
MEANING OF BIRTH

The next day passed with more raucous festivities. Small events were set up all around the palace grounds but only one thing was on everyone's mind: the Dragons' Fight. For all the fun and games, this was what the festival was really about. They celebrated the event, but it was always a tense few hours leading up to the fight itself. By the end of the day, they would have the omen for how the next year would go. Would Fai win and bring prosperity to Ryushima, would their crops flourish and their trade prove fruitful or would Yami win and bring torment with famine, natural disasters, and more? It was impossible to predict and that's what made people worry. They couldn't intervene in the fight as it would go against hundreds of years of tradition. But, they couldn't escape the inevitable consequences of the battle's result. None knew why the fight had such an impact on their way of life, but there was little they could do to prevent it. So, while they waited for the time to come, they tried to push it to the back of their minds as they partied.

As the sun began to drift towards the horizon, everyone made their way to the arena. Over time, the arena had become the location of the tournament, but initially it had been designed to play host to this specific annual combat. It was placed far enough away from the palace to ensure it remained safe from any harm, and powerful magical barriers protected the people from the dragons' fierce attacks.

Once everyone was seated, King Lee rose from his throne to speak. "We are here once more. I pray this fight goes as we wish it to." With a deep breath he raised his sword to the sky and called out, "*ARPHE MICAOLI VOVIN, EF OD PASDAES VANGEM!*"

A swirling vortex began to form in the sky. Bright blasts of fiery light seemed to crackle through the dark cloud. The atmosphere around the arena grew dense and heavy as a powerful force began to batter the arena. The vortex drew in more and more of the clouds around it, speeding up until it was all a blur. Then with a cacophonous roar, two hulking dragons burst through the vortex shattering it into puffs of smoke. They were locked in vicious combat, clawing and biting at each other as they plummeted to the earth like a chaotic black and white meteor. They crashed into the ground in a shower of fire and mud and only then did they separate.

The two dragons were majestic if terrifying creatures to behold. Hideki had grown used to the sight of dragons thanks to Mjölnir, but his Vardr was like a baby in comparison to these colossi. From Rosalina's explanation, Hideki knew that the white dragon was Fai and the black dragon was Yami, but even with that knowledge he was shocked at how truly diametrically opposed the two were. While Fai's body was truly white as snow with the kindest blue eyes, Yami was pitch black with eyes of burning crimson. Where Fai was of a slender build with elegant golden markings working their way down the length of his body, Yami was incredibly bulky with sharp blood red lines running down his underbelly. Then there were the wings. Fai's scales gradually morphed into feathers as they cascaded down the wings, creating a soft almost angelic quality. Yami's wings were bat-like with deep purple webbing stretching between spiked protruding bones. As Fai looked at his brother with concerned determination, Yami bubbled over with sheer rage.

The two dragons circled each other for a moment and Rosalina caught sight of Yami's eyes. The flaming irises, the slit pupil, the horrifying stare. She'd known she knew those eyes from somewhere. As she looked into them the realisation dawned on her. It was Yami. Yami was the one who'd prevented Hideki from awaking. It was Yami she'd made a deal with. She started to worm her way into her seat as she began to expect the worst. Hideki was going to find out what she'd done. She knew he would. What would he think of her after that? What would her parents think of her? What would the people think of her? She had to tell him the truth. It had to come from her. There was no other way.

As the dragons charged at each other and began clawing and biting away, Rosalina made her way over to Hideki. "I need to speak with you."

"Does it need to be now?"

"Yes… It does."

Hideki looked at her and saw how worried she appeared. "What's the matter?"

"There's something I need to tell you…"

"You can tell me anything, Rose."

"Well… I… I did something terrible when you…" Her breathing quickened as she started to panic. "I'm sorry… I'm so, so sorry…"

Gently grasping her shoulders, Hideki tried to sound reassuring as he asked, "What did you do?"

"I –" She was cut off before she could say anything more as the audience began to scream. The two whipped their attention back to the battle and saw Yami bludgeoning Fai to within an inch of his life with his mace-like tail. "No, no, no, no… This can't be happening. They fight but they always stop when one is defeated. Yami's going to kill Fai but there's nothing we can do to stop them! We can't get involved!"

Hideki frantically searched the faces of the crowd for any sign of action, but all he saw was horrified resignation. They all saw this as a bad omen; a sign that their lives would be hell forever. He shouted at King Lee, "Your Majesty, stop the fight!"

With a heavy heart, all the king could respond with was a saddened, "I can't…"

Hideki looked back at the dragons. Fai was howling out in pain, looking frantically from his brother to the crowd in what was clearly a plea for help. Hideki couldn't let this continue. It wasn't right. He knew the people of Ryushima might hate him for it, that Rosalina might hate him for it, but he couldn't sit by and watch such a beautiful creature be so brutally murdered. He quickly kissed Rosalina and said, "I love you, Rose," before running down towards the battleground.

He was halfway to the dragons before Rosalina had time to respond. She began to panic even more. What was he doing? She saw him leap over the railing yelling "STOP!" He was trying to be a hero and stop the fight. Why was he doing it? She knew why. This fight wasn't right and she knew it. They all knew it wasn't right but centuries-old traditions are difficult to break. Her next thought was one she couldn't stomach. What if Hideki died? She couldn't bear that. She started to run after Hideki, but before she could get any further down the stairs she felt the protective hands of her mother on her shoulders. They couldn't intervene, it was not their place to. She tried to wrestle free, but her mother's grip remained firm.

"STOP!"

Hideki's cries finally caught the attention of Yami. The dragon turned his attention away from Fai and slowly moved towards Hideki. There was a moment of silence before the dragon let loose the most terrible roar of laughter. It was a cacophonous blast of screeching booms which rocked Hideki.

Hideki began to shake in fear but he stood his ground and from a distance nobody could see quite how scared he was. Yami licked his lips as his eyes flickered with demonic glee. "I never thought I'd have to deal with you again little boy." His monstrous head rose and scanned through the crowd. "How's that princess of yours doing? She seemed awfully fond of you despite knowing nothing about you." Yami picked her out and laughed once more. "And she was so willing to bargain with your memories to wake you up too."

"What do you mean?" Hideki's hand tightened around the hilt of his sword.

"Little Princess Rosalina made a bargain with me. An important piece of your memory for you to wake up. That gaping hole that you can never seem to fill? You can blame your princess for that one."

"That can't be true... She'd never..." Hideki froze. She wouldn't do that to him, surely. She couldn't be the reason. He looked up at her in the stands and saw her crumple to the floor in tears. So it was true. "That doesn't matter now." As he said those words he wasn't sure whether he meant them. He loved Rosalina dearly, but this betrayal hurt deeply. Could he ever forgive her? His heart pounded as he thought everything through. Could he? Could he? Could he? Yes. "She did what she thought she had to do. If she hadn't made that bargain, then I wouldn't be here now. I wouldn't have found my home or fallen in love."

167

Yami's expression snapped from one of malicious glee to murderous fury. "Well then, I will just have to do what I should have done the second you entered this world." The dragon leant back on his haunches and leapt towards Hideki.

Before Yami could reach Hideki, he was slammed out of the air by Fai who had managed to recover some of his strength. "Leave the boy out of this Yami. I am your opponent." His rich voice was like that of a wise kindly grandfather, gravelly with the gravitas of age. His eyes glowed for a moment and his wounds began to heal.

In a furious rage, Yami soared into the sky circling the arena before raining fire down upon the stands. The barrier held for the moment, but the people cowered as the flames encompassed the area around them. Then, Yami rammed into the barrier at full speed and it dissipated entirely. Those without magical abilities began to scream and desperately tried to run away as Yami looped back around and brought more fire down upon them. The cloth covering the structure fizzled away and the wooden roof began to blacken and crack as the flames wrapped their tendrils around it. Everyone who could pointed their weapons to the roof and let out a cry of "*ZUMVI.*" A torrent of water surged into the air to dowse the flames and though it worked, everyone was all but blinded by the steam and smoke. They coughed and spluttered as Yami swooped in, mace-like tail at the ready to bludgeon and skewer as many people as possible.

Fai had recovered enough of his strength to fly and he slammed into Yami once more, knocking him off course and sending the pair careening into the nearby gardens. While the two dragons were momentarily occupied, Queen Sakura whirled her staff around and cried out, "*I call upon the winds to remove this threat, Disperse!*" The smoke was swept away and everyone could catch their breaths.

Granny Bea chose now to launch a spell of her own with a firm tap of her own staff and a call of, "*I call upon the heavens, heed my call, defend the innocent with your almighty light, Holy Barrier!*" As she spoke, all could feel the great power that emanated from her voice. Her staff glowed a wonderful yellow before sending forth an enormous barrier that enclosed the area around the stands.

"Everyone, stay calm. Everything is going to be alright." King Lee tried his best to make the people feel safe but considering even he didn't believe the words coming out of his mouth, he doubted anybody else would.

A tremendous explosion drew everyone's eyes to the gardens where they saw the two dragons bursting from the inferno. As they sped into the sky, they peeled away from each other, and spiralled up to try and gain the advantage. They let forth bursts of fire that span around them as their aerial ballet continued. Eyes aglow they both launched tremendous fireballs from their gaping jaws which collided mid-air and sent embers skittering to the ground. One minute they'd draw close and be

169

tearing shreds off of each other, the next they'd return to their fraught chase until one caught up with the other. Then Yami decided to switch his focus back to the arena. He honed in on Hideki and charged through the air towards him.

It was in this moment that Hideki realised something. Rosalina and Granny Bea were always talking of inevitability. That the choices you make in life lead to inevitable conclusions. His involvement in this fight was inevitable from the moment he was born. The choices he had made, the people he had met, the person he had become, they had all led up to this.

He ran towards the oncoming dragon, sword at the ready. As Yami swooped down, Hideki used his momentum to slide under the dragon and cut through some of the scales on its underbelly. Then Yami landed and whipped his tail around. Steam was rolling furiously from his nostrils and a fiery foam was dripping from his maw. In his anger his aim was a little off and this allowed Hideki to jump onto his tail. As soon as Yami felt the weight of the young man on his body he began to violently smash his tail to the ground but Hideki would not let go. In a fit of rage, the dragon flicked his tail towards the air and this was just enough to dislodge Hideki's grasp and send him flying towards the stands.

As Hideki had been fighting, Rosalina had been preparing herself. When Yami flicked Hideki her way, Rosalina twirled her staff and launched a series of spells. "*I call upon the heavens, heed my call and shield him with your light, Great Barrier! Light,*

shine down upon this soul and restore him to full health, Healing Circle!
Spirits of the Raging Fire, lend him your strength, Keenness!' In quick
succession, her staff glowed yellow, green, and red, and the
light of the mana rapidly flew towards Hideki. He soon felt
some of his energy return and his strength increase and he
could see the ripple of the protective barrier around him.

He struck the barrier protecting the stands and gently
rolled down to the ground. He picked himself up and readied
himself to attack. Yami stampeded towards him despite being
hammered by fireballs coming from Fai. Upon reaching Hideki,
Yami swiped him into the air and attempted to crush him
between his clawed feet but he couldn't get through the barrier.
Hideki used this moment to swing around one of Yami's claws,
run along his arm and clutched on to one of the spikes running
down Yami's back.

Yami roared in frustration and leapt into the air. Fai
tried to follow but Yami brought his tail thudding into Fai's
skull, sending the white dragon plummeting back down. As
Yami flew higher and higher, Hideki started to gradually make
his way up the dragon's spine towards its head. As he climbed,
the dragon soared ever higher, breaking through the clouds.
The air around them grew thin and Hideki knew he needed to
end this soon or he would pass out from the lack of oxygen.
The wind battered him as he struggled upwards, but he refused
to give in. He was not going to die like this. Finally, he reached
Yami's head. Clutching on to a nearby spike, Hideki raised his

sword and tried to stab through the dragon's skull. It got caught in one of the scales but Hideki couldn't push any further. He was struggling to breathe and the air around him was particularly frosty. Up above he could see the stars shining in their multitudes. It was so beautiful up here. He brought his attention back to Yami and started to pry the scale away. It finally ripped off and fluttered away in the breeze. With the scale gone, Hideki raised his sword once more and with all the strength he could muster he rammed it through the fleshy skin and straight into the beast's brain.

Yami's crimson red eyes went black and his wings stopped beating. The two seemed to hang in that moment for what felt like a lifetime before Yami's head dipped forward and they started to nosedive. All Hideki could do was hold on. He was too short of breath to perform any spells, so even if he wanted to summon Mjölnir, he couldn't. As they fell, Hideki knew that there was no way he could survive a crash landing from this height. So, this was it? Well, at least the people of Ryushima would no longer have their bad omen. They were free from that curse. But what about Rosalina and everyone he'd come to care about so much? They'd be heartbroken. As Hideki closed his eyes for what he thought would be the last time, one thought stuck in his head, *I'm sorry I couldn't stay any longer, I'll love you all always.*

CHAPTER 20
MIRRORS

One minute Hideki was plummeting down to earth, the next he seemed to slow down. He opened his eyes and looked up to see the brilliant white scales of Fai. With every inch of his being, Fai was clutching on to Yami's corpse and slowly but surely easing the descent. His wings beat furiously to maintain control, but though the speed was dramatically lessened, Fai didn't have enough strength left in him to change their course. As the ground drew closer towards them, Hideki realised where they were going to land: the palace courtyard. He could see swathes of people fleeing to the palace but as soon as they spotted the falling dragons they froze. It was impossible to tell whether Hideki had been victorious or not from where they stood and that thought terrified them.

Soon enough, Hideki and the dragons crashed into the courtyard, kicking up stones and rocks as they ground to a halt. Yami's head struck the great tree, Yggdrasil, and a deep fissure formed in its crystalline trunk. Fai let go and gently landed on the ground. As the dust settled, Hideki felt relief as his feet hit the stones of the courtyard. He'd survived.

Fai solemnly nuzzled Yami's neck as he said, "Brother, I hope you are now at peace. She can no longer harm you." Tears fell from the dragon's eyes as his grief started to take hold. "I'm so sorry it had to come to this. No matter how violently we opposed each other, you always were and always will be my brother."

A crowd began to form in the courtyard as the people finally realised that the fight was over. They gazed at the broken stonework, the cracked Yggdrasil, and the silent corpse of Yami. There was a swell of happiness which quickly descended into melancholy. They had worshipped this once great creature and here it lay, dead.

"I will make sure She pays for everything She did to us, don't you worry, Yami."

"Who's this She you keep mentioning?" Hideki asked.

Fai's head lifted with great effort to face Hideki. "The Fallen Goddess. She snatched our beloved mother from us. She drove Yami to madness with dark, malevolent thoughts. She pitted us against one another and has enjoyed every second. She was behind that assassination attempt on Princess Rosalina's life. She was the reason you came here, Hideki. She's been planning something for a very long time and finally it is coming to fruition. It is inevitable." His eyelids flickered and he groaned in pain. His perfect white sheen began to dim. "As is my own death."

"But we can heal you!" Hideki said. Rosalina finally reached the front of the crowd and nodded fervently. Hideki continued, "And even if our spells aren't enough, we can try something else, anything else!"

"I could attempt to use Resurrection. I don't know the incantation or the principles of it, but we could figure it out!" Rosalina began to twirl her staff but the mighty dragon wearily shook its head.

"It is not meant to be, young princess. No spell or medicine you could concoct would ail an old broken heart. Yami and I were born together, and so shall we die. From the moment of our birth our destinies were intertwined. We are like mirrors; two opposing sides of the same whole. There can be no darkness without light, but there cannot be light without darkness. The balance of the universe must remain in equilibrium or it will implode upon itself. And so, my heart must give way and I shall join my brother on the other side."

"I'm sorry. I am so, so sorry." Hideki said. This was mostly directed at Fai, but it was in part aimed at the people of Ryushima. "I didn't intend for it to end like this. I thought that if I got involved I could bring happiness to everyone. I'd never have–"

"It is as it was always meant to be, Hideki." Fai's wings drooped as more of his energy drained away. "I have one request before I fade away. Give the Fallen Goddess hell for me. You found the strength to defeat my brother, so maybe you could prevent the destruction she seeks to cause. It's a lot to ask of one so young, but ask I must."

"I'll do it."

The dragon seemed surprised at the speed with which Hideki responded, but as weariness ran through him he knew he didn't have much longer. "It'll be an arduous quest and one from which you may never return, but what will be will be. To reach the Fallen Goddess you must return to the cursed plains of Helheim." This shook Hideki's resolve for a moment but he quickly overcame his panic. "The Fallen Goddess can be found at the ends of the universe in the Temple of Creation, not far Wonder's End."

Hideki's tears fell anew. "That's where I grew up…"

The dragon weakly nodded. "And that is where you must return."

"But how do I get back to Helheim without dying?"

"The burning ashes of the great Yggdrasil. Use it as our funeral pyre and you will open up a gateway there. Yggdrasil is a world tree. It connects the worlds together and the only way to cross through is to destroy the tree."

If the people of Ryushima hadn't been crying and in shock before, they were now. In one night they were losing the creatures they revered as gods and the tree that was the symbol of their unity. It felt as if their perfect little world was shattering around them and there was nothing that anyone could do to put it back together again.

Hideki spotted King Lee and with the King's sorrowful nod, he knew what he had to do. "I will do everything in my power to complete your task."

Fai's breathing slowed, his almighty chest heaving as he tried to keep going for just a few moments longer. "I... have... something... of... yours... to... return... Place... your... hands... on my... scales..."

Hideki did as he was told. As his hands touched the smooth surface of the dragon's scales, he saw Fai's eyes glow a magnificent blue and felt a surge of mana run through his body. The hole in his heart seemed to vanish instantaneously. He remembered everything. "Yuuko."

With a relieved final exhalation, Fai closed his eyes and fell into the eternal sleep of death.

Chapter 21
Intertwined

Nobody said a word. The courtyard was silent apart from the gentle tinkling of Yggdrasil. People stared dumbfounded. People bit back heaving sobs. Nobody could believe what had happened. They looked from the corpse of Yami to the corpse of Fai and with one tremendous wail came the major outpouring of grief. Their gods were dead. They were inconsolable. Where could they go from here? The future was no longer set and that terrified them.

"Ok. That is enough." Granny Bea's voice echoed around the courtyard as she forcefully strode to Fai's rigid body and whipped around to face the people. Their wails diminished to a quiet blubbering. "We can weep and mourn in time. I'm certain that we will grieve for a long while yet, but now we need to be strong." But how could they? Their guiding lights had been snuffed out. "We have faced turmoil before. We have lost loved ones. We have struggled through illnesses. And yet we are still here. We have lived and we will continue to live. Time beats on, never stopping, never failing. We are but a grain of sand amongst the storm. But what can one grain of sand do? Nothing? Everything? That is the question we must answer. As Fai departed he left us with the knowledge that some greater evil wishes to end us. We cannot allow that. We are a kingdom of hope. And so we shall forge onwards. We shall face the challenges that assail us and we will be victorious."

Some began to wipe their eyes and find a kernel of resolution deep within their souls. Others began to burn with anger. "He's the cause of it all." "He killed the Almighty Dragons!" "If he hadn't turned up this would never have happened." Shouts broke out around the crowd and a few of the larger men started to move ominously towards Hideki.

The King was about to speak up but Granny Bea slammed her staff to the ground with an almighty bang that silenced the men. "If you harm that young man you will have to answer to the most powerful warriors in Ryushima. Don't test us." One of the men took a step forward and Granny Bea shot him a brutal glare. "Before he died Fai asked Hideki to defeat this Fallen Goddess. I understand your anger, but we must treat the wishes of our departed god with the respect they deserve." She ushered Hideki towards her and gently placed her hand on his shoulder. "You did what you thought was right and we will make it out of this ok. But you've accepted a terrible quest and I can only pray for your success. Still, I have faith in you. King Lee has faith in you. Queen Sakura has faith in you. Princess Rosalina has faith in you. Your fellow Riders have faith in you. And the people of Ryushima have faith in you. Don't you?" She stared down the crowd who seemed hesitant to respond. "Don't you?" Her glare made them acquiesce and they yelled their affirmation. "Good." She looked over to the king. "Now, Lee, I think we have some arrangements to make."

King Lee nodded. "If everyone would head home and rest, we can begin to tackle the issues that face us in the morning. As it stands, we are all emotionally drained right now and that is not healthy for any of us. I will speak to you all tomorrow and then we can begin to think about the path we all shall walk."

There was a murmur of agreement and people filed out of the courtyard towards their homes. It was a sombre walk that felt more like a funeral procession, but they knew that none of them were in a fit state to do anything productive right now.

As the courtyard emptied, only the royal family and the royal guard remained. The torn bunting lay limply on the cold ground and seemed to epitomise how they all felt: destroyed and empty. After Granny Bea's passionate speech a few moments ago, she suddenly looked a lot older as lines of worry wrinkled her face. Her confidence had clearly been an act, but it had done its job. She gently embraced Hideki, whispering to him, "It'll all be ok, you'll see." Then she hobbled off with the king and queen to discuss what they were to do.

Hideki and Rosalina hurried themselves inside and quickly sequestered themselves in Rosalina's room. They couldn't bear to face anybody right now. As soon as the door was shut they crumbled.

"What the hell have I done? I've ruined everything!"

"You haven't done anything, Hideki! I'm the one who ruined everything. I made that stupid deal with Yami and now look where it's got us. I'm sorry, I'm so, so, sorry."

They fell into each other's arms and dropped to the floor. Despite the tears they felt comfort in their intimacy. Gradually their breathing slowed and the panic subsided.

"You did what you had to do, Rose. I forgive you."

"But I bargained your memory away –"

"For my life. I would not be here if it weren't for that decision, Rose. We both know that."

"I'm so sorry Hideki."

He gently wiped the tears from her eyes. "Remember what you told me all those months ago? Stop apologising." He smiled at her and she laughed.

"You cheeky little..." Rosalina moved herself into a slightly more comfortable position on the carpet and finally shook off the shock she'd been feeling. "So, what now?"

Hideki thought carefully for a moment. Rosalina was right. What now? He'd made a promise to the Almighty Fai to give that Fallen Goddess hell. He had to follow through with it, no matter the price he might have to pay. "I have to return to Helheim. I accepted this quest and so it is my duty to fulfil it." As he spoke he began to see the ramifications of this decision. "I may never return, but that is the price I must pay."

"You can't think like that, I won't let you."

His response was a solemn resigned smile. "I have to do it alone, and if this Fallen Goddess is as powerful as I suspect she is then I may not even succeed. But I have to try."

This seemed to spark an idea in Rosalina's mind. "You don't have to do it alone." Her eyes lit up as she looked into Hideki's inquisitive stare. "I'm coming with you."

"You most certainly are not. You're the princess of Ryushima! The people need you! And anyway, there's no way your father will allow it."

"You made a promise to my father to protect me at all costs. That means you are not allowed to abandon me here. If I go with you then not only will our chances of victory improve, but you'll also be able to keep that promise. So, I'm going with you and that's all I have to say on the matter." She gave him a grin that signalled check and mate.

He answered with a droll eye roll and a muttering of, "Well I guess I can't argue with that," which ultimately brought Rosalina's fist colliding with his arm.

They laughed and in spite of all the sadness it felt good. It felt like the first step in moving forward. After a brief moment of silent reflection, Rosalina remembered what Hideki had said before Fai passed away. "Yuuko. Who were they?"

"She's the woman that Yami forcefully removed from my memory. After Ramona left, I was just a husk, but then I met Yuuko. She arrived from out of the blue and took me under her wing. She taught me everything I know: how to fight with a sword, how to use magic, all of it. She was so kind to me. And when I said I had to escape from Helheim, she understood and let me do what I had to do. I wonder what happened to her after I left and why Yami chose to remove her from my memory. Maybe I can find out when I return to Helheim."

"She sounds like a lovely woman, Hideki, I'm glad you finally remember her."

"So am I."

There was a hasty rapping of the door followed by the entrance of Diana, David, and Arthur. Diana let loose a sigh of relief when she saw that Hideki and Rosalina were ok. "Why on earth did you go running off like that? We were all worried about you! Don't ever do that again!"

"Hideki and I just needed to get away from everyone, Diana. We needed to just talk through some things on our own."

"You guys sure know how to create drama, don't you?" David quipped. "Half the palace is freaking out and the other half is frantically trying to clear up, it's pandemonium out there. A bit daft when you think about it, there's nothing any of them can do until tomorrow so there's no point in worrying until then, y'know?"

Arthur nodded in agreement. "That's probably the best way to get through this. It's still a shock though. If it weren't happening in my kingdom and featuring my best friends it would probably be sorta gripping entertainment. A bit melodramatic and cheesy, sure, but either way…" After plonking himself down next to Hideki, he elbowed him in the ribs saying, "I'd certainly read about it."

"Be quiet Arthur," Diana snapped. "So, Hideki, what's your plan for that quest?"

"Well, initially I was going to go by myself…" This was met with concern and it looked as though all three were about to leap down his throat. "But then Rosalina said that she was coming with me and that I had no say in the matter. So, I suppose the plan is for the two of us to go it alone. I don't want to see any more pain and suffering than is necessary."

"You two will not be going by yourselves." Diana's voice was firm and commanding as she said this. She looked down at Arthur and then up to David and they both smiled knowingly at her. "We're coming with you."

"We're a team, Hideki." Arthur said, clapping Hideki on the back. "We've not had the chance to fight alongside one another, but we're a team nonetheless, and if we can kick arse by ourselves we can definitely do it together."

Grappling Arthur and Hideki into headlocks, David added, "And better yet, we're a family and that means that nobody gets left behind or forgotten. We look after our own no matter the circumstances. Ain't that right, Di?"

"It is indeed."

Rosalina lifted herself up from the floor, "So, we're all decided? We'll head to Helheim and grant Fai's dying wish." The others drew towards her and she placed her hand in the middle of the little circle that had formed. "We're in this together until the end."

David immediately placed his hand on Rosalina's. "I'm in, come what may."

Diana followed suit. "Of course."

Arthur added his hand to the mix. "I can't let you guys have all the fun now can I? That just wouldn't be fair."

Hideki felt a swell of emotion in his chest which he quickly had to quieten down before it overwhelmed him. "Thank you everyone." He placed his hand on top of everyone else's. "I guess this means we're stuck with each other until the end, right?"

"You're damn right!" Arthur cheered a little too loudly.

Rosalina giggled and made her pronouncement. "We are all agreed then. Together we shall defeat this Fallen Goddess whatever the cost. We will protect and defend each other until our final breath and our fates shall be forever intertwined. Let us fight onward to a brighter tomorrow."

With a valiant cheer they raised their hands. They started to laugh at the pomp of it all and came in for a group hug. This was their little family and they were going to do everything in their power to complete this quest.

CHAPTER 22
TO BE FEARLESS

"We can't send an entire army with him, Lee, there'd be no one left to protect the kingdom! I know you're trying your best here but that isn't a solution that's going to help anyone." Queen Sakura exhaled harshly as she tried to expunge her frustration. She looked with exasperation at her husband and Granny Bea who returned their own irritated gazes. They'd been debating how best to proceed for the better part of three hours and had gotten nowhere; one minute they thought they were getting somewhere but soon enough they realised how useless that plan was and they were right back where they started.

"I honestly don't know what to do Sakura. We can't send Hideki off on his own, but we can't afford to risk anyone's life on a revenge quest. And even if we did ask anyone to join him, I can't see anybody putting their lives on the line anyway." He slumped down in his chair and scratched away at his beard. "It's never simple, is it Mother?"

Granny Bea chuckled to herself before speaking, "That's life for you, Lee; one bloody thing after another." As her fingers impatiently rattled on her staff to some unknown tune, she stared at the door. Suddenly, she stopped. "Perhaps the decision is not ours to make."

"What's that supposed to mean?"

"It means that maybe someone else has already made the decision for you. We all make choices in our life that lead us down an inevitable path. Those choices make us who we are. We are changed by the people we meet, and there is no escaping that path we walk down." Granny Bea stood up and walked to the door just in time for a polite knocking to be heard. "There is only inevitability."

She opened the door to reveal Rosalina, Hideki, and the other Riders of the Light. Rosalina spoke out first. "Father, we need to speak with you about that quest."

With concern, King Lee ushered them all in and the door was firmly shut behind them. He guessed where this was going and he didn't like it one bit. "What did you wish to say?"

It took a few moments for Rosalina to pluck up the courage to say what she needed to. She'd been so certain earlier, but now as she stood before her father, mother, and grandmother, she didn't know whether she could go through with it at all. It'd break their hearts. But it had to be done. "We will accompany Hideki on his quest through Helheim." There it was. Out in the open. There was no turning back now.

The King raised his voice protectively but even though his fist slammed down on the arm of his chair he remained seated as if in defeat. "You most certainly will not."

"I most certainly will, Father." She clasped Hideki's hand for a bit of reassurance and continued on. "This Fallen

Goddess has killed our Almighty Dragons. She tried to have me assassinated. She clearly wants to create mayhem in Ryushima and we cannot let it stand. As a team, we have the best chance of defeating her. Hideki, Captain Diana, David, and Arthur are all incredibly adept warriors and I'm one of the best healing mages in the kingdom. Together, nothing can stand in our way."

"But you are all far too young. We cannot put such a burden on you and we cannot allow you to risk your lives. Rosalina, you are the heir to the throne. If you perished, the kingdom would be thrown even further into turmoil. If any of you died, Ryushima would lose some of its greatest hopes for the future." King Lee's fist clenched tighter and tighter as he spoke, desperately willing himself to persuade his daughter but he knew that look in her eyes. It was fierce and determined. It was the same look she'd given him when she'd taken Hideki into her care. This was her uncompromising position. Nothing he could do or say could change her mind.

Queen Sakura moved over to the king and gently rested her hand on his shoulder. She'd seen the look too and knew that there was no point in arguing. "If that is what you all choose, then while we disagree, we will support you every step of the way. Just make sure you return to us otherwise I'll force my way into Helheim and kill you myself, got it?"

This defused the tension in the room and everyone relaxed a little. Granny Bea leant in close to Rosalina and Hideki before whispering, "She'll have to beat me to it."

"You can't make it a race, Mother, otherwise I'm going to have to get in on the fun," quipped the King.

Granny Bea tapped her staff on the ground as she let out a jovial laugh. "Well, I'll be going there sooner or later, so I might as well make a trip of it before then. Do a bit of reconnaissance, find a lovely patch of land to build my dream home; that sort of thing." She clapped Hideki on the back as she said, "I know you said it was a barren wasteland and all that, but I'm sure I can spruce it up a little bit."

"Mother!"

"Well it's true. Death is inevitable for all things, it's just a case of understanding when one's time has come. And when it does come you must be fearless." She huddled the Riders and Rosalina together before loudly pronouncing, "You must now be fearless in the face of adversity. Give that Fallen Goddess the hell she deserves."

The king lifted his hand up to the queen's as he said, "So the decision is made. You will all go to Helheim. Now go and get some rest because in the morning preparations must begin."

And so they did. The palace became a hub of activity as every possible little thing was taken care of. The kitchens began cooking and baking food that would stay preserved for what they assumed to be long enough to complete the journey. The smithies and tailors began the intricate process of constructing new armoured outfits for the Riders and their princess, carefully weaving spells of protection into the metal and the fabric. All of the knights were brought together to train alongside the team to improve their co-operative battle skills and ensure they were ready for anything. The mages worked tirelessly every night to strengthen everyone's weapons, forcing spell after spell into them. When the people learned of the plan, they were understandably concerned but they all knew not to question such a decision. The king and queen would not put their daughter in such danger were they not sure it was the only course of action.

As the Riders and Rosalina trained, they were fuelled by an intense fiery passion which would not abate. They had to be the best they could possibly be. They needed to have perfect control of their mana. They brought forth their Vardr and pushed their endurance to its limit. Days turned to weeks. Rosalina pushed herself to master Restoration and started to find herself getting closer and closer to it. She was managing to shift mana to the others but only in tiny increments. It was frustrating work but she was improving. Hideki flung himself into every challenge with more verve than ever before, so much so that Diana had to have words. After about a month had passed, everything was ready. It was time for their quest to begin.

Chapter 23
Heaven's Mirror

The solemn air hung heavily over Ryushima as the final preparations for the dragons' funeral were made. Anxious mutterings fluttered to and fro as the people began to truly realise the enormity of what was about to take place; this was their final farewell to their gods and could very well be the last time they saw their beloved princess alive. The dragons' corpses had been lain so as to enclose Yggdrasil between them and side by side in their eternal sleep they looked at peace.

Hideki and the Riders descended from the palace bedecked in their magnificent new armour. Hideki was fitted in a new leather jerkin which was protected by interlocking leaves of a greenish metal which the mages were adamant nothing could break through, and his undershirt, though visibly unarmoured, was imbued with the strongest protective magic known in the kingdom. His dark brown trousers seemed to have the same interlocking leaves as the jerkin though these were hidden inside the fabric itself and seemed far lighter. He also had a new set of boots almost entirely encased in the greenish metal bar the leather cuff and the soles. His sword hung in its scabbard from a multi-pocketed belt and when he'd surveyed the outfit he almost laughed at how heroic it made him look. It was as if he was someone important, and considering he was in a relationship with the kingdom's princess and their current champion, he realised that right now he was someone important.

As they made their way to where the funeral procession would start, Hideki noticed that little had been done to Diana's or David's outfits bar merging their chest plates into the fabric of their flowing coats and making the shoulder plates and hip plates sit closer to the body and move with it. Hand in hand in their opposing red and white and green and black armour they looked like they should never work as a couple and yet they seemed stronger than ever. Arthur was, however, more armoured than before with a muddy yellow chest plate worked into his jerkin along with armour-plated gloves, a lighter closer-fitting version of the trousers Hideki was wearing and the same metallic boots though Arthur's were of the same muddy yellow as his jerkin.

Excitement and dread surrounded them as they walked. Hideki knew what to expect on the other side, but he didn't know exactly how he felt about having to return to Helheim. He also wasn't sure how the others would react to seeing such a desolate place after living in the opulence of Ryushima all their lives. Could they cope with it? Either way, they would have to. They'd all made a pact to follow through with this and there was no turning back.

Eventually they reached the start of the procession path where Rosalina and the rest of her family were waiting. When Hideki looked at her he couldn't get over how beautiful she was, even if her warm smile was replaced with a look of anxiety. In preparation for the journey a new dress had been made for her. Thousands of tiny blue scales wove their way around the bodice and sleeves, meshing like Hideki's leaves to form an impenetrable barrier, before gradually fading away down the length of the skirt which housed carefully embroidered renderings of the Almighty Fai and Yami on either side. She shifted nervously in her armoured boots, fiddling with a sapphire phoenix necklace which hung from her neck. The queen nestled Rosalina in her arms while both desperately tried to hide the tears in their eyes, but they both knew exactly what the other was doing. The king in his mourning regalia wore a notably grim expression as he tried to maintain a calm and composed exterior.

It seemed that only Granny Bea was capable of smiling. "Grieve as needs must, celebrate the lives that have been lost, pick yourself back up and continue on living. That's my mantra when it comes to these sorts of things." She stroked Rosalina's arm before subtly holding King Lee's hand. "Life and love is just like a cherry blossom. As the petals fall, you never truly know where they're going to end up. They collide with many other petals on their journey, but the unpredictable nature of life means they often must part. No matter what happens, it is always beautiful. The only way to stop those we love fading from our lives once they are gone is to remember them; to never leave them behind. Whatever happens from here on out, just remember that, Lee. You too Rosalina. Nobody gets left behind."

The people of Ryushima began to gather behind them to create a mighty procession. A lone violin softly sounded and everyone walked forward. The violin was soon joined by a plethora of other instruments from the band around it and as the people moved they were surrounded by the melancholy music. Everything else was silent. The overcast sky hung in the dew that rolled solemnly off the blades of grass beside the path on which they walked. A faint breeze caused some people to shiver as they fumbled in their pockets for handkerchiefs to dry their eyes. The procession slowly but surely made its way to the courtyard where everyone filed in and created a complete circle of grief around the two dragons and Yggdrasil.

As the music faded the king proclaimed, "Before we begin, I would like you all to partake in a moment of silence with me in honour of our departed gods." The people of Ryushima followed this order and bowed their heads and closed their eyes in a collective nod of respect and mourning for the dragons. When complete silence had descended and only the tinkle of Yggdrasil's leaves could be heard, so many thoughts rushed through the crowd. Why did this have to happen? What did this mean for Ryushima now? Was the princess going to survive the journey to Helheim? Would any of them? How long did anybody have left if even the Almighty Dragons, all-powerful creatures, were fated to die? Am I a bad person for being grateful we are free to choose our own future? How would I feel when this is for someone I care very deeply for? I just buried my father last month, can I cope with this funeral? Will it ever be possible to regain those idyllic years gone by?

Clink. Clink. Clink. Clink. The breeze ran through Yggdrasil's boughs and knocked loose a few emerald leaves which plummeted to the courtyard floor and shattered into dust. The sound caused people to open their eyes and quake at the imminent demise of the Great Tree. The king hushed the crowd as they began to mutter and readied himself to speak.

"People of Ryushima, today we lay to rest a piece of our history. The Almighty Dragons, Fai and Yami, have protected Ryushima for centuries, bringing with them both prosperity and turmoil. They were part of our identity, our kingdom's namesake, and now they have passed on into eternal slumber. Their passing comes as an awful surprise to us all but now is not the time for us to fall apart. Our kingdom has survived worse and will continue on, taking with us the memories and the knowledge our Almighty Dragons brought down to us. As our tears fall and we mourn the loss of these magnificent creatures, let us take inspiration from their will to fight. They were prepared to fight each other for what they believed in for so many years no matter how much pain they suffered, returning again and again to the battle. As the river of time ran on, Yami clearly became corrupted by a greater force and lost sight of who he truly was but in death we can remember him as he should have been. In death, we can avenge the wrongs done through him by holding steadfast to our ideals that Fai upheld for so long. Family. Trust. Love. As we bid farewell to our Almighty Dragons, we see my beloved daughter and the Riders of the Light set off on a journey to Helheim, the afterlife where Fai and Yami must now reside, to stay true to our champion Hideki's promise to Fai. This Fallen Goddess will suffer for the pain she has wrought and when we have had our revenge we shall head proudly into a future of hope and opportunity."

He paused to let the sentiment sink in but it did have another purpose, it put off what could be the last time he ever saw his daughter again. He waited, clinging on to the moment with every inch of his being, desperately wishing it never had to end but he knew that it must. The petal can't dance in the wind forever; it must always land somewhere. *"BRGDA NOTHOA PERIPSOL DOH."*

A ring of mages on the walls of the courtyard raised their staffs and yelled in unison, *"IALPIRGAH OIAD."* A stream of flames surged from the staffs, merging into an ever-closing circle which cast a burning orange glow on the ground beneath. When all of the streams had combined together, they rained down upon Yggdrasil and the two corpses in a swirling inferno of a pillar. As the pyre roared the tree began to react in a manner none had seen before; iridescent flowers bloomed into life across Yggdrasil, drawing in and exhaling a brilliant white light. Fai and Yami's scales brightened along with the flowers for a moment before they disintegrated from view. The ashes they left behind were picked up by the pillar of flame and Yggdrasil appeared to breathe them in through the flowers, emitting a stronger and stronger light. The mages held off on shooting more fire and the torrent of flames began to subside leaving the still glowing Yggdrasil seemingly unharmed.

The king looked in confusion at Granny Bea who merely shrugged in response. "How are they meant to –"

He was cut off as the flowers shot forth beams of that blinding light into the sky, briefly turning the tree into what appeared to be an almighty stag of pure light. The ground beneath them shook, rumbling as Yggdrasil's roots flexed beneath the courtyard's surface, booming as they dragged mana from deep within the earth's core to the tree's trunk. The crack that had formed when Fai and Yami crash-landed in the courtyard grew larger. An invisible force seemed to chip away at it, making it wider and wider until it began to take the shape of a door. Tiny symbols of angelic script pulsed across the surface forming words that no one could decipher. The light beams twisted down towards the door like weaving branches ushering a visitor into a dangerous wood, imbuing it with more mana from the sky above. Yggdrasil let forth a crystal-clear chime to signal that is was ready. It was time.

Chapter 24
The Opened Way

Queen Sakura softly pushed Rosalina's hair away from her eyes and in no more than a whisper said, "You look after yourself, sweetheart. I want you back safe and sound."

With a tremor in her voice, Rosalina responded with, "I will, Mother. I'll see you soon." They hugged each other tightly and refused to let go.

"I believe in you." King Lee said as he wrapped his arms around the two of them. After a brief pause to build up the courage he turned to Hideki and the other Riders, "I believe in all of you." He held his arms out further and ushered them towards the hug. They all dutifully obliged and were soon joined by Granny Bea who wasn't about to go unrepresented in this group embrace. "Do Ryushima proud and come back with your heads held high." He squeezed them all tightly with every ounce of love and compassion he had to offer and then he let them go. Goodbyes could only last so long, and the longer they lasted, the more they hurt. "Now go on, begin your quest." His confident voice faltered as the urge of paternal protection swelled within him, but with a deep breath he brought it back under control. "That's an order."

"I love you, Father."

"I love you too, my darling Rosalina."

Hideki gently held onto Rosalina's hand as she slowly walked away from her parents and grandmother. As they moved, Hideki shouted back to them, "Thank you so much for everything. I promise I'll keep her safe."

"You damn well better." Granny Bea yelled back. The King and Queen could only nod as they clung to each other for support.

They eventually reached the door and Hideki turned to face the crowd. "When I arrived here in Ryushima, I couldn't believe how beautiful it was. The way everything just beamed through vibrant colours and it was all overflowing with the joy of life. If there's one thing I want to achieve in my life, it's to make sure Ryushima stays this wonderful. I apologise profusely for the deaths of Yami and Fai, but I will do everything in my power to avenge them. And when I am finished, I'm going to come back and serve this kingdom however I can. We're all coming back." One by one he nodded at Rosalina, Diana, David, and Arthur; he saw their excitement, their worry, their pain, and their determination. He turned back towards the door and began to push it open.

It was cold and smooth to the touch as one would expect of a crystalline tree, but the mana coursing through it left Hideki's fingers with an odd tingling sensation. It was almost as if Yggdrasil was examining him, analysing every cell in his body, almost as if trying to figure out whether he was worthy of entry. The tree chimed again and the door shifted. Thin root-like grasping tendrils crawled out through the crack and reached out towards Hideki and the others, stretching further and further from the pitch-black tunnel which was appearing behind the door. The tendrils couldn't reach far enough so they resorted to swaying in and out of the inky abyss, writhing with an erratic rhythm.

Hideki held out his sword and calmly used "*IALPON*" to light a small flame at his sword's tip. He aimed it towards the tendrils and they shied away from the fire, but it did little to light the blackness that lay behind them.

"Well that's not terrifying in the slightest," said Arthur, "Do you remember anything like this when you made the journey here?"

"Not a thing. One minute I was in a temple in Helheim, the next I was here. I wasn't really in a fit state to be paying much attention."

"Fair enough." Arthur's eyes darted around nervously, "So, are we going then?"

Diana let out an aggravated huff and rolled her eyes in just the right position for Arthur to catch every last bit of sarcasm oozing from the glare and then without fear she strode past the tendrils and into the tunnel. As she strode in they could just make her out in the shadow but then she was gone. The only indication they had that she was still okay was when she called back to them, "Are you coming or what?"

After that they all followed her in to the point where no one could see a thing. The only sounds they could hear were their footsteps and breathing until Yggdrasil chimed once more and the door slammed shut behind them. "Well, this was a smart decision, wasn't it?" quipped David, who they all thought was at the back of the line though at this point it was impossible to tell. "No wonder you didn't remember anything about this, Hideki, it's boring as all hell. I for one will not be recommending this as a holiday destination when we get back home."

"David, are you sure now is really the time for jokes?" said Rosalina, still a little shaken after saying goodbye but trying to hide it from the others.

"Well, what else are we going to do? Trundle along this tunnel in silence until we reach the other side? Because that's going to be oh so fun."

"Well, maybe if we just keep talking to each other as we go then not only can we make this more bearable we can also make sure we don't lose anybody." Hideki said from somewhere.

"He's got you there Rosalina," came Diana's voice from way in front.

"And anyway, something interesting may happen when we least expect it," came Arthur's.

Almost as soon as he had said that their footsteps began sending glowing ripples through the floor, rolling out to what appeared to be the walls and falling back in on themselves. The ripples collided and spiralled together in a bluey-green dance that made them feel like they were walking on water despite the floor most definitely being solid. Arthur stretched out to touch one of the walls and it sparked into life at his fingertips; a plethora of luminous flowers bloomed in his wake before more wormed their way ahead of him and began looping round the tunnel in pulsing waves. In the floral light they could now see one another and their looks of baffled amusement.

"For once you putting your foot in it has proved useful, Arthur," David joked.

As the lightshow spurred them on they could hear a low beating hum like a heartbeat. Thump thump. Thump thump. Thump thump. The roof above them began to sparkle with thousands of tiny star-like lights which tinkled and chimed just like Yggdrasil had always done and glowing water streamers flowed down the walls as the sound of strings soared through around them.

"Do you feel that?" Rosalina asked. "There's so much mana in here... It's beautiful." She took a deep breath in and was greeted by a lovely pastoral aroma filling her nostrils. "Could Helheim have changed at all, Hideki? I can't imagine such a beautiful tunnel leading to somewhere so awful."

"It could have done, but I doubt it. Helheim was always filled with a lot of mana, more than I ever encountered in

Ryushima, but it was still so dead. The mana was there but it just hung lifelessly until you formed it into something." He gazed around the tunnel in amazement until a small memory in the back of his mind was unlocked. "Hershel and Claire used to tell me that Helheim was so wonderful before the life was drained from it. Perhaps this," he gestured at the floral pulse around them, "is what it used to be like."

"That would be lovely. Hopefully one day it'll look like this again."

The tunnel stretched on before them and they continued to walk, admiring the spectacle that surrounded them, talking about anything that came to mind, laughing at how insane this quest was, and just generally trying to keep away from the fact that they must be nearing Helheim and then they would see what the afterlife looked like. Hideki knew what was coming and was not thrilled to be returning but he knew that it was his duty to finish this quest. The floral pulsing got slower as they pressed on and the beautiful twinkling chimes faded as the stars began to go out. A cold breeze rushed through them when they saw light at the end of the tunnel; it did not feel welcoming in the slightest. They could still feel the mana around them but the magic was slowly dying the closer they got to that light. A sense of foreboding gripped them, they started to tremble, and then they were through the tunnel and out into the depressing reality of Helheim.

CHAPTER 25
THRESHOLD

The first thing that struck them was how tranquil it felt. Through the dull greys and browns of the dilapidated ruins they could see a vast desolate wasteland that stretched all the way to the horizon, but the silence around them and the gentle breeze carefully brushing through the murky weeds created an odd sense of resigned peace. The open doors they'd walked through slammed shut behind them and a few stones crumbled away from the wall around it, dislodging clumps of moss as they rolled. There was an odd smell in the air too, something approaching that of a musty old book; at once showing signs of decrepitude while at the same time being oddly comforting. It was a truly odd sensation looking around this ruined temple as despite its visual rot it was possible to sense a latent energy in the air just wanting to burst into life. If the sky overhead was a lovely clear blue, the flora a true green, and the dusty ground around them a sandy colour, the ruins could have drawn in people from far and wide. But sitting as it was, drained of any hint of life beneath the dark cloudy sky, it was merely depressing.

"It hasn't changed a bit," said Hideki. He didn't really want to be back here again, but there was a strange hint of nostalgia in his heart and he was somewhat glad that things hadn't changed.

Rosalina slid her hand into his and clasped it tightly. "So, where do we go now?"

"Well, when Fai passed away he told me that this Fallen Goddess could be found in the temple not far from Wonder's End where I grew up. It took me a good few weeks to make it here, but that did include following up on any rumours in my attempt to find this place. If my memory serves me correctly then we may be able to make it there in a week, maybe two at the most." Hideki rummaged through his memory for the fastest route back to Wonder's End and was relieved to find the information ready and waiting for him, he had been worried about having forgotten too much about Helheim and leading everyone on an endless goose chase but clearly everything was still where it should be. "There's a little village about two days away which we should probably head to first. It's only small, but they get messengers running through every other day so they tend to hear all the latest rumours going around Helheim. They might have some information on this Fallen Goddess. It took me all my time finding the village, and it turns out that despite it taking me weeks, I was actually only several days away from where I started. It's just a straight hike from the village to Wonder's End if the landscape's still as flat as ever."

"Well, that doesn't sound too bad, if anything, it's just a road-trip through the afterlife. Nothing can go wrong with that, right?" Arthur joked.

"Hideki, do you remember what attacked you before you made it to Ryushima?" Diana cut in.

After mulling it over for a few moments, Hideki settled on the rather enigmatical, "The fields of Helheim overflow with many monsters and demons." Following the rather quizzical looks he received from everyone he went a little more in-depth. "Hershel and Claire always used to say that when the lifeblood of Helheim was sapped away it gave rise to the demons. They come in so many different shapes and sizes; wolves, apes, vultures, ogres, mermaids, chimeras, almost anything you could imagine in your worst nightmares. But their numbers seem to ebb and flow at random so it was always impossible to figure out when and where an attack might happen. Wonder's End never seemed to suffer too badly, but I do remember hearing tales of poor souls being devoured in the most gruesome of fashions."

"Thanks for cheering us up, Hideki," David said sarcastically.

"We'll be fine. I managed to make it here on my own back then, there's five of us here and we've trained a lot, nothing is going to be able to stop us." Hideki took a deep breath before saying, "Let's go." One foot went in front of the other and the team followed him as they left the crumbling ruins and began their journey through the wasteland.

As they walked they passed the odd drooping tree and small patches of flat tufty grass, but for the most part all they could see was the dusty expanse looming out in every direction. There didn't seem to be any landmarks of any kind and so there was some confusion as to how Hideki knew exactly what direction he was heading. When asked, he'd respond by pointing out humorous figures in the cracks that had long since ingrained themselves into the earth; the little dancing man, the laughing dragon, the thing that sort of looked half-way like a cat, the solitary dying willow tree weeping as its leaves miserably swept the ground, the random boulder that stood firm amid a ring of tiny pebbles, and so on.

"You must have been so bored, mate, how many of these things did you name?" Arthur asked, making sure to elbow Hideki in the process.

"Of course I was bored, I'd been walking for weeks, I was going out of my mind so I did just about the only thing to maintain some sanity and that was spot things in the land around me."

They continued to walk for another hour or so until their stomachs started growling and at that point they knew they needed to have a break. After quickly setting up camp, which at this point equated to a campfire, they delved into their food pack for bread and a few other bits and pieces to put together a reasonable lunch. They'd brought about two months' worth of provisions with them, most of which had spells of preservation cast over them, so they were in no doubt that they'd be able to make it to their goal and back in that time frame; the only issue was carrying it all, though between the five of them they were able to lug around all the food and gear.

David was just in the middle of spreading some jam over his slice of bread when he saw Hideki leap to his feet and draw his sword. "What's the matter?"

Hideki scanned the horizon before pointing his sword directly at the cloud of dust storming towards them. "That's the matter."

"It's never bloody simple is it?" moaned Arthur.

Rosalina added a curt, "Indeed," before raising her staff. "What's coming, Hideki?"

"I'm not sure."

The dust cloud drew closer until the hulking forms of six gigantic ox-like beasts became visible, their hooves pounding the cracked earth with enough force to split it apart wherever they trod. Their eyes glowed red through the dust, leaving a crimson streak in the air as they charged. Stinking matted fur hung like twisted ivy over their backs and their horns split off at multiple angles for the sole purpose of maximising their chance at skewering prey.

As they drew nearer Rosalina felt mana begin to surge through her body; she'd been preparing to use a spell but hadn't figured out quite what to use just yet considering the beasts were still a considerable distance away. Water. She needed to use a water spell. Why did she know she needed water? Words began to stream into her mind and she twirled her staff around. As it moved droplets of water were flung from the surface of the crystal ball and the words froze in her mind's eye. *"DOOLAP PIR, ADRPAN TOL HAMI DODSIH, ENAY DE EGO ZUMVI, SUSANOO!"*

As soon as the words left her lips the clouds quickly darkened nearby, grower blacker and blacker until they burst and let loose a torrential downpour beneath. Slicing through the rain came a glinting sword carried by a large man with fiercely bushy black hair and a cascading beard. The Vardr, Susanoo, landed in the giant puddle that had formed beneath him and as the droplets fell Rosalina could see his webbed feet through his wooden sandals, the sleeve-like fins hanging from his arms beneath his simple white shirt and swaying around his red hakama. Despite his skin seeming typically human from a distance, it was in fact composed of thousands of tiny scales and on his neck underneath the mounds of swirling hair were a set of gills to allow him to breathe underwater. With a horizontal slash of his sword he unleashed a great wave that ploughed across the dusty earth and crashed into the beasts with the force of the ocean. They stumbled and crashed but quickly righted themselves and resumed their charge.

Hideki and the others were just about to summon their own Vardr when Susanoo held up his hand to stop them. With a deep booming voice, he said, "Stand down little ones, these nameless beasts are mine." Then, before they could object, he leapt towards the beasts taking his storm cloud with him. Every bound he took sent wave after wave at the creatures, with more slashes from his blade letting loose even more; by the time they reached each other the beasts were encased in a violent tempest with the wind howling around them. Their charge stopped and they collectively tried to spear Susanoo with their horns. Their attempts failed as Susanoo deftly parried them and with one swift cut he slit their throats and they all crumpled to the ground in a growing pool of thick oozing blood. With another slash from his blade the beasts dissolved into water and washed away the blood into the earth's cracked surface. He turned and checked around to make sure that there were no more dangers present before stating, "My work here is done," and then he vanished as soon as the storm cloud cleared.

"Where the hell was he when you nearly got assassinated?" Arthur asked. "And why do you guys get to be special with getting two Vardrs when we're stuck here with our poxy one?"

Rosalina surveyed her staff and the events that had just taken place. Was this how Hideki had felt when he summoned Jörmungandr? His half-smile seemed to indicate that it was. But then, why hadn't Susanoo come to her rescue back then? Did she just not have enough mana to sustain his summoning? Even though she'd felt safer in this situation than that assassination attempt, Susanoo chose now to appear. Mana. It had to be the mana. That influx of power was fuelled by the mana around her jumping at the chance to come alive. There was so much hanging in the air that one tiny flicker of determination or panic was enough to set them on. Hideki must've been born with some of that Helheim mana coursing through his veins and that would possibly explain how he had summoned two Vardr in Ryushima when nobody else had managed it. She explained as such to everyone and with a shrug and a sigh of "Well that sounds reasonable enough to me," from Arthur, they batted the dust off their blankets and resumed their lunch with a newfound appetite though Rosalina was the only one who had actual done any work and even then, it was her Vardr, Susanoo, who'd done all the fighting. Still, they needed the break either way and were just grateful to have calm once more to fill their stomachs and ready themselves for more inevitably long walking.

Chapter 26
Hand in Hand

Hours ticked by as they crossed the empty landscape with little more happening than a brief glimpse of what appeared to be a wolf with multiple tails prowling through the wasteland, pausing to look at them with big wise eyes, and then running off in the direction they were heading. As they walked, Hideki and Rosalina held hands, as did Diana and David, leaving Arthur feeling more than a little aware of how he was without someone to love or to love him. There was no intention to make Arthur feel like that, the two couples had just drifted together as they kept moving forward and it was just the most natural thing in the world. Arthur held back behind them in an effort to hide his frustrations, largely because he knew that they couldn't help being in love and it was hardly their fault that he was the odd one out on this quest; so he just kept quiet and they nattered away.

"When Yuuko took me in she was always commenting on how lovely the town was, how cosy it was, standing like a beacon of hope in the dreary world. I never really saw what she meant back then because I'd never left Wonder's End, I mean, why would you when the whole town thinks you're a devil child and there are dangerous monsters waiting out there in the wilderness? But, I suppose, thinking about it now, home was lovely in comparison to all this," Hideki looked wistfully at the horizon, hoping to see Wonder's End waiting for him up ahead though he knew it was still many, many miles away.

"Well, I suppose that's not too difficult to manage," Rosalina said with a giggle. "But, you know, if this place was just green fields, I expect it'd be really peaceful and lovely in its own way."

"Yeah, you could plant a few trees and a meadow of flowers, really liven the place up; you could probably try your hand at a bit of gardening, eh, Rosalina?" David joked.

Diana punched him in the arm, "No need to be a fool."

"When we get back to Ryushima, maybe I will," said Rosalina.

It was at this moment that Hideki looked back to see Arthur with a glum look on his face. "Are you ok, Arthur? You look a bit down."

Arthur flushed in embarrassment and quickly tried to regain some of his confident façade but realised it was a wasted effort as they could all see through him. "It's nothing... Staring out at all this nothingness is just de-moralising is all."

"You're telling me! I had to live here for eighteen years before I got free of it and now I'm back again." Hideki waited for Arthur to catch them up and clapped his arm around him. "It's alright to be a bit miserable looking at this you know. We've just got to try to have a laugh as we go. There's not

215

much else we can do really. Now come on, give us that cheeky grin of yours. This ship only runs on happy faces."

Arthur laughed. "That sounds completely ridiculous."

"It did its job though, right?"

With his mood lifted somewhat for the time being, Arthur nodded and they all continued on until nightfall. By that time they were all ready for some more rest so they set up camp, this time with some sturdy tents fortified by magic and a campfire which was likely to burn all through the night thanks to the surplus of mana coursing through the air. They all sat around it as they ate a hefty dinner of various meats and vegetables which David cooked on the fire. The night sky above them was as overcast as ever and the lack of starlight left them feeling isolated in the world as they huddled round the fire.

Out of nowhere, Diana said, "I'm proud of you all." Arthur nearly spat out a mouthful of food when she said this but he managed to stop himself and swallow it down. "I think back to when you all started training under me and you were all so fresh-faced and unsure of what you were capable of. Now look at us, off on a quest to slay some all-powerful goddess. We really do know how to pick our challenges, don't we?"

"Well, if you hadn't have pushed us so hard we'd probably be sitting with our feet up nursing the killer of all hangovers right now, or at least I would," said David. "We never really had time for that engagement party, did we?"

"No. But we'll have time when we get back," she said with a surprising note of uncertainty in her voice. "I love you, David, don't ever forget that."

"I love you too, Di." He rested his hand on hers and squeezed it reassuringly, "And yes we will have time when we get back. Nothing's going to stop me from marrying you, you're not getting away from me that easily."

She greeted this with a wry smile and a soft look at the others. She didn't show it often, but it was clear just how much she cared about them all. It was only really in times like this where she let them in. Rosalina had figured out many years ago that Diana's stern personality was more of a defensive shield than anything else. She didn't want to get hurt, but she didn't want anyone else to suffer and so she had to be strong. It was how she coped with the world.

"You'll find someone too one day, Arthur," Hideki said with a smile to Arthur who he'd noticed shrinking a little bit as Diana and David talked.

"Who says I need anyone?"

"No one," said Rosalina, "but Hideki is right that if you want someone one day, you'll find them. You'll be fine."

"Well thanks for the pep talk I suppose." Arthur put his bowl down and, feigning sleepiness, yawned, saying, "I think I'm gonna hit the hay, I'm knackered." He then quickly ducked inside his tent so they wouldn't see him cry.

David followed, realising something was wrong, and immediately embraced his little brother as soon as he got into the tent. "What're you crying for you pillock?"

"It's nothing, David, just let me go to bed."

"Well, I'm hardly leaving you like this now, am I? I'm your older brother so it's my responsibility to make sure you're ok. So, tell me what's wrong."

"I can't."

"Can't or won't?"

"If I tell you, you'll think I'm an idiot and you'll hate me."

"Well, you're my little brother so I already think you're an idiot," David said, ruffling Arthur's hair, "and since we're related, I'd never be able to hate you. I love you too much for that."

Arthur looked up at David with his big amber eyes filled to the brim with tears which were ready to burst. "I shouldn't be here. I'm not as strong as any of you, I'm the odd one out, and I'm jealous of you and Hideki with your perfect relationships that don't go wrong no matter what happens. I'm just the scrawny one who doesn't matter."

"Well, if you don't matter then I clearly don't. I just stick in the background and fire arrows at things unless otherwise necessary. And you seem to forget that none of us would've let you come if we didn't think you could stick it. You're stronger than you think you are, just think about your fight with Hideki; you kept him on his toes all the way through and there's no way I would have been able to wield that halberd as effectively when I was your age." David glanced towards the door of the tent as the fabric fluttered as though someone had drawn in close to it. "And no relationship is perfect, Arthur. You can try and do everything you can to make it perfect, but it's simply not possible. Me and Di may seem secure together, and we are, but that doesn't mean we don't have our arguments or I don't hurt her or she doesn't hurt me. Plus, we've been together for so long now that we've worked through any problems we have faced to get to where we are now."

Arthur wiped some of the tears away with the nearby blanket. "Really?"

"You're damn right really. And if you think that Hideki and Rosalina are so perfect, if you give them a few more years together, you may find that they start to escape the immediate throws of love and become more realistic about their relationship. In all likelihood, they'll probably last in the long run. When I look at them, I see how me and Di were back then. But that doesn't mean it will happen. You can't second guess life or love. And as Hideki said, you'll find someone someday. Trust me."

"Are you sure?"

"Of course I'm sure, you idiot." David squeezed Arthur tightly. "I love you, Arthur."

"I love you too."

"Are you alright now?"

"Yeah, I should be. Thanks David."

"You're very welcome little brother. Now, I'm going to get back to the others and then we'll probably head to bed too. See you in the morning, Arthur. Sleep tight."

When morning came, Arthur bounded out of his tent with newfound cheer and woke everyone up. They set off just before whatever counted as the sun here rose behind the clouds and as they strode on they could see a hazy lightshow happening on the grey canvas. The day passed much like the last, treading across the endless wasteland, praying for something new to turn up to talk about and being disappointed at how flat and dead everything continued to be. Nothing happened for hours on end bar the reappearance of that strange wolf for a few brief seconds.

Eventually they came upon what amounted to an oasis; a small pool of muddy water surrounded by tufts of mossy grass and a tall blackened tree. It was nothing special but enough to break the tedium for the time being. But no sooner had they paused for breath, they could feel an odd rumbling beneath them. They quickly drew their weapons in preparation for the battle they presumed was imminent.

"Don't move," Diana ordered as she spotted a clawed hand scratching around the earth for its prey. With a swift lunge she skewered the hand and as the creature roared in pain it broke through to the surface and scowled with its gigantic translucent eyes. Its pale ashy skin was mottled with bruises along its gangly arms and it violently gnashed its razor-sharp teeth at them. It yanked its hand backwards through the rapier blade and freed itself, howling a blood-curdling scream as it did so before hungrily licking at the oozing black blood around its wound. More of the creatures surfaced and quickly surrounded the group, twitching in an otherworldly fashion as they drew in ever closer.

Then Diana coughed and on that signal the group leapt into battle, slashing away at the creatures, launching whatever spells were possible at such short range along with defensive barriers and anything else that would help them. More creatures burst from the ground to replace their felled brethren and they just kept coming no matter how many the group slew.

A violent screech ripped through the air and before anyone had time to realise what was happening, Diana had been snatched from the ground by some gigantic raven with a serrated beak, losing jagged feathers as it lifted itself and her into the sky. Diana tried to lift her legs up to either kick the raven or to get some kind of foothold from which to escape but the raven gripped her arms far too tightly and held her at such a distance that she just couldn't stretch that far.

"DI!" David yelled before screeching, "*PLADPH ORS,*" and launching the shadowy arrows towards the raven. They hit their target and burrowed deep beneath its feathery flesh but bar a slight dip it didn't falter in its flight. David cursed as he fired arrow after arrow at the raven until he realised that he needed to use Ziz. *"ARPHE PERIPSOL, VPAAH ZONG, ZIZ!"* The mana surged through his bow but just as he was about to fire the arrow to finish the summoning, one of the ashy creatures leapt onto his back and caused him to lose the arrow. In anger he grabbed the creature's bulbous head and with one hand flung it down in front of him before shooting it straight through the eye. He cursed again as he spotted Arthur beginning to struggle against the horde. He couldn't save them both with Ziz. The Vardr was quick and powerful, but it could probably only reach one of them and by the time he rushed back the other would probably be dead. Hideki and Rosalina seemed to be coping for now but time was of the essence. He needed something huge right now.

He could see his bow glowing an earthy brown and the mana began to surge into him; he needed this power and whatever help it could bring. The words formed in his mind and he shouted them so loudly he nearly made his voice hoarse, *"CORONZON CAOSGO, TORZU, BEHEMOTH!"*

No arrow needed to be fired as the small pool of the oasis bubbled and frothed as something made its way to the surface. The ashy creatures froze as they felt the rumbling through their feet; they knew something gigantic was coming and it terrified them. As Arthur, Hideki, and Rosalina made the most of this opening, a massive hole opened up where the oasis had once been with the earth crumbling into the pit. Loud pounding thuds echoed as something climbed its way out of the hole. Thud. Thud. Thud. Whatever it was sped up as it climbed. Thud thud. Thud thud. Two tremendous ebony horns came striking up into the air followed closely by an almost reptilian face that resembled an elephantine ox with thick leathery skin the colour of soil. The gigantic beast's front feet stretched up over the side of the pit with sharp retractable claws on the soles digging into to the ground to give it some leverage to lift its mighty bulk up and out. The Vardr was bigger than anything any of them had seen before, standing taller than the Almighty Dragons, maybe even the palace; and as its bountiful muscles flexed from the effort a powerful tail like a cedar tree came flicking out of the pit. Behemoth reared up on its hind legs before thrusting its humungous feet down into the earth and knocking all of the ashy creatures onto their backs. Thankfully this was the turning point needed for Arthur to regain the upper hand which meant that now David could focus all his efforts on Diana.

"Please, help me rescue Diana!" David said, leaping onto Behemoth's tail and clambering up to his back. "That raven's got her." With a much stronger vantage point, David hoped he would be able to do a bit more himself to get Diana back, so he was more than a little surprised when Behemoth opened its cavernous mouth and let loose a beam of pure earthy mana which left a gaping hole in the demon's chest.

As it died, its claws let go of Diana and she began to plummet. As she fell she spotted more of the demonic ravens hurtling towards her and David atop the monolithic Behemoth. He needed to defend himself and Selene wasn't going to be of much use with her blazing towards the ground. She needed wings right now. "*VPAAH!*" The windy wings grew from her back and she tried to slow her descent but they just weren't strong enough at the speed she was falling. She needed something more powerful. The mana around her surged into the wings and she began to see words in her mind. Perfect. "*ARPHE MOMAR BASGIM, ILMO, HELIOS!*"

The sun began to break through the clouds as the brilliant white mana swirled into the sky, the rays searing the already scorched earth in such a fashion that it seemed as though the very sun itself were charging down towards them. Then with a whinny, a majestic horse burst through the clouds sporting white feathery wings and a mane of blazing flame. It galloped through the sky beating its wings as it flew, shining like the very sun itself. In seconds the Vardr, Helios, had scooped up Diana on his back and seared through the air towards the ravens. From atop her new steed, Diana was in her element. She raised her rapier and lay waste to them before David and Behemoth could get in any more attacks. "That's much better. You are a lifesaver, Helios, I presume."

"You are very welcome, Mistress Diana. I am just glad you summoned me in time," Helios neighed in response.

With the aerial threat neutralised, Diana and David descended to help destroy the remnants of the ashy creatures and once they were certain that no more were lurking beneath the surface they bid farewell to Behemoth and Helios. Clearly this quest was determined to force their hands and make them waste as much mana as possible before they reached the Fallen Goddess; but that wasn't going to stop them. With new Vardr on the team, nothing would.

Chapter 27
Pieces of a Broken Heart

They trudged on for another day, thankfully without incident, until they came across a small abandoned village. "This isn't right…" Hideki looked around the village and was horrified to see the shattered windows and roofs with gaping holes through the thatch. "What the hell happened here?" Had the village not been in a shambolic state, it would have been rather quaint. A little collection of houses circled round a simplistic but large stone well with lush but murky grass filling in the area between. Considering the overgrown ivy working its way through and around the houses, it was clear that nobody had lived here for many months. "Those poor people." Hideki ran into one of the houses and spotted a notebook strewn on the table carelessly as if the owner had left in a rush and forgotten it in their hurry. He picked it up out of curiosity and turned it over in his hands; the leather cover was well worn and slightly damp to the touch as though a leak had dripped down onto the notebook since it had been abandoned, and when he flicked through the pages while some stuck together it was clear from the neat, dense writing that its owner thought quite deeply about things.

"Does it say anything interesting?" Rosalina asked.

Hideki turned to the first page and read, "My name is Andrew Freeman and this is the story of why I died." That was all it said, so he tried to turn the page only to find that it was firmly stuck to the other pages behind it.

"They always leave off at the good bits, eh?" David said with a sly grin.

Hideki flicked further through the notebook as best he could and came across the date he'd walked through this little village. "A young man came through the village today asking all sorts of weird questions about trees and portals and gateways back to life. I tried my best to point him in the direction of those ruins I'd heard rumours of from one of those cheapskate merchants, but he's wasting his time. It's impossible to get back once you're dead. I tried to get back once but it's impossible. You can exert your presence in the places you once lived and for the people you once knew, but you can't get back. There's no body to return to. Still, I hope he finds what he's looking for. He seemed like a genuine enough guy when he spoke to me, but then again I was never the best judge of character when I was alive. The rest of the day was pretty uneventful outside of little Ollie running off and Brittany storming after him and giving him a right telling off. It's times like these when I wonder why I keep on writing when most of the time nothing new happens, and then I remember that's it's the only thing keeping me sane."

"Do you remember meeting him at all?" Rosalina asked.

227

"Not really. I was in and out of here like a flash, I was just too desperate to get away from Helheim."

"Does he say anything else in that notebook? Anything about what happened here?"

Hideki flicked through the fresher, unstuck pages and came across an entry that looked pretty important. "WARNING. There's a monster lurking on the horizon. Must warn everyone. Can't write much today. Need to fortify the village in case it attacks."

"I'm guessing things didn't end well for them," stated Diana.

"The monster has vanished for the time being, so everyone is annoyed at me for panicking them, but I know what I saw and I know it's still out there. They're saying I'm going mad. They're saying I'm still grieving my own death. I know that's not true. I made peace with that long ago. I protected you and now I need to protect my fellow villagers. They might not believe me, but I must help them to survive. I still miss you, even after all this time. I wonder, do you miss me? Do you ever think about me? Probably not. One minute I was there, the next I was gone. Maybe one day we'll meet again but make sure it doesn't happen too soon, ok?"

"Sounds like he really cared about whoever he was writing to. Poor guy…" said Rosalina.

"Little Ollie and Brittany disappeared during the night. We all heard the awful wailing but when I ran out to see what all the fuss was about, there was just a massive hole where the front of the house had been and all of their belongings in tatters. God knows what happened to them, and to be honest, it doesn't even bear thinking about. I tried to tell the villagers that it must have been the monster but even now with the evidence right in front of them, they don't believe me. I tried pointing out that we haven't had a merchant pass through the village in weeks but they just passed it off as though maybe they were on holiday or something. *Idiots. Nobody goes on holiday. We're dead.* We just do what we do because it's how we pass the time. Those merchants wouldn't stop doing that job for anything unless they thought it was too dangerous to pass through the village. Why must the villagers all be so pig-headed about it? Do they want to die again? Do they never want to see their loved ones again? Because that's where they're heading."

Arthur's ears perked up at hearing this. "What does he mean 'die again'? Is that even possible?"

"Well, considering my parents just vanished, as did Lara and Ramona, and Yuuko always said that sometimes the afterlife wasn't as eternal as everyone hoped it would be; I think it's definitely possible. I'm pretty sure the demons and monsters feed on souls, and once the soul is gone, your very existence has ended."

"That's awful," muttered Rosalina.

"That's life," said David.

Hideki continued reading the notebook aloud, "The folks from across the road went missing last night. They were all so adamant that nothing was out to get us but look who's suffering now. Part of me is filled with the joy of schadenfreude, but then the other part is terrified about what's going to happen next. What does this monster want? Our souls? Does it enjoy toying with its prey? Is it eating them? Taking them somewhere else? None of it makes any sense. Maybe I should leave this little village. If this monster keeps coming, then it'll inevitably come after me at some point and I'd rather not find out the answers to all the questions I have about it. I'm going to try persuading people to come with me tomorrow, but I think I can already tell just how well that will go. Still, it's worth a shot. It's not like I can fight off that monster, I'm only human after all, and it's not like I ever ended up in a fight apart from, you know, that one. So, I'm just going to have to take as many people with me as I can. Wish me luck!"

"About a third of the village said they'd join me. That's certainly far more than I was expecting, but then I suppose they're all frightened about what that monster will do to them. If we get out now then maybe we'll never have to worry about it ever again. We set off in the morning and I've decided that I'm going to leave this little notebook behind. It's served me well and I've written down everything that's happened from the day I died to now and should anyone find it, they'll hopefully realise that they need to get out of the village immediately. It isn't safe. That monster will probably set up its home here once it's done devouring everyone who stays. And if you are the one to find this notebook, I pray for your safety and hope you can escape before it is too late."

"Goodbye, little village. Goodbye, trusty book. Goodbye, my love. Yours and forever, Andrew Freeman."

"That poor guy," Arthur said.

Diana was already making sure they had everything before heading towards the door, "If what he said is true, we need to get out of here. Now." She walked outside and could hear an awful scratching coming from inside the well. It was very much akin to nails on a chalkboard although horrifyingly crossed with a man's piercing scream. "Too late, it's here."

Chapter 28
Unfinished Battle

The pungent stench of rotting flesh oozed from the well and was so potent that it was possible to see a nasty purple mist spurting forth as the creature breathed. In. Out. In. Out. In. Out. A gigantic hand clasped over the edge of the well and took root as the demon began to lift the rest of its humungous body up. It let out a guttural scream that rumbled all the way through its stomach, violently ripping its way through the demon's gravelly vocal chords and bursting out to release a sound that made the ears bleed. Then its head was visible; a misshapen forehead attached to two deep-set baggy eyes and a protruding jaw that featured very prominent jagged teeth. Its rotting flesh squeezed through the well shaft and just kept going. Its decaying body was covered in awful infected welts, sharp bony spikes, and what appeared to be moss and fungi growing from under its armpits and covering its groin. Then it was out of the well, standing impossibly tall above them. It must have been a good eighty feet high and Diana quickly realised that the hole in that nearby house had been caused by the demon's fist. How had anybody missed this monstrosity on the horizon? And for that matter, how had it been so stealthy?

With a powerful swipe, the roof that had been shielding them was gone. They'd seen the demon move its arm towards them, but they didn't have time to process how quickly it had demolished that roof before it was gone. So, that was how it had managed to catch all those people off-guard. "Attack it from all sides and try to keep your distance," Diana ordered as they sped out of the house and tried to put as much distance between themselves and the demon as possible. In unison they started firing spells at the monstrosity, everything from fireballs to thunderbolts to earthquakes; anything to bring it down but nothing worked. The demon just screeched in frustration and started batting away the houses around it as it looked around for the little ants attacking it.

"It must be resistant to magic," yelled Rosalina.

"Bloody typical," yelled Arthur in response. "Maybe if we tripped it up? David?"

"On it!" David aimed his bow at the demon's leg and fired an energy arrow that remained tethered to the bow with a rope of mana, then before the arrow had even struck the demon, he shouted, "*VPAAH*," and the wings sprouted from his back. The arrow hit its mark and David leapt from the ground and started circling the demon. It tried to reach out for him but David was too low to the ground for it and just a little bit too far away for it to catch him. The mana rope went round and round its legs until it looked like it was about to topple over, but to everyone's horror it bent down and sliced through the mana rope with one of its nails before picking up the thread and pulling David in with it. He cursed to himself and let the mana trail go before retreating to a safe distance.

The demon felt the rope go loose and let out a moan of disappointment that it wouldn't get to eat the little ant on the end of it. Its rotting head lolled from side to side as it searched for when the little ant had gone when it spotted Arthur charging towards it, halberd swinging like a murderous baton. It went to slam its hand down to squash Arthur flat, but it just missed by a few inches and Arthur was able to spear the top of its hand with his halberd. The demon withdrew its hand, with Arthur clinging on for dear life to his weapon, and started shaking it to try to get rid of the pain.

"Arthur! What are you doing, you idiot?" David yelled at him.

"I'm slaying the giant!" came Arthur's gleeful reply though it was clearly tinged with worry at his rash decision. In a moment when the giant stopped shaking its hand, Arthur began to climb, using his halberd as both a springboard and a climbing axe. With one hand firmly on the halberd's shaft, Arthur jumped as high as he could before yanking the halberd out and slamming it into the demon's wrist before he fell. With each jump, the giant howled. But Arthur's plan hit a major snag when the demon's other hand came around to squash him as he made his way up the arm. "Oh buggery hell!" A bit of quick thinking led to Arthur dislodging his weapon and flinging himself at the giant's oncoming hand; his halberd went straight through the skin and hooked itself onto bone. The demon recoiled in pain and scowled at its hand, lifting it up to see the ant. It spotted Arthur and howled so loudly that Arthur began to feel incredibly woozy as the purple mist viciously attacked his senses. The demon's hand moved perilously over its opening jaw and Arthur cursed loudly as he realised what was happening. The giant was going to eat him.

Not like this. He was not dying like this. Could he use Gloriana? Nope. She was too small to deal with something this big. Could David summon Behemoth? Or Diana summon Helios? Or Rosalina, Amaterasu? Or Hideki, Mjölnir? They could, and they were clearly about to but he knew he needed to do this himself. He needed to get himself out of this mess with his own abilities and power. The mana around him surged into him as he thought this and the words began to form in his mind. "Hell yes!" he shouted out before yelling at himself in his head for being so blasé when he was potentially about to get eaten by a terrifying rotting demon giant. Then words wrote themselves clearly in his head and he shouted them as loudly as he could, "*ARP LN AMMA A-C-LONDOH, NAT OD BNG CAOSGO, BRAN!*"

A tiny crow flew down through the clouds and charged towards the giant. Arthur cursed his bad luck. This is it. I am actually going to die like this. Why did I have to lumped with the small Vardrs? He looked more closely at the crow as it

235

zoomed towards him. It seemed as though rather than aiming with its beak it was performing some sort of drop kick. Then the crow's body began to grow and morph at a rapid pace. The talons became toes, the feet became much more human, the wings became gigantic muscular arms beneath a feathery cloak and a rugged face with a particularly impressive beard appeared beneath a hood that took the appearance of the crow. It grew and grew and grew until it was the same size as the demon and then the Vardr's feet collided with the demon's face and knocked it to the floor, sending Arthur spiralling into the air.

"Careful there, little Master," he said with a full and jolly voice. He picked himself up from where he had himself landed and plucked Arthur out of the air and set him safely on his shoulder. "The name's Bran. Bran the Blessed," He said, pointing to himself. Then he turned his attention back to the demon. "Ugly looking feller ain't he? Not seen anything that hideous since a fool nicked my bleedin' cauldron."

At this point the demon giant was getting back up and snapping its neck back into place. It scowled and grumbled at Bran before running towards him flailing its arms in an outpouring of frustration. Bran stood and waited like a tremendous immovable statue and when the time was right he grabbed the demon's wrists and headbutted it. It tried to pull away but Bran's grip was too strong. "No one is eating my little Master here; you hear me?" He placed his foot quite firmly on the demon's stomach and began to push down on it as he pulled its wrists towards him. "I don't think you'll be needing these." With a horrifying crunch, the demon's arms came clean off leaving a trail of tarry blood as they flew through the air and crushed one of the houses. Bran glanced at the house with embarrassment, "I did not mean to do that." Then he returned his attention to the demon, I did however mean to do this." And with that he punched the demon giant in its misshapen face and the force tore its head from its neck. The monstrosity crumpled and quickly oozed away into the ground as if it had never been there, only the wanton destruction of the village stood as testament to the fact that it had ever existed. "Well, I think that went rather well, little Master, don't you?"

"You mate, are one awesome Vardr. Why couldn't you have turned up when he first attacked us?" Arthur responded with a relieved grin on his face.

"We appear as and when we are needed. Lovely Gloriana was needed when you were a little lad and she's served you well ever since as far as I'm aware. Now, you have more mana and you needed me, so here I am. Gods you humans ask some silly questions."

"No, I asked why you didn't turn up when – Never mind, thank you, Bran. You are a life-saver."

"You're damn right I am," Bran said as he carefully placed Arthur back on the ground. "Now, seeing as that's done, I really should be off. Got a kingdom to run, you know." Bran shrank back to his crow form and shot back through the clouds as Arthur waved goodbye.

The team regrouped in the wrecked village and Rosalina made sure to heal Arthur up in case he had sustained any injuries, but he seemed mostly ok. In the end, he was just so happy that he didn't feel weak or defenceless anymore. He had two awesome Vardrs, just like everyone else and he was the one that had taken down that demon giant. Not Diana, not David, not Hideki; him. He'd honestly never felt better. With a loud exultant cheer, he jumped into the air as he excitedly shouted, "HELL YES, THAT WAS AMAZING!"

CHAPTER 29
DON'T THINK TWICE

With the demon vanquished the little village was left to rest in peace. Maybe one day some people would return to it and restore it to its former beauty, but there was little Hideki and the others could do when there was nobody left. As they departed, they could feel how much calmer the atmosphere was around it and after what could have been a fatal encounter, the peaceful silence was much appreciated. The awful smell of decay had also faded away until all that remained was the almost comforting aroma that reminded them of musty old books and grass.

"Don't you ever do something rash like that again, d'ya hear me, Arthur?" David said as he rushed to catch up with his ecstatically bouncing brother. "You could've been killed."

"We all could've been killed, but I saved the day didn't I? That's all that matters."

"What David is trying to say, Arthur, is that he wouldn't know what to do if you got yourself killed," Rosalina chipped in.

"You lot are all I've got, so I ain't planning on losing any of you anytime soon, especially not you Arthur." David said.

"Yeah, yeah, alright," said Arthur with a reluctant sigh.

They walked on in silence for a while, needing time to work off the stress of combat and needing a bit of time inside their heads, away from the caring but prying eyes of each other. They were all thinking about what would happen if somebody died on this quest. They'd all kept it locked away in the furthest recesses of their mind, but after so many close calls on the journey so far, it was becoming an all too real possibility. They only reason they'd survived this long had been the miraculous appearances of the Vardrs. David for one knew that he wouldn't cope if either Diana or Arthur perished, and he'd probably die too should both be killed. Diana thought that she would be able to cope with any of the others dying, but deep down she realised that she'd be overcome with grief and lock herself further and further away from those she cared about. Arthur figured that he'd crumble without the rocks that were his friends and family to act as a support, and that was not a reality he wished to envision. Rosalina was surprisingly at peace with the idea. This was their duty. They had taken on this quest knowing full well the potential consequences and nothing could change whatever was inevitably going to happen. She would mourn and grieve, but then she must fight on and finish the job. That was her duty. Hideki on the other hand was very conflicted. On one hand, all he'd known for eighteen years was death and Helheim, so he was well aware of what death entailed for any of them and while it wasn't exactly pleasant, it could be so much worse. On the other, he was terribly frightened to lose the people he'd grown so close to. He could cope with dying himself, but he couldn't bear to see them vanish from his life.

The silence lasted for so long as they worried about one another until Hideki finally broke it. "You know, whatever happens on this trip, I don't regret a thing."

"How so?" asked Diana.

"Well, if I hadn't left Helheim, I never would've met all of you, I never would've fallen in love, I never would've known that a world could be so much more than this," he gestured at the wasteland around him as he spoke. "Maybe I made a mistake when I stepped into Fai and Yami's battle, but it's meant that I'm finally going to make something of my life; I'm going to save the universe from this Fallen Goddess and then we'll all be free to live how we choose. If I can succeed in that, then what is there to regret?"

"Never falling in love? Never being able to step out of your brother's shadow? Constantly trying to be something you're not?" Arthur suggested, before clarifying, "Those are the things that I regret. Maybe if I didn't care so much what other people thought none of it would matter but it does."

"You're not the only one, Arthur," said Diana. "In some way, we all portray the person we think others wish to see rather than the one we wish to be. I'm the calm, cool captain whose sternness allows her to make tough decisions; but at the end of the day, I just want the world to be at peace so I can settle down and fill my time with something other than constant battle. Rosalina, I'm sure you feel the same, being forced to be the elegant, perfect little Princess because that is what is expected of you, when all you really want is to have fun while you still can." Rosalina nodded fervently in affirmation. "We're only truly ourselves when we're alone because subconsciously we care about how others perceive us. That's not a fact we should regret or be ashamed of, Arthur. That's just life."

David interjected, "But when you think about it, we are what we portray ourselves to be. It's like a self-fulfilling prophecy. If you're cracking jokes even if you don't feel like that's you, it doesn't stop them from being funny and you become a bit of a joker. Bit by bit you become that which you portray yourself to be or something like that. That calm, cool, steeliness, Di; and that elegance, Rosalina; and that confidence, Arthur; they are part of you. But you're all more than that. You're all squishy and insecure underneath, but there's naff all wrong with that. You are allowed to be more than one thing at any one time. Try thinking about it like this. The you you portray to others is the you you wish others to perceive you as. Part of that is what they want and part of it is what you want. Simple right?"

"Kinda," Rosalina said with a giggle. She sighed deeply and smiled at them all. "Good grief, we're hopeless, aren't we? We get in a few battles that could have gone badly south and we start getting all introspective and philosophical. It's silly when you think about it."

"Well yeah," said David, "all philosophy is a bit silly when you think about it. Life's ridiculous. It makes very little sense and then it's over and then you're here and it still doesn't make any sense. What more can you expect?"

"A bit of consistency?" Arthur suggested.

"Life cannot be consistent. It's got to have its ups and downs otherwise nobody would ever grow as a person, you'd just stay the same drifting endlessly through an unchanging existence. It'd be dull and as awful as life can be, it's better to live than to exist." Diana said.

"I can attest to that," Hideki added. "That's all I did as a kid: exist."

"I suppose you're right," Arthur concluded.

"Hideki, do you know how much further Wonder's End is? I'd say the sooner we finish this thing the better, otherwise we're all going to be driven insane by melancholy," Rosalina said as jokingly as she could.

"A few more days should probably do it. But if that village was destroyed, then I have no idea what might have happened to Wonder's End. We're just going to have to hope for the best really. There's not a lot else we can do but keep walking." And that was what they did.

CHAPTER 30
A BROKEN WONDER

"Is that wolf creature showing us the way or something?" Arthur asked. "That must be what, the third, fourth, fifth time we've seen it?"

Just ahead of them, the five-tailed wolf gazed at them knowingly as it gently rapped the ground with its paws. They hadn't really noticed it before, but the wolf's fluffy white fur almost glowed beneath the murky clouds overhead. Its ears twitched. It quickly scanned the horizon and then it set off towards whatever it had heard.

"Well, he does seem to be heading in the direction of Wonder's End, so maybe he is. It's nice to think that we've got some sort of guardian here to guide us, eh?" Hideki replied once the wolf had vanished from sight. "Come on, I don't think we're too far away now. That tree," he said pointing to the crooked thing, "was the first real landmark I came across after I left so we should see Wonder's End in the distance in the next hour or so I would've thought."

The hour passed and they could finally see buildings looming ahead of them, a surprisingly large swathe of homes that very much formed a town rather than a tiny hamlet or a village. Even from this distance it was clear that the place was well settled and Hideki was surprised to see that it had expanded more since he'd left. Clearly, with him gone they'd all felt more comfortable and invited all their friends and family from across Helheim or once they too had passed and then built houses for them all. How would they all feel when he walked back into the town with the others? If they hadn't already died, they'd probably die from the shock. After all, it wasn't every day that something long-thought removed returned. Thinking about it more carefully, Hideki grew worried. They wouldn't accept him with loving arms after all this time, but would they try to attack him and the others out of fear? Should they have avoided Wonder's End entirely? But then the team would have no idea where the Fallen Goddess's temple was located and they wouldn't be able to complete their quest. Hideki's breathing quickened as they drew closer and closer to his childhood home. They needed to do this, but the reality of his past grew ever more real as though the faded dream had shifted into a painfully sharp focus.

The walk to the town felt as though it were going in slow motion; with every step they technically drew closer but it didn't feel like it, and the longer it took, the more time Hideki had to worry about what would happen when he entered the town. Rosalina's hand slipped reassuringly into his and then they were into the town.

A few people were stood chatting outside their door having a lovely time, but for the first time, Hideki realised that their skin was a pallid grey and despite efforts to add a bit of colour to their faces and clothing, nothing had worked. Hideki's skin in comparison was vibrant, his clothes retained their majesty from Ryushima and it was the same for the rest of the team. One of the people, an elderly woman, caught a glimpse of them out of the corner of her eye and after a double take saw Hideki and screamed. The other two, a couple of middle-aged men, whipped around to follow the elderly woman's line of sight and immediately shouted, "Everyone get inside, now!" One of the men ushered the woman into the nearby house while the other eyed them up and went to grab a weapon from the inside of the door.

"We're not here to cause trouble," Hideki said in a vain attempt to defuse the situation, "We've just come to rest and find out some information, nothing more."

"I don't give a monkey's," the man said as he revealed a spiked baseball bat. "Get out of our town now you demons or we will destroy you."

Diana stepped forward and noticed the man flinch backwards a bit. "Well that's hardly any way to treat a bunch of weary travellers including the Princess of Ryushima."

"Ree-oo-what-now?"

"Ryushima, that's where we're from," Rosalina stated with no small hint of offense.

"I don't care where you're from, demons, just stay away." The man flailed his bat around as if to push them back but they refused to budge.

"We're not demons, we're people like you." Hideki noted the man's disbelieving scowl and quickly understood that his best bet was to reveal who he was. "My name is Hideki, I was born here in Wonder's End and I lived here until a year or so ago. Don't you remember me?"

"The devil child?"

"If that's what you want to call me, then yes, the devil child. But I am not a devil or a demon and I never have been. I don't want to make a scene or cause any trouble. We'll be gone before you know it and I'll never darken your doors again. I don't want to be here as much as you don't want me here, ok?"

The man's eyes widened and he seemed to be very conflicted in how to deal with the situation. Thankfully for him, a group of the townspeople appeared wielding their own weapons and with the mob behind him he regained some courage. "The devil child has returned and he's brought some new playmates with him."

Arthur, David, and Diana were all about to say something but Rosalina stormed up to the man and, though she only came up to his chest, he cowered away and his bat hung limply in his hands. "I have had just about enough of this devil child and demon nonsense," Rosalina snapped, "Hideki is one of the kindest and most caring men I've ever known and I'm so

247

happy he escaped this hell-hole and found his way to the kingdom I call home. He's made me happier than I have ever been and he is most certainly not a devil child. And we are most certainly not demons. We've spent the entire journey here defending ourselves from demons and monsters, and why in the name of all that is good in the world would we do that if we were demons ourselves, hm? Why would we be stood here having a conversation if we were demons? Surely if we were, you'd already be dead." She pushed herself forward and further into the man's face, "Now call off your little mob and let us pass through in peace, please, or we will be forced to use force." A little flicker of self-deprecation rushed through her mind. Forced to use force? Really? Very threatening. But she kept up her glare and the man eventually backed down. With a growl, Rosalina made her command one last time, "Call off the mob."

The man shrank away and ushered everyone else away. They obliged with no small hint of confusion and disappointment, some of them had been raring for a fight and though quite a few recognised Hideki and were ready to cause some pain, they knew when they were outclassed.

With the mob gone, Hideki let out a long sigh. "It looks bigger but it hasn't changed a bit. Still the same broken town it always was."

With a twinge of trepidation, the group entered into the town proper and saw the remnants of a marketplace frantically packing away their wares and people scurrying into their houses; anything to get away from the monsters they thought were coming. When the stall-holders spotted Hideki and the others they quickened their pace, finished packing and ran away as quickly as their legs would carry them.

"Of course," Hideki mumbled.

"Don't feel too down about it mate, they're clearly small-minded and terrified of anything and everything. From the looks of things, they'd bring an army to take on a cute little bunny rabbit if it looked at them funny," Arthur said with the best smile he could give considering the circumstances.

"What about Hershel and Claire?" Rosalina asked.

"What about them?"

"Well, might they know anything? You're always talking about them and telling us about their stories. Hopefully they stuck around and we could ask them a few questions."

"They were always like the grandparents I never had, so hopefully they didn't succumb to that stupid curse everyone thought – thinks I carry around with me."

The lonely buildings stood high around them, the thick dark wood adding some decoration to the simple white walls and thatched roofs. With the sky still permanently overcast, the towering houses just felt oppressive as it became increasingly clear people were looking down at them from the windows; too scared to come outside but too curious to look away. It was something Hideki had experienced his entire life and having it here again just made him feel sick to his stomach. There was no need to stare at them as if they were escaped beasts prowling the land for prey. They were people, human beings.

"It's this one."

They stood in front of a house unlike any of the others; one that was clearly much older and yet much more looked after, the door was painted a relaxing pale blue with a smiling knocker in the centre and two little flower pots stood either side of it with well-maintained miniature trees. Hideki knocked and waited. Would they come? Were they still here?

The door opened and a small wrinkled walnut of a woman stood there with her sharp piercing eyes hidden behind a pair of wiry glasses. It took her a moment of scratching her head through her long white hair and batting off some flour from her flowery apron to realise who she was looking at. "Little Hideki?" He nodded and she quickly hobbled towards him and locked him in a tight embrace, completely forgetting that she still had flour all over her. "Hershel! Hershel! Get down here! Hideki's come back!"

A brief sound of rushed clomps sped down the stairs and an equally wrinkled old gentleman appeared at the door, smiling warmly with his small beady eyes and looking with intrigue at the others that stood around Hideki. He tipped his flat cap in greeting before focusing on Hideki. "Welcome home young man, you best all get inside quickly."

Claire nodded fervently and hobbled inside gripping on tightly to Hideki's hand and the others followed with warm "Thank you"s to Hershel as they passed him. He stuck his wrinkled head out of the door, searched the street for any danger, and pleased to see that no one was approaching the house, he closed and locked the door as securely as possible. Nobody was causing harm to any guest in his home.

Chapter 31
Records of Memories

They were quickly ushered through the wood-panelled hallway; walking past an old grandfather clock which had been sculpted to look like a dark mahogany temple to time, barely having time to notice the very well-worn floral carpet and the candle-esque light fixtures that hung from the walls. When they were in the sitting room and told to make themselves at home on faded cream armchairs they were able to take everything in a little bit more. Bookshelves with every text imaginable covered the walls leaving only room for the windows at the front of the house and a wide glass door at the back which opened out into a small garden. It had that comforting smell of old books which made them feel safe and relaxed.

Claire had hobbled away to the kitchen with Hershel and promptly returned with a tray of cups, saucers, a jug of milk and two teapots steaming with freshly brewed tea. "You must all be absolutely parched!" She set the tray down and sorted out the tea for everyone, passing each cup and saucer out with a plucky, "Here, get this down you, it'll do you good. I always find that a nice cup of tea always calms me down and brings out the best in you, isn't that right, Hershel dear?"

"Quite right, my love." Hershel regally settled himself down into his chair by the window and Claire sat down in hers on the other side of a little table. "It's a pleasure to see you again, my boy; though we didn't expect it to happen quite so soon." He looked at them all closely with his beady eyes and stroked his chin thoughtfully. "Hideki, would you care to introduce your companions so we can converse in a simpler fashion?"

"Oh, yeah! This is Rosalina, she's the princess of the kingdom where I ended up and we're kind of – no, definitely together right now; this is Diana, she's the captain of our little group, this is David, he's Diana's fiancée, and this is Arthur, David's brother and my best friend."

Claire tapped Hershel's arm in excitement, "Oh our little Hideki found love! Isn't it wonderful Hershel dear! And friends too! I'm so happy for you sweetheart. I was worried when you went off on your own, I know Yuuko was too, but it looks like you've done just fine."

Hideki started at the mention of Yuuko's name, "Is she still about? I'd love to be able to speak to her again, after all there's so much I need to thank her for and so much I need to apologise about."

Hershel looked sadly at Claire before stating, "She vanished not long after you left, just like all the others. I'm sorry, my boy."

"Oh." Hideki could feel tears welling in his eyes but wiped them away when he felt Rosalina's hand on his.

"You know, none of you seem to be dead, you're brimming with too much of that mana for that. So, what are you doing here now and like this?" Claire asked.

"We're on a quest, Mr –" Diana began to say before she was cut off.

"Hershel. Just call me Hershel. Same for my darling wife, just call her Claire. You're all friends of Hideki and therefore you're all friends of ours."

"We're on a quest, Hershel. Someone called the Fallen Goddess has committed many atrocities where we live. She tried to have Rosalina assassinated, she drove one of our gods mad which ultimately led to the death of both him and his brother, she messed with Hideki's memories, and apparently much more. Before he passed away, one of our gods asked Hideki to avenge him and his brother. That's what we're here to do. We're here to find this Fallen Goddess and defeat her."

"Isn't that a bit dangerous for a small group of young'uns like yourselves?" Claire probed.

"We're more than capable of looking after ourselves, if you don't mind me being blunt," David responded.

"Have you heard anything about this Fallen Goddess or the temple she calls home? It's supposed to be near here somewhere…" Rosalina asked.

Hershel thought about this for a moment. "I can't say I have. How very peculiar." He lifted himself up and began roaming the bookshelves in search of something that may come to his aid. "I've certainly never heard anything about any Fallen Goddess, but I've read about a few temples in my time. Now where is that book that spoke of those mythic temples? You remember, Claire? The one that historian explorer wrote after he spent the best part of a century trying to find everything there was to find in Helheim. I can't say it was hugely illuminating in the grand scheme of things. The gentleman had no literary flair whatsoever and the main gist was that he never actually found anything, just rumours and stories. He was clearly terrible at his job, but maybe he might come in handy now. What was it called again Claire?"

Claire picked herself up too and her eyes darted through the bookshelves looking for any titles that stood out to her. "Thor's Hammer: Fact or Fiction? A Comprehensive Guide to Old Norse Mythology? The Art of Puppetry in Helheim? Seriously, Hershel dear, I question why you keep some of these books when you've still not even managed to read half of them."

Hershel tipped his hat at her, "One never leaves a challenge undone."

Claire tutted and they both stood staring at the bookshelves. Hideki and the others didn't quite know what to do with themselves as the old couple went about their

255

searching; it was always more than a little awkward when your host got pre-occupied by something else, but Hershel and Claire were so warm that they appreciated anything they could do to help. The same idea seemed to come to both Hershel and Claire at the same time as their eyes lit up and they aimed their fingers at a large muddy red volume in the very middle of the shelf with a proclamation of "That one!"

Hershel eased the book out and carefully rested it on a specially made stand and began flicking through it. "Alexander's Magnificent History of Helheim: An Archaeological Journey of Epic Proportions; I'd forgotten how arrogant the author was too." He ran his finger through the index at the back as he asked, "You say this temple you're looking for is near here, correct?" Hideki nodded and Hershel whipped the book's pages back and forth until he found mention of a temple in the vicinity of Wonder's End. "Ah, here we go. 'The people of the town speak of a temple not far from Wonder's End.' I'm not quite sure who he has been speaking to, because we've lived here for centuries and nobody has once said anything about a temple nearby. Anyway... 'It's apparently big and very dangerous, and anyone who enters never returns.' I'd forgotten how long he took to get to the point with these things. 'One lady, who requested anonymity, said the temple stood due North from the town but suggested that I'd never find it.' So, just keep heading North from here is probably your best bet. How did he end this anecdote again? Ah, yes. 'I went searching and though I found a broken archway that could have passed for a door, I never found that temple.' So, absolutely useless." He nodded contently and slammed the book shut.

"I wonder who that lady who spoke to him was as those directions while simple seem oddly definitive," Rosalina said.

"Probably someone trying to mess with this 'amazing' Alexander," David muttered.

"But what if she was telling the truth?" Hideki said, trying to puzzle the whole thing out. "The guy found a broken archway. Maybe the temple was hidden? If there's any sort of evil hiding in there, it's hardly going to want to be found, right?"

"Indeed," was Hershel's firm response as he carefully put the book back in its place. "So the question is, how do you make the temple appear?" He thoughtfully scratched his chin while he mused over the question. "Unless it was previously destroyed and the archway is all that remained of the temple, I suspect the answer lies somewhere in that archway. Think of it like a puzzle. Maybe you need a special key and inserting it into the archway reveals the temple, or perhaps some guardians will lie in wait which need to be defeated, or perhaps the archway is itself a puzzle and needs manipulating in just the right way so as to unlock everything. Without the archway here, it's impossible to figure it out. There's too many variables."

"But, Hershel dear, I assume they all know how to use a bit of magic. Yuuko spent enough time teaching Hideki to last a lifetime and if I'm not mistaken by all of your weapons, you're all trained warriors. You don't need to figure it out for them. We're old dear, frightfully old. We can carry on with the books and the home and the thrill of learning new things even now, but we're not strong enough to leave the village to help. You know that just as much as I do. So don't get any ideas about going off on an adventure."

"We'd never ask that of you, Claire," Hideki said, gently grabbing her hand. "This is a quest we have chosen to accept and it is our quest alone." He also grabbed Hershel's hand and he looked between the two of them as he said, "Thank you so much for your help and for everything you've done for me over the years, you are truly amazing and I am so glad I got to know you."

"One always does the best he can and one always finishes that which he begins. No other way is proper." Hershel stated with a wrinkled grin. "Stay until nightfall, we'll make sure you're all fed and rested for the rest of your journey and then when it is quiet, you should be able to get out of Wonder's End without anybody noticing, ok?"

"Thank you for your kindness, Hershel; you too Claire," Rosalina said.

Claire beamed with pride, "Oh you all look so noble. I've got a good feeling about this quest, I think it's going to go perfectly well. Now, who wants a bit of dinner?"

Chapter 32
Time of Judgement

After they'd had their fill, they all sat around the living room and pondered over the next few days until they became aware of an insistent scratching at the door. At first it was merely inquisitive but as they didn't move toward it, the scratching got more and more frantic until it was a constant irritant in their ears. Hershel hoisted himself out of his chair and hobbled to the door. On opening it, he was greeted with a white five-tailed wolf which rushed past him and into the living room before he had a chance to react.

"You?" Hideki said with a cocked eyebrow. This was quite clearly the same wolf that they'd seen throughout the journey and though it was a surprise, he wasn't particularly shocked to see the wolf again. "What do you want boy?" He held out his hand to pet the wolf but it scoffed and turned its great furry head away.

Close up, it was clear that the wolf's white fur wasn't merely glowing, tiny particles of light continually sparked along the snowy hairs causing the wolf to shimmer and glisten. "I will not be treated like some pet," the wolf said petulantly. Its voice was deep with a hint of a growl and washed over them like rich velvet, it landed with a gravitas that demanded their attention.

"Your journey is almost over Hideki, Rosalina, Diana, David, Arthur."

"How do you know our names?" Arthur asked after almost jumping from his chair at the wolf speaking.

It rested its huge wise eyes on Arthur and its mouth turned up into an unimpressed snarl. "I know quite a lot about all of you, but now is not the time to be asking questions. Now is the time to escape from here." It signalled the door with its head and turned around to leave, expecting them to follow.

"Who, or what are you?" Diana asked. "How do we know we can trust you?"

The wolf's tails stood on end and its ears twitched as it turned around and growled at them. "None of that is important, you must make your way to the Fallen Goddess now or you will certainly perish."

"If we're going to trust you mate, you need to give use some answers. We've been attacked enough in this place to know it's not the smartest move to leave a safe haven when you're not prepared all so you can follow a strange wolf with more tails than it should have," David said with a not unusual amount of sarcasm. He folded his arms and stayed resolutely seated with a smirk across his face.

The wolf bared its teeth at David and looked as though it were about to bite him, but after quick glances at them around the room the wolf stopped and sat down on the floor.

261

"If that's the way you're going to play, I will not be responsible for your inevitable deaths."

Rosalina opened up the questioning by repeating what Diana had asked a few moments ago, "Who or what are you?"

The wolf rolled its eyes before answering, "I have been called many names over the millennia, but the one I have come to be most fond of is Yggdrasil. As to what I am, not even I know the answer to that question. A spirit? A demon? A god? One day I hope to find out what it is that I am, but for now, you'll have to settle for the creature which will show you the way to that vile woman and her treacherous lair."

They all stared at each other in shock at this before Rosalina managed to address it, "Yggdrasil? Like the World Tree?"

The wolf seemed particularly un-enthused by this question and with a wave of his paw uttered a simple, "If that is where it comes from, so be it." Clearly no more headway would be made there.

Hideki took up the probing and went in a different direction, "And just who is the Fallen Goddess? Where did she fall from? Why is she so dead set on hurting innocent lives?"

Yggdrasil huffed and puffed as it tried to figure how best to convey the multitude of thoughts that were playing on its mind until it finally settled on, "There is no time. We must be moving. And the answers to those questions would take far too long, just be content in knowing that her ultimate goal is the destruction of humanity and be done with it. I can be as omniscient as I like, but even I cannot guess as to her motives. She's a bitter, twisted monstrosity who the universe needs protecting from."

"But that doesn't tell us anything new! We already know she's evil, what we need to know are notable weaknesses, how she fights, what her temple is like, that's what will be useful," Arthur moaned.

Yggdrasil stood up and padded about the room to release some of its frustration. Hershel remained by the door and Claire sat transfixed in her chair. Both were all but paralysed by fear of this creature that had barged into their home. What surprised them more than anything was how calmly the children were talking to it as if it were the most normal thing in the world. Then Yggdrasil spoke again and they shrank back into themselves. "She may have fallen from grace but she is still a goddess which means she's all but undefeatable. She is omniscient and omnipotent, capable of creating and destroying anything at will; she can warp the very afterlife on a whim." Hideki, Rosalina, and Arthur grew notably afraid at this statement and Yggdrasil noticed. "What did you expect? You're taking on a goddess. Gods by their very nature are all but immortal."

"But then how can we kill her?" Diana asked without missing a beat.

"Through a miracle or through the only way dictators ever fall: the power of the many is capable of overthrowing the power of the one, as long as they have the right leader." Yggdrasil crept closer to Rosalina and rested its large head on her lap, looking up into her eyes with piercing intent. The sparkling fur was remarkably soft to the touch, almost heavenly really, and when Rosalina ran her fingers through Yggdrasil's fur she felt her mana stores increase in capacity. "You'll know what to do when the time comes, young Princess."

"What do you mean I'll know?" she asked with concern.

The wolf let out a rumbling laugh before answering, "Exactly what I said." Having the wolf laugh in her lap caused Rosalina to giggle as the fur sent tickling tingles all through her body and the whole situation was just so clichéd that she couldn't help but be amused.

"Why speak to us now when you've been keeping an eye on us since we got here?" was Rosalina's next question.

The wolf pulled away and began to inch towards the door. "Because had I interrupted your journey then, you would have been in far more danger. At least here we are away from prying eyes and ears." Yggdrasil suddenly began to sniff at the air and darted towards the door, nearly knocking down Hershel as he ran. "Say your goodbyes, you need to leave now, her army is coming."

"She has an army?" Arthur gawped.

Through an angry growl, Yggdrasil snapped, "Of course she does, she's a goddess. Now move!"

They all leapt to their feet and rushed towards Yggdrasil with Claire and Hershel hobbling up behind them. "You all take care of yourselves, children. We wish you the best of luck!" Hershel said, doffing his hat a little as he did so.

"I don't want to be seeing you again anytime soon, Hideki dear; the same goes for all of you too. Get back home safe and sound; and know that we'll always keep an eye on you from here."

As Yggdrasil's growling grew more intense, Hideki ran back to Hershel and Claire and grabbed them into a tight embrace. "Thank you so much for everything you've ever done for me. Look after yourselves too, ok?"

"We will."

Yggdrasil sniffed the air once more and darted through them all towards the back of the house. "Out the back. We need to leave out the back." Its head whipped around and sent a flurry of sparks into the air as it did so. "Block the doors, Hershel and Claire, don't let anyone in and you will remain perfectly safe." It waited for them to nod their understanding before pushing open the back door and leaping through the little garden to a fence at the back. When the group caught up with him, Hershel and Claire blockaded the back door and when they were out of sight, Yggdrasil stated with absolute urgency, "We need to get out of here now."

Chapter 33
Leap The Precipice

Shouting could be heard not too far away, harsh guttural bellows that struck you down with fear, and it was quite clearly getting closer. The words were unintelligible, just a gibberish string of sounds between various different voices and it became immediately clear to Hideki and the others that Yggdrasil was telling the truth. They needed to leave Wonder's End now. After a brief sniff of the air and a twitch of the ears, Yggdrasil pushed open the gate and set off at the fastest run it could go which would allow the team to follow; something that it found aggravating but realised it had no other option but to do. Humans just weren't built for running at the same speed as a four-legged animal, especially not one the size of Yggdrasil.

The buildings stood high above them and as the shouting stretched out around the town to come from all directions it became a frantic race through the streets. The houses became more overbearing and oppressive than ever before, staring down upon them like a monolithic trap. They whipped around down one street and then down another and each looked all but identical to the last. They had very little clue how Yggdrasil knew which way it was going, but from the slight sniffs and twitches of its ears it was clear that the wolf grew ever more certain of its path. They headed straight through two crossroads before Yggdrasil realised something was coming and zipped back down the same cross roads before taking a left. Then right, then left, then right; the streets stretched on and on and thankfully they had yet to meet whatever was searching for them.

"What are we escaping from, Yggdrasil?" Hideki asked as they surged around another corner.

The wolf stopped and nodded ahead as it began to turn back the way it had come. Humanoid creatures were roaming the street just up ahead, were it not for the glinting blood red eyes shining through a horned and tusked ghostly white mask, they could've been mistaken for the normal residents of Wonder's End. They carried a varied assortment of weapons, some of which Diana, David, Rosalina, and Arthur had never seen before, but either way they were clearly out for blood.

One of the nameless demons caught sight of them and the mouth on the mask opened wide to allow it to howl its orders at the others before galloping towards them at a tremendous speed.

"Run, run, RUN!" David yelled as the demon drew nearer. Hideki and the rest were already ahead of him by this point and David had to play catch up. "Don't leave me behind to deal with those abominations myself!"

"David look out!" Arthur cried as one of the nameless demons leapt down behind David and was about to crush him in its arms.

"*AVAVAGO!*" Rosalina roared and the violent lightning struck the demon with such force that it was no more than a frazzled lump of dust sitting atop the earth.

More of the demons appeared and as the group continued to run they tried to get in as many pot-shots as possible to cut down the numbers of their foes. "*ZUMVI!*" "*IALPIRGAH!*" "*OZONGON!*" "*BALZIZRAS!*" "*TELOCH!*" Soon they were followed by a trail of scorching flames, cutting winds, violent seas of water, blinding explosions of light, and the awful cries of death as the demons were struck down into the dust. But more just kept coming.

"Is everything in this bloody world never-ending?" moaned Arthur after he launched forth a particularly violent "*AVAVAGO!*"

"Just keep running!" Diana yelled.

And then they were out of Wonder's End and still running as fast as they could. Looking back at the town it was possible to see the demons swarming all over it like bees in their hive; there were so many that their white horned masks seemed to coat every possible surface of the town. Hideki had to breathe deeply and pray that Hershel and Claire would be ok as it looked as though no one could survive facing down that many demons. Yggdrasil hadn't lied to them so far so he was

268

filled with hope that they would make it out just fine. For Hideki and the others, the outlook was much bleaker. In escaping the town they'd bought themselves a momentary reprieve and managed to get out of sight of the demons, but soon the demon swarm would realise they were no longer there and expand their search at which point they'd be sitting ducks. The landscape was flat as far as the eye could see apart from a tiny speck in the distance. No matter how quickly they ran, they'd be spotted before they made it to the temple in which case they'd be forced to fight.

Yggdrasil stopped and its fur stood dramatically on end, it stood rigidly for a moment as its five tails fanned outwards before they split off and each tail formed its own wolf of solid glistening light. In unison the five wolves said, "I'll create a distraction, it should hopefully buy you enough time to get a big enough head start. Whatever you do, don't stop moving. If you do, they'll catch you and you will die. Reach the temple, due North; perform that miracle and defeat that vile goddess. Go!" One by one the wolves set off in different directions and once they'd gone far enough they howled and the demons leapt from the town in five hideous clusters and flew off towards each wolf.

"This is it. No turning back now. Let's go!" Hideki said and started off in the direction of the speck on the horizon with the others in tow. Whatever happened from now on was inevitable. They had chosen this path and while there was no

269

way of knowing how it would end, they knew that it had the potential to change the universe forever. The weight of that thought bore heavily upon them but they could not dwell on it. If they did, it was far too easy to lose confidence and spiral into a lake of self-doubt in which they would drown. Best just to focus on what was in front of them. That speck was perhaps an hour or so away at a run, and hopefully the demons wouldn't be back until they were over half-way there. This could go smoothly, or it could go so, so wrong. In the pit of Rosalina's stomach there was a deep sense of foreboding, but she couldn't quite pinpoint why.

Chapter 34
Blinded by Light

They sped towards that tiny speck as quickly as their legs would take them. They had to make it there. They had to. The barren wasteland seemed to stretch interminably ahead of them, that speck never getting any nearer. It was just there. That's all they needed to do. Yggdrasil had distracted the nameless demons for the time being and they needed to make the most of it. Onwards. The overcast sky grew darker and darker above them as though it were about to rain in what must have been the first time in centuries.

"Something doesn't feel right," Rosalina said as they ran. She searched around the landscape and noticed that the ground around them seemed lighter than it was further afield, and as she looked up she realised that a hole in the clouds was causing a beam of sunlight to highlight them. Even though they kept moving forward, the light simply followed them. "They're going to spot us."

Diana dropped to the back of the group and shouted ahead, "Just keep moving. Don't look back." She herself chose this moment to check if the demons were following them and she was frustrated to see that Yggdrasil had barely bought them any time at all. Thousands of the nameless demons were streaming over the walls of Wonder's End and heading straight for them with more coming from the directions where Yggdrasil had run off to. What were their options now? Either they kept running and outpaced the demons, which currently seemed unlikely as they seemed to be gaining on them every second; they fought them as a group which could work but then if they all perished no one would be left to take on the Fallen Goddess; and the last option… One of them could try to buy the others some time. With the help of the Vardrs and powerful spells that covered a wide area, one of them could potentially stem the tide enough for the others to make it. It had to be her. Hideki was the one who took up this quest and he was damn well finishing it. Rosalina had to survive for the sake of Ryushima. And David… She couldn't bear to see him die protecting her, and she couldn't bear for him or Arthur to be apart. As much as she loved David and wanted to spend the rest of her life with him, she felt that it was her duty to protect everyone.

David quickly glanced back to see Diana stop running and turn to face the oncoming horde. He dropped behind the others and ran back to her. "Diana, what are you doing? Come on! We have to move!"

"Someone has to buy us some time and it has to be me." For the first time in her life Diana felt truly vulnerable and afraid. She could feel her voice quake as she said it and could feel the tears welling up in her eyes. "You go, and you look after them all."

David's hands frantically shook Diana's shoulders as he tried to force her to move, "What are you talking about?"

"That horde is going to catch up to us one way or the other. If one of us stays behind, then perhaps we can slow down those demons enough to give everyone else a fighting chance. It's the only way." She gently stroked his face, wiping away the tears that had begun to roll down his cheeks.

"I'll do it instead; I can't let you do this Di!"

Diana bit her lips and regained some of her ardent steeliness. "You need to look after Arthur and do your duty to protect Rosalina and Hideki. This… This is my duty." David shook his head at this but he could tell that Diana's mind was made up and there was no changing it now. "I love you." Diana kissed him on the lips, a slow lingering kiss that both realised could very well be their last.

"I love you too." David hesitantly drew away while still clinging on to her hand. "Whatever you do, don't die. We've got a wedding to plan when we get back home! And I can't exactly marry myself can I?"

Diana laughed. "I'll just have to see what I can do."

There was a brief moment where neither wanted to move but then Diana signalled that it was time for him to go and he sped off to catch up with the others. She took the time she needed to catch her breath, draw in as much mana as she could and prepare herself for the challenge that was surging towards her like an ungodly torrent. The others would be heartbroken, and she could just about hear Rosalina's cries of "Diana, don't do it!" and Hideki's yells of "Just run!" but she had made her decision.

How many of these demons could she destroy before she either died or passed out from mana exhaustion? She didn't know, but she would by the time this was all over. Gripping the hilt of her rapier tightly she drew the crescent moon and called out, "*PAMPHICA, A GRAA ORS, YOLCAM VANGEM, SELENE!*" As Selene was in the process of appearing, Diana whipped around and drew a circle in the air above her as she yelled, "*ARPHE MOMAR BASGIM, ILMO, HELIOS!*" Two Vardr at once was a risky strategy, but what other choice did she have? At least this way she had more firepower behind her and that way she could cause some serious damage.

Selene and Helios were now next to her and nodded knowingly at one another while they waited on Diana's orders. "Destroy as many of those things as possible. Do whatever you have to do but whatever happens slow them down." And with that she charged forward with blistering fury toward the demons, her two Vardr galloping alongside her.

The tsunami of nameless demons was met with a swarm of gigantic meteors, blazing tornadoes and huge swathes of magic as they clashed with Diana. Their masked mouths opened and howled with tremendous force as many of their lives were snuffed out in an instant. But the swarm soon filled in the gaps that had formed and they quickly surrounded Diana and the Vardr. For the moment the plan seemed to have worked and the demons' attention was solely on them, but Diana knew it wouldn't last for long.

Up close and personal Diana realised that the nameless demons all had subtle variations in their masks and the robes that almost seemed to glide through the air as they moved. One had a thin blue crack through one of its eyes while another had multiple red splotches all over its chest and yet another had a solitary purple circle right in the centre of its forehead. No time to focus on that right now. A small group tried to jump her from all sides but with a quick spin her rapier sliced through them all and they shattered into dust. At least they died quickly, but that left the question of how powerfully did they hit? While Selene and Helios moved off, trampling and slicing through any demon that stood in their way, Diana was caught off guard by a demon slamming a club into her back. The force of the blow sent her flying into some of the nearby monstrosities and were it not for her quickly whipping her feet up and using one of the demon's face's as a springboard she probably would have been skewered on one of its tusks which she now realised were viciously sharp. So that was how hard they could hit. They were in essence glass cannons, terrifyingly powerful but very easy to take down. That certainly made things interesting since she couldn't really afford to be hit too many times by these demons.

And so began her dance of death. With her entire body working on high alert she ducked and dived through and around the many blows that came her way, slashing her rapier around her like a ribbon whirling in a pirouette. Selene launched a ferocious beam of energy that shimmered like stardust and utterly eviscerated a huge stretch of the demons running towards Diana; this was quickly followed by Helios' neighing and his subsequent stamping which crushed many more demons beneath his flaming hooves. This gave Diana a moment of respite which she used to launch some of the more powerful spells she knew, "*NAPEAI VEH AVAVAGO!*" She quickly drew a lightning bolt in the air and then the instant she held her rapier aloft it was struck by lightning and began to crackle fiercely with electricity. With numerous swipes she was able to send forth waves of electrical fury which sliced through scores of the mob.

Diana was too focused at the time to notice but the violent bursts of magic surrounding her were filling the land with intense colourful glows. The blazing tornadoes that were whipped up by Helios were leaving a scorching red flickering through the air and Selene's starlit moonbeams and meteors were bringing a multitude of whites and yellows into the mix. In the chaos this colourful mana was helping her as she slid under another attack but it couldn't maintain her level of focus forever.

That slightly sadistic glaze flowed over her as she realised she was enjoying the thrill of this battle. Part of it made her feel sick but as long as she did her job then maybe the others could make it.

"*DODS IALPIRGAH!*" With a swift picture of a flame in the air, Diana's rapier was ablaze and as she swung it around the flames extended like some demonic whip cutting through the abominations like butter. How many had she killed now? Dozens? Hundreds? Thousands? She couldn't tell. All she knew was she had to keep fighting until she could fight no more. Ahead. Behind. Two on both sides. North West. South West. Her rapier flew from nameless demon to nameless demon without mercy. Everything it touched crumbled to dust and it filled Diana with some degree of hope. She could kill every last one of these monsters and then she could re-join David and the others and all would be well. But when another demon sent her flying she knew she couldn't celebrate yet.

As the demons kept coming at her she was wondering how much longer she could keep this up. Their number seemed nigh on endless and she'd killed so many not even counting the damage that Selene and Helios were still causing. She knew that the toll of all her magic and maintaining Selene and Helios' presence was beginning to affect her. She was noticing that her movements were getting increasingly slower and she was dodging by less and less of a margin each time one of the demons swung for her. It was only a matter of time before she… A demon's sword broke through her defences and created a sizeable gash in her chest plate and would have done more damage had Diana not driven her rapier through a purple slit in its throat. "*GRAM ZUMVT!*" Rain started to fall through a gap in the clouds and increased in power until it was a raging waterfall that plunged every demon surrounding her into squelching piles of ooze.

Everything around Diana was complete and utter chaos. She was beginning to struggle to remain focused and found herself resorting to whatever tactics she could to keep fighting. Forceful kicks were enough to shatter the demons too but she was now trying to keep her distance. How long had it been since she'd started fighting? She couldn't tell any longer. It was probably only a few minutes, ten at the most, but the madness of the combat left it feeling like an age. Selene and Helios were still going strong around her and she had to keep going to keep them going.

Another demon got a blow in and dropped her to the floor. She sprang back up as quickly as she could but she could feel the bruises forming beneath her armour. There was the possibility of using a healing spell to help out but she really didn't have the time to pull it off. The demons were already thinning around her and it became clear that a very large portion of the swarm was moving on. Her plan had clearly bought the others some time and hopefully it would be enough. Just keep fighting. She plunged her rapier into the chest of one of the demons before retracting it and all but decapitating the demon that tried to jump on her. Just keep fighting. Her rapier cleaved another demon into two halves of crumbling dust. Just keep fighting. She could no longer hear Helios' powerful hooves. She was running out of mana and fast. Just keep fighting. She parried another demon's sword and disarmed it before kicking it to the ground. There were maybe only two or three left and Selene had also vanished from sight. Just keep fighting. Her sword cut through one and then another and then another and she couldn't see any more of the demons other than those running off into the distance.

She collapsed into the dust of her enemies and looked at the unstoppable torrent that surged towards those she had been trying to protect. "I did what I could," she said to herself. "Please make it home safely." Her eyes closed. She didn't have the strength to keep them open anymore. A soft breeze scattered some of the demon dust over her but she didn't care. All she could think about was the light that seemed to stretch out in front of her. It was so warm, so caring, like a mother's embrace. Her final words that day were, "I'm sorry… David…" And then she said no more.

Chapter 35
Scorched Feathers

David stopped running. The explosions and the brilliant crackle of magic had ended. Something was wrong. Suddenly he felt dead inside. Tears welled in his eyes as he turned to face the oncoming horde and couldn't see any hint of Diana, Selene, or Helios. She couldn't have left him. Not like this. She couldn't leave him like this.

"David, why've you stopped?" he heard Arthur ask.

"She's gone…"

"No…" he heard Rosalina cry as she too came to check on him.

"I'm so sorry, David," said Hideki, though David paid him little attention.

An infernal rage like none he had ever felt before erupted from him in a terrifying battle roar. "I'm gonna kill every last one of those bastards." He let the tears stain his face as he readied his bow and started towards the horde with deathly intent.

"David, we can't lose you too!" he heard Arthur wail.

"And I can't live without Di. You're all more powerful than you think you are. Now you go and you kill that bitch. Di did what she believed was her duty and now it falls to me to finish what she started. Now go!" Anger didn't suit David, but his pain and his rage was beyond uncontrollable. It took everything in his power to remain calm as Arthur, Hideki, and Rosalina reluctantly began to run once more. He could hear all of them sniffling as they tried to maintain some level of composure but that wasn't his concern right now. His concern was that these monsters paid for what they had done. Once the others were out of earshot he let the fury consume him. He didn't care if he made it out of this alive, he just needed to have the strength to fight, to protect those Diana had given her own life to protect.

He readied his bow and called out with a vehement growl, "*ARPHE PERIPSOL, VPAAH ZONG, ZIZ!*" The arrow flew and he called once more, "*CORONZON CAOSGO, TORZU, BEHEMOTH!*" The clouds parted and the earth shattered, and Ziz and Behemoth stood majestically before him. He pointed at the swarm that was nearly upon them and shouted so loudly his voice nearly cracked, "Obliterate."

Behemoth's humungous feet crushed hundreds of the demons as it walked and tripped many others up as the shockwaves of its force upon the ground shook the earth around it. David leapt up onto Ziz and as the Vardr soared into the air, he saw the true scale of what they were facing. In the distance the dull cracked earth was coated in a thick layer of the demon dust and it seemed as though the demons covered every inch of the ground beneath him for what appeared to be thousands of metres in every direction bar where his poor little brother was running for his life.

As he began firing off arrows at the demons while Ziz buffeted them with razor sharp winds and skull crushing shrieks, David could feel his life flashing before his eyes. He saw Arthur as a baby and remembered how proud he was to have a little brother; he saw all the times they used to play fight in the garden and how, even though David won every single time, Arthur was never disheartened; he saw the moment he first encountered Diana and the butterflies that accompanied it; he saw the day he found out his mum and dad were never coming back from their trip to the nearby village of Leoholm and the difficulty he had explaining that to Arthur; he saw his first date with Diana; he saw the day he first became a Rider of the Light and the pride that swelled in his chest back then; he saw the day he found out about Hideki and the plentiful jokes and queries he had made; he saw his proposal to Diana and felt the overflowing love he had for her; and then he saw the moment he left her to take on these monsters all by herself. He couldn't forgive himself. He should've fought and died by her side. They were a team; a partnership. They were going to be together until the end. Well, if he did his job now, they would be once more.

The time passed slowly about him; each demon slain by his energy arrows crumbled into dust at such a pace that each particle seemed to shatter separately; Behemoth's trunk-like tail swept through swathes of the demons as though in an elegant ballet but the force of the movement was clearly unbelievable as the demons were crushed beneath its weight; Ziz's winds were whipping up hundreds upon hundreds of demons into a swirling vortex of death in which they were shredded limb from dusty limb. In his rage there was this unbelievable clarity with which he saw everything and it urged him on even more.

"*FABOAN GIXYAX!*" His arrow bubbled with a poisonous purple tinge and when it struck the ground it caused many of the demons to melt from the spurts of acid that erupted from the violently shaking and disintegrating earth. He whipped his bow around and roared, "*TELOCH PIADPH ORS!*" The arrow this time was pitch black and were someone to look closely at the mana arrow they would have seen tiny white skulls peppered through the feathery tail. David launched the arrow and it split into hundreds more arrows which rained down upon the battlefield, spearing many demons through their masks and ripping straight through them before setting off on their own deadly mission to kill as many demons as possible. The flurry of pitch black arrows darted from demon to demon with such force and ferocity that there was very little they could do to defend themselves. All they could do was die.

The bloodlust David felt grew ever stronger. These monsters had taken away one of the people he held most dearly and he couldn't let a single one survive. He didn't want to stay on the periphery of the battle either as that wouldn't satisfy his need for revenge. For one normally so collected and light-hearted, he knew this wasn't like him but as his heart was breaking his mental restraints and his inhibitions were shattering. He spotted a small clearing near to where some demons were being skewered by Behemoth's tremendous horns, "Ziz, drop me off there. I need to get close and personal with these bastards."

Against its better judgement, Ziz descended and as it aimed for the clearing it clawed at the heads of the demons with its talons, shredding them down to dust. David jumped off and then a lot of the demons chose to focus on him. Most of them had crimson diamonds on their masks and clambered towards David with malicious intent. Their horrifying mouths opened and screamed some note of recognition before they leapt forward to attack. At such close range, David knew he'd put himself in unnecessary danger but he didn't care, he needed to feel the demons' dust crunching beneath his feet as he put his arrows through their skulls. With more speed than he'd ever mustered before he shot one and then another and another and another. He was a whirling hurricane of arrows which would not end until every last demon was dead. "Come on! You want us dead? Do your worst!"

The gigantic form of Behemoth crossed over him and he could just about make out Ziz zipping down through the air and drilling through the demons before he was suddenly launched into the air by one of the demons and slammed back down by another. The blows winded him badly and as he tried to get back up the demons swarmed around him, all but encasing him in a shell of their cloth robes and horrific white masks. They moved in closer and closer, their tusks and horns making the manoeuvre act like some sort of demon iron maiden. He was mere seconds from being crushed when the top batch of demons was lopped clean off and Ziz plucked David out of their clutches before they could do anymore. It was only then that the realisation of quite how close to death he had been hit David. Even one mistake in battle can quickly be the death of you. He'd always known it to be the case but hadn't understood how true it was until now.

As he hung from Ziz's talons and the Vardr destroyed more of the demons with its shriek, David wondered exactly what had happened to Diana? Had the demons actually beaten and killed her? And if they had, what had they done to the body? Did they even do anything to the bodies they killed? He stopped that train of thought right there as it was too much to bear. Had she used up too much mana and collapsed after the demons had passed her? That was probably more likely as David too was beginning to feel the strain of his mana exhaustion. All he could hope was that Arthur and the others would finish the quest and reunite his and Diana's bodies so that they could rest in peace together.

How much strength did he have left in him? The demons' numbers had thinned considerably since he had begun fighting but there were still many thousands remaining, perhaps a third or so left of the original horde. Maybe two more powerful spells?

A lightning bolt of pain suddenly shot through his left arm. He looked down to see a massive gash down its length and he could suddenly feel the warm blood gushing over his hand and bow, dripping down into a few of the remaining demons' gaping mouths. When the hell had that happened? One of the demons' tusks must have caught him when Ziz yanked him free of the crush. He tried to lift his bow up but struggled to move his arm at all. He let loose a string of profanities. Not now. He hadn't finished the job. He hadn't avenged Diana. If he couldn't use his bow, he couldn't fight effectively. Quick. Think.

He twisted the bow so he could grab its string and with it aimed at the ground he pulled the bowstring as tightly as he could from that angle. It was all or nothing now. He searched deep inside himself for every last scrap of mana and then he yelled as loudly as he could through the pain, *"YOLCAM LAS IALPRG VEH DONASDOGAMA TASTOS!"*

The arrow flew true and struck the ground like a meteor, smashing through it and drawing forth violent eruptions of lava which very quickly spread across the battlefield, engulfing all it touched. And then the lava exploded into a raging inferno that lit up the sky.

I've done all I can, Di, I'll be with you soon, David thought before his eyes closed and his body went limp in Ziz's talons. Behemoth had disappeared but Ziz managed to cling on to its material form just long enough to wrap its wings around David and crash into the ground so no further harm came to him. As Ziz vanished into the ether, David's body rested on the dusty earth next to his beloved fiancée, his hand rolling from his chest and into hers. And there they would stay.

Chapter 36
Vector to the Heavens

They heard the explosion before they saw the red haze it cast through the sky and in that moment, they realised that David was no more. Tears streamed down Arthur's face as he ran. Stupid David. Stupid Diana. Why did they have to try and be the heroes this time? Why couldn't they have just all stuck together and faced whatever came as a team? Surely that would have been better than this. Anything would have been better than this. Arthur cared deeply for Hideki and Rosalina but right now he felt lonelier than he'd ever done before. It was the adrenaline more than anything that was keeping him going. If he stopped to think about what he'd just lost, then he'd never be able to continue, so he just focused on putting one foot in front of the other as quickly as he could.

"We're nearly there!" Hideki huffed, "We're going to make it!"

Rosalina's expression had become one of grim determination as her heart steeled itself from the sorrow and the anguish; her eyes were wet with tears but she refused to let a drop fall. She was hurting right now; her limbs ached from running and she desperately wanted to let everything out, but now was not the time and Arthur was hurting inside far more than she ever could. "She's going to pay for this," she spat out through gritted teeth.

Why was he even here? Arthur thought once more. He wasn't powerful like Diana, he wasn't calm and collected in battle like David, he wasn't very good at healing magic like Rosalina, and he didn't have the courage or confidence Hideki had so thoroughly mastered. He was easily the weakest link. He should've been the one to sacrifice himself first, not Diana, not David. What use was he going to be in the final fight against that Fallen Goddess? Since arriving in Helheim he'd realised he wasn't as weak and defenceless as he had thought he was, but he was under no illusions that he was outclassed by everyone else. But, maybe if he eradicated the remaining demons... The idea took root in his mind. If he could defeat them all then he would have proven his worth on this quest. The idea sprouted and began reaching for the sun. If he did it, not only would he have protected his dearest friends, he would also have avenged his brother and his captain. The idea blossomed and he was certain now.

Hideki clocked what was going through Arthur's mind and he tried to put a stop to it, "You can't sacrifice yourself too, Arthur! We need you!"

Rosalina's hands trembled, "Don't you dare, Arthur. Don't you dare!"

"What happens if we get to the temple and those demons overrun us? We'll have fallen at the final hurdle. We can't let that happen. So somebody has to get rid of those remaining demons and I'm the only one left that's expendable." Arthur's tears had long since dried and he grew increasingly pragmatic as the time of attack drew closer.

"You're not expendable! Nobody is ever expendable! Every single life has meaning!" Hideki yelled at his friend. "Don't you ever think you're expendable."

Arthur laughed, "Oh come on, Hideki. All guards and protectors are expendable. Our duty is to risk our lives for the cause we commit to. We're not getting into an argument now. You two are finishing this quest and that's final." He drew his halberd down at his side and traced a semi-circular arc around him as he quietly uttered, "Let nothing pass while the world yet breathes, protect all beyond it from harm, Impenetrable Wall!"

An all but transparent surface appeared in front of him and when Hideki and Rosalina tried to walk towards Arthur they found that they couldn't get near. A wall of pure mana stood between them and nothing could get past it while Arthur had breath in his body. It was the same spell his parents had used all that time ago to build the protective shield around the training grounds and the arena. He was only young when they passed away, but he remembered watching them maintain the barriers on so many occasions that he'd long since learned the incantation and method for its construction. There was part of him that had imagined following in his parents' footsteps when he grew older but clearly that wasn't going to happen now. So, as part of what he suspected to be his final act, he used a spell he'd wanted to perform for so long.

"I'm sorry, guys. Now go and finish what you started. I'm going to deal with everything here."

"But why not create the wall behind you and come with us?" Hideki asked.

"Because then you'd be able to stop me. Goodbye, Princess; Goodbye, Hideki; thanks for having me along for the ride." He turned away from them and as they stood completely dumbfounded and heartbroken he lifted his hand up to wave back at them. Despite the fact he knew he was going towards his death, he couldn't help but think how cool and heroic he looked right now.

He didn't look back to see whether Hideki and Rosalina had started off again, he just focused on the task ahead. Either way, might as well go out with a bang. "*CACACOM OD FIFALZ QTING, EXENTASER TOHCOTH, GLORIANA! ARP LN AMMA A-C-LONDOH, NAT OD BNG CAOSGO, BRAN!*"

"Why are you throwing your life away, Master Arthur?" Gloriana asked as she flitted into existence around him, "You had such a bright future ahead of you!"

"Because I'm not like the others. I'm not as good at anything as they are, but even then I can still do something; I can fight until the bitter end and give my friends the best possible chance of success. And I can prove to myself that I
291

was strong enough for this journey all along. I'm fighting for my friends and myself." His shaking body betrayed the fear that currently coursed through him, but Gloriana and Bran, who had also appeared, either didn't pick up on it or tactfully chose to ignore it.

"We're behind you all the way, young Master Arthur," the tremendous giant said. "There are only a few thousand of those ugly ants left. Tough odds I'll bet, but not impossible."

Gloriana plucked a small bouquet of flowers out of thin air and carefully attached them to Arthur's armour. "I know you've never been particularly fond of me, Master Arthur, but please accept my gift. No matter what, you'll always be my Master and I am so proud of the man you are today." She didn't go into the details of the flowers that made up the little bouquet, but she had filled it with what she saw to be the most important plants and flowers for the coming battle; an eglantine rose to heal wounds, a dandelion for overcoming hardship, a nettle for protection, a peach blossom for long-life, a pear blossom for lasting friendship, and a peony for bravery and honour. It was not perhaps the most aesthetically pleasing array of flora she'd ever created, but they would hopefully do their job of keeping Arthur safe.

Arthur gently stroked the stems of the bouquet and gratefully said, "Thank you Gloriana, I'm sorry I've been so awful to you over the years. Now, shall we fight together one last time until the bitter end?"

She nodded promptly and the great Bran followed suit, though his height made the gesture difficult to see from the ground and he resorted to an affirmative, "Of course, young Master Arthur."

All too soon the demons were upon them and the chaos ensued. Demons were crushed, demons exploded, demons were chopped in two; they were flung into the air by whipping vines, they were lifted up and, much to Arthur's distaste, eaten by Bran, they were subject to the brutal blade of Arthur's halberd swinging about with wild abandon and tearing them limb from limb, killing dozens with a single blow. Eventually a group of the demons managed to reach the wall Arthur had constructed and no matter how much they scratched and clawed and bludgeoned and smashed and screeched, the wall remained strong.

Arthur realised that they couldn't make it through while cleaving three demons in half at the waist, or what he assumed to be their waist, and couldn't help remarking, "Why the hell didn't I do that before Diana decided to sacrifice herself? God I am such an idiot!" Still, he couldn't insult himself too much. When you're running for your life, your brain doesn't necessarily make the smartest of decisions and it wasn't like Diana or David made the suggestion either. They were all as bad as each other really. As he dodged out of the way of what would have been a particularly nasty bludgeoning blow to his skull, he was drawn to the thought that, as Granny Bea and

Rosalina always said, everything in life was inevitable. The choices they'd made had led them here; this was the only way this quest was ever going to end for them.

The black clouds overhead finally burst and the heavens opened, drenching everything in its path. Bran paused a moment as he let the rain wash off some of the dust that had accumulated on his face and hands, appreciating this brief reminder of home. Gloriana meanwhile was dancing around through the raindrops and wreaking havoc as she scattered her flowers over the demons and obliterated them in petal explosions.

Further into the fray, Arthur was whirling his halberd all around him, slicing through not only the demons but the very rain itself. Despite being intently focused on the battle at hand, he wondered how epic the entire battle looked. All this rain and dust and the petals, the three fighters of vastly different sizes taking on a common enemy in various different ways and hopefully looking badass while doing so. It was either an artful spectacle in combat or an incomprehensible mess but that didn't really matter as nobody was there to watch it anyway.

More and more of the demons were turning back and trying to make a move on Arthur but Bran's humungous size meant most struggled to get close, which allowed Arthur to take his pick of whatever demon he wanted to kill next. But he could ultimately only fight for a little bit longer. He had nowhere near the amount of mana or stamina as the others and it was beginning to show. The sweat was dripping down his neck and his back, though it could've been the rain, and his muscles were beginning to ache from the exertion.

There were maybe only a few hundred of the demons remaining and Arthur remembered a spell he'd been told never to use. It took too much of a toll on the body and had only ever been used by those with a death wish in the past. Well, Arthur knew he'd probably collapse from mana exhaustion soon anyway so why not go out with the biggest bang he could summon. He'd protect his friends and avenge his loved ones in one final attack. It'd be the most powerful spell he'd ever used. Well, here went nothing.

"GEMPH PAMBT OD OM TELOCH OLNA DOX!"

Chapter 37
Blood and Darkness

They stopped running. A lone archway stood right before them and then they heard a colossal explosion behind them. They turned around to witness an enormous dome of exploding fire erupting and engulfing the horizon. They quickly realised what had taken place. None of the demons were capable of escaping that final blaze, even as it struck and shattered the barrier which Arthur had constructed. By the same logic, there was no way Arthur could have survived.

"So long, my friend," Hideki said in tribute as he tried to maintain his composure. His hand slid into Rosalina's and they both gripped on to each other tightly. It was now just them against the world.

Rosalina nodded and with a deep breath muttered, "We should finish what we came here to do. We can mourn later." The pain was too great to comprehend right now and so her only defence was to follow Diana's example and shut away her emotions for the time being. She struggled greatly with this, but as she spoke she finally managed to sever the ties to her emotions until there was time to grieve properly.

Now that the imminent threat had been defeated, Hideki and Rosalina's pace slowed. They gave themselves time to catch their breaths, to restore what mana they could before the final battles, to get a proper grip of themselves and the situation they found themselves in. They were alone now. No friends. No allies. Just them against a goddess. Could they do it? Neither of them was sure now that Diana, David, and Arthur had seemingly perished on this final stretch. Hideki began to doubt his abilities while Rosalina questioned whether she could have done more to save everyone. This moment of respite had the potential to make or break their resolve.

The stone archway stood a few feet away; two winding pillars holding up the arch from which sprouted a gothic spike. Rosalina could just make out the faded remnants of angelic script at the top of the arch itself but it was all but illegible. The broken remnants of a wall rested to the side of the archway, crumbling away at the top, but clearly the author of that book had fabricated at least some of his tale as the archway itself was relatively intact. There was little out of the ordinary about the arch other than its isolation from any sort of ruins and when Hideki circled around it, he couldn't spot anything that seemed out of place about it. Perhaps what was odd was the fact that it was only worn around the angelic script. Actually, now that they thought about it, the archway looked as though it could have been new bar that one tiny detail.

Hideki ran his hand around one of the pillars, feeling the grooves for any indentations that could signal a secret button but he didn't have any luck in that endeavour. Rosalina meanwhile was focused upon the angelic script above her head. There must be something there, a spell of some sort. She felt a sardonic laugh swell in her chest, oh those doors and their magical incantations. It would be just like the stories she'd read when she was younger. If only 'open sesame' would work here.

Then she noticed something about the script, some of the worn angelic letters looked remarkably similar in shape, almost like a warped L while others looked like a curved X. The more she looked at the script the clearer it seemed to become. Well if that's *MED* then maybe they could be *GAL*, which would make *ODO OD*; so 'Open and' what? That faded squiggle could be *TAL*, which would make the next word *OM*. So, 'Open and know'. But what could that last word be?

"Rose, look at this," Hideki said, pointing out hundreds of weeping faces that adorned the foot of the pillars as though the weight of the archway rested solely upon their shoulders. "I wonder what they mean?"

"Woe. *OHIO*."

"Come again?"

Rosalina held her staff out at arm's length and spun it around once before pronouncing loudly and clearly, "*ODO OD OM OHIO*."

Nothing happened for a minute or so and Rosalina began to doubt that she'd found the solution to the puzzle, but then the earth beneath their feet began to rumble.

"What did you just do?"

"Open and know woe. That's what the angelic script on the archway says, and clearly that's the incantation you need to solve the puzzle. Or at least, that's what I thought it would do anyway. It could've been a motto or a warning or anything, but it was worth a shot. And it worked anyway, so it's all good, isn't it?" Rosalina waffled on as she tried to stem the momentary rush of panic that accompanied the quaking earth.

"Well, it seems to have worked, certainly!"

Structures burst through the ground and the temple rose like an exhalation. A set of stairs stretched upwards from the archway to a large plateau on which the temple grew, its magnificent spires reaching higher and higher towards the cloudy heavens. Terrifying gargoyles were wrapped around the top of these spires and every few seconds seemed to twitch ever so slightly. A row of robed figures glared down at the earth above the temple's entrance as though their sole purpose in life was to cast judgement upon any who dared to enter. From where Hideki and Rosalina stood gawping they couldn't exactly see how enormous the temple was, but they figured it must be pretty gigantic. The intricacy of its design was unbelievable as each ridge, spike, engraving, window, and sculpture was placed and formed with such precision that it seemed as though the carved creatures could come alive at any moment.

"We've made it, Rose! We've really made it!" Hideki said with what enthusiasm he could muster as they climbed the steps to the plateau.

"We have indeed," Rosalina replied, allowing herself to smile for the first time in hours. "But we can't let our guard down yet."

"Definitely not."

They'd finally reached the plateau when something cracked above them, the sound of stone violently tearing itself apart.

"What was that?" Rosalina asked.

The cracking grew louder and more violent before dusty shards of rubble clattered to the floor around them. They looked up as a monster let loose a vicious blood-curdling howl. One of the gargoyles, a great demonic bat-like beast with wings that stretched across almost the length of the temple, was contorting and writhing as its stone shackles crumbled off its leathery skin. The beast had deep black eyes like bottomless pits which flitted quickly from point to point, though it was nigh impossible to tell that they were moving. It howled once more and Hideki realised that the reason the howl sent shivers down his spine was because it was so oddly formed through the beast's protruding jaw and tusk-like canines making it sound particularly grating. The beast briefly clawed at its face to remove the remnants of the stone and then it stared intently at the two of them down below.

"We're going to have to beat that thing, aren't we?" Rosalina asked.

"Yup."

Both of them quickly tried to formulate a plan of attack but Rosalina was the first to finish hers. "I'll take it down, you save your mana and watch my back, ok?"

Hideki nodded, "Ok."

"Might as well go big from the start and end this as quickly as possible," Rosalina said as she twirled her staff through the air. The gargoyle figured out what she was doing and dropped from its perch, nosediving towards them at tremendous speed. *"DOOLAP PIR, ODO MADRIAX OD TORZU, NE EXENTASER, AMATERASU!"*

Before the gargoyle reached them, Amaterasu swooped down from the heavens and plucked it from the air, her talons tearing through the sinewy membrane it had for wings. The gargoyle howled and tried desperately to free itself.

"BALZIZRAS! AVAVAGO! IALPIRGAH!" Rosalina fired off spell after spell and while they all hit their mark, the gargoyle didn't seem to have suffered a scratch bar where it was being held by Amaterasu.

"DOOLAP EGO OLPIRT, PHAMAH TOLTORG LN VBRAH!" The light that swelled in Rosalina's staff was blinding, almost as if there truly was a star shining away in the crystal, then it went supernova and the mana burst towards the gargoyle like a comet and exploded in its chest. Amaterasu let go milliseconds before the attack landed and after righting herself launched her own barrage of attacks with her blazing feathers.

301

Suddenly, Hideki was rushing behind Rosalina yelling her name. Next thing she knew, the ground was no longer beneath her feet. She looked up to see another huge gargoyle. There was another one. Why was there always another one? Hideki was clearly about to summon Mjölnir but Rosalina shouted down to him, "Don't waste your mana! I can handle this!" She turned her attention to Amaterasu, "If you could deal with that one, Mother Ammy, that would be most appreciated." The phoenix cawed in acknowledgement and set to work keeping the original gargoyle occupied. "And as for you…" The water was already swirling around her staff as she yelled, *"DOOLAP PIR, ADRPAN TOL HAMI DODSIH, ENAY DE EGO ZUMVI, SUSANOO!"*

The mighty warrior cut through the storm-clouds and landed on the gargoyle's back. The weight caused them to drop out of the air. As they plummeted, the gargoyle lashed out in every direction, at Susanoo, at Rosalina, at whatever it could reach with its claws. At one point it caught Rosalina along her leg, slicing through her dress and drawing blood. This evidently caused the gargoyle glee as it started to laugh, but it quickly stopped when Susanoo sliced off its wings, grabbed Rosalina, and left the gargoyle to plummet to the ground.

However, the two monsters were not going to give up that easily as they started launching fireballs through the air in a highly erratic manner. From the ground, Hideki's view of the battle was completely obfuscated. Even though he desperately wanted to help, there was nothing he could do.

With Rosalina in his arms, Susanoo leapt from foothold to foothold across the face of the temple cutting through every fireball he could with the watery blasts from his blade while Rosalina attacked with every powerful spell she knew. It was a cavalcade of elements lighting up the sky and bringing more colour to Helheim than it had seen in a very long time. The gargoyles just refused to die. Even when the gargoyle which was now without wings smashed into the ground, it just picked itself up and started to climb up the temple.

Hideki managed to make it to the great gate of the temple and was grateful to find that the doors were open and they would easily be able to get in. It filled him with trepidation, but at least it was one less thing to worry about. Then he heard one of the gargoyle's howl once more before the lifeless broken rubble of its body smashed into the ground in front of him.

"One down!" Rosalina yelled from up above.

More rubble came tumbling down.

"And that's two!"

Susanoo landed and placed Rosalina gently down on the ground.

"Thank you, Susanoo. You too, Mother Ammy!" Rosalina said with a smile as they vanished into the ether. She started to walk towards Hideki but stumbled and fell.

"Rose!" Hideki rushed to catch her and made it just in the nick of time.

Rosalina winced in pain as she looked down at her gashed leg. She took a deep breath and said, "It'll be fine. It's just a flesh wound. Nothing a quick healing spell won't fix." She quickly used Healing Circle on herself and began to feel a lot better as the wound stitched itself together. "See? Nothing to worry about."

Hideki held her and kissed her, "Are you sure you're ok?"

"Yeah… Just give me a second." She took another deep breath as she collected herself and then asked, "Could you help me up, please?"

Tentatively, Hideki pulled her up and Rosalina could see that his face was still clearly full of concern. He made it even clearer when he asked her, "Are you going to be able to continue?"

She started to walk forward and found that it was quite a bit more difficult than before. There must have been some sort of nasty magic in that gargoyle's claws, she thought. She managed a few steps normally and then she had to limp. "I'll be fine. I just need to walk it off."

He didn't believe her and she didn't believe herself, but they both needed it to be true right now. They were so close to the end now. They couldn't stop. Even though she couldn't move so quickly now and had used up quite a lot of her mana already, Hideki still needed her to finish the quest. And so, arm in arm to give each other support, they entered the temple and readied themselves for what they knew would be the final battle.

Chapter 38
The One Ruling Everything

Cold stone stretched out before them as they walked. The dull marble floor beneath their feet felt particularly foreboding as every now and again a pulse of mana seemed to flow through it. Above them the ceiling was not visible; all they could see was a dark starry sky with billions of tiny little gems peppering the firmament. There were no windows. There was no light apart from the glow afforded by the starlight above. Carved statues stood at intervals along the corridor; some were like totems of various monsters, others seemed human, others still were terrifyingly an amalgamation of the two. Their eyes followed Hideki and Rosalina intently, constantly watching, constantly staring.

In their hearts, they knew that they would soon be face to face with this Fallen Goddess. What would she be like? Some hideous witch? Would she even have a corporeal form? It wasn't until they began to think about it that they realised they had no clue what to expect from a goddess. After all, if she was that powerful, how had they managed to make it this far? If she had wanted to stop them, then surely she could have killed them off in an instant long before they had ever made it here.

Something just didn't feel right about the whole thing and they both knew it.

A great chamber opened up in front of them and Rosalina gasped in horror. Millions of crystalline chambers coated the walls. In those chambers were the bodies of people. They hung lifelessly and yet clearly in pain at the same time. Hideki had to take in a deep breath to calm himself as the cogs in his mind began to piece together the mystery of Helheim. His parents. His guardians. The people who had vanished without a trace. They were here. This was where they had vanished to. You didn't die in Helheim unless a monster destroyed your soul, so those that had vanished had had to be somewhere, and that somewhere was here. The only thing Hideki couldn't figure out was why. They couldn't be here by choice. So why were they here? And why were they all locked away and in such visible pain?

They stepped tentatively into the chamber. They had a job to do. As horrifying as this was, they had no choice in the matter.

An icy laugh echoed out through the chamber sending chills down Hideki's spine. The laugh echoed out again, but this time it seemed much closer than before. Hideki and Rosalina looked at each other to make sure they weren't going out of their minds, and then the laugh started up again.

"Oh, you poor pathetic little mortals, whatever are you doing here?"

That voice… Hideki recognised that voice.

"Turn back now before it is too late."

"Show yourself!" Hideki yelled out.

"Oh, my dear sweet Hideki, don't you recognise me?"

"Show yourself!"

"How's this?"

Hideki leapt out of his skin as the goddess' face appeared right beside him as if from nowhere. He let go of Rosalina and whipped his sword out of its sheathe as he turned to face the goddess. That thin angular face, the crisp black hair, the fiery red eyes, and that voice coming from those pursed lips. His sword dropped.

"Yuuko?"

With a lithe flourish and a smouldering wink, the goddess's voice, laced with biting sarcasm, struck him, "Hello sweetheart."

Hideki was paralysed with shock. He couldn't move. He couldn't speak. His hands just trembled as his eyes grew wet with tears. He just couldn't compute what he saw before him. It couldn't be possible. Not Yuuko. Not the lovely lady who took him in and taught him everything he knew. Not the person who had rescued him from his childhood solitude. This couldn't be real.

"Who are you?" Rosalina asked for him. Her horror had made way for that steely determination to rise to the fore, she could not let this 'goddess' get away with hurting Hideki like this.

Yuuko glanced her way with tutting disdain and a fiercely arched eyebrow. "Who do you think I am, little Princess?"

Indignation rose in Rosalina's chest. "You're the one behind it all, aren't you? You're the one bringing despair to the world."

Yuuko's slender hand rose, lifting up a long black sleeve which seemed to be coated in blue flames along the edge. Her hips shifted in her richly embroidered black and golden gown and her malicious eyes rested more firmly on Rosalina. "Perhaps."

"Don't get enigmatic with me. We've just lost three of our closest friends to get to you and I am not in the mood for worthless ambiguities. Are you really Yuuko or are you taking the form of the woman Hideki called Yuuko?"

Yuuko's eyes widened with excitement for an instant. "We are one and the same. I am the goddess and she is me."

"Why?" That was the first and only word Hideki could manage. "Why?"

Yuuko glided past them and through to the centre of the chamber. "Because humanity has reached its end." She pointed at all of the trapped souls around her. "In the beginning was a word, and that word was with the gods. The gods built the universe, and in that universe, they placed mankind. The gods dreamed that one day the universe they built would thrive, but man had another plan. They cheated. They lied. They turned the power of the gods on one another. They cared not who they hurt in the process. The gods in their sorrow left their universe to wither and perish at its own hand and vanished. But not I. I was exiled by the gods because I wished to end that which we began. The depravity of humanity will not die of its own accord, it must be crushed and obliterated by those that created it."

Hideki had gathered himself together by now as his shock turned to intrigue. "You haven't answered my question."

Yuuko laughed. It was elegant and captivating and yet cold and emotionless, as though she had rehearsed it over millennia. She moved around the chamber with terrifying speed, vanishing from sight and appearing somewhere else in an instant. "The gods always had a kernel of hope that their beautiful creation would find peace one day, a kernel founded on a few good souls who managed to achieve great things. That is why I thought I would give humanity one chance. A trial to see if they deserved to live. That is why you are here."

"What do you mean?" Rosalina asked.

Choosing to ignore Rosalina, Yuuko honed in on Hideki. "My dear sweet child, everything that has ever happened to you, every person you have met, everything you have done has brought you here to me at this moment. It was inevitable. Your mother and father were just so wonderfully sweet together, and their desire for a child gave me the perfect opportunity to set this trial in motion. I allowed your birth. I trained you. I sent you away to Ryushima, pathetically perfect Ryushima, with its perfect King and perfect Queen, its perfect Princess, its perfect existence. Your time there inevitably changed you into who you are now, and now you are ready to take on this trial for humanity. To see whether every last one of you should vanish from the face of the universe."

"But surely that is no longer your decision to make? The gods abandoned us to our own devices, so it is up to us to decide our future." Hideki felt tricked and betrayed and sick to his stomach, but every inch of his being was telling him to keep fighting, to win. "None of us are perfect. We clearly weren't made that way. But we try. The people of Ryushima do everything in their power to do good. They may not always manage it. Sometimes their fear turns into anger and hatred. But they try. And if you try to do good then you do. The ripples become a wave, and that wave can bring about wonderful change. We hope and we dream and we try. That's how I've made it here. Because I believed we could make it, and the people I care about believe in me. You aren't going to take it all away from us."

Yuuko drew a finger to her lips, "Quiet now, my dear sweet child. You may try to stop me, but that's exactly what I'm going to do, take it all away." She slowly stretched her hand out in front of her as violent flames began to surge from her

311

fingertips. "I am immortal." The flames knitted themselves together, weaving along to form a burning scythe. "I am omniscient." She gripped the scythe and swung it behind her as her other hand stretched forward. "I am omnipotent." The flames enveloped her hand in a burning inferno as she started to inch closer and closer to Hideki and Rosalina. "Your only hope for salvation is to defeat me in battle and neither of you stand a chance. Say goodbye to your pathetic universe."

Hideki and Rosalina took one swift look at one another.

"We wouldn't be here if we didn't stand a chance," Rosalina said as calmly as she could.

"And even if the odds are small, a chance, no matter how miniscule, is more than good enough," Hideki continued.

"You may think that humanity is beyond salvation, but we know it isn't." As she spoke, Rosalina readied a spell in her staff.

"For everyone back home, for everyone we've ever loved or cared about, you are going to pay for what you've done." Hideki shifted his stance and readied his sword.

In unison, they began their attack as they yelled, "Now!"

Hideki's sword collided with Yuuko's scythe and just as she was about to unleash the fireball from her hand into his face, Rosalina roared, "*EGO ZUMVI!*" A torrent of water burst forth from her staff and came crashing down on Yuuko and Hideki as a terrifying waterfall.

Yuuko's flames were extinguished momentarily, but she shrugged the water off as though it were a light drizzle on a Summer afternoon. Her scythe let Hideki's sword free for a moment before engaging it in a more advantageous position thereby allowing her other hand to ready a spell and launch it towards Rosalina.

"Barrier!"

The spell bounced off the shield and skittered off into one of the crystalline chambers, cracking it right down the centre. A bright blue liquid seeped through the crack and began to gush down towards the ground. As Yuuko and Hideki engaged in close-quarters combat, Rosalina was firing every spell she could think of at Yuuko while Yuuko responded with spells of her own using her free hand. Lightning, fire, water, earth, ice, darkness, light; every magical element known to man swirled around the arena, ricocheting off magical barriers or exploding upon contact with another spell and more and more of those chambers cracked or shattered and let forth their glowing liquid. Soon their arena was surrounded by a moat of the ooze.

Yuuko clicked her fingers and suddenly the whole moat was ablaze. There was nowhere to run. Nowhere to hide.

Every strike and every spell was countered. It seemed that no matter what they tried, Yuuko knew their every move and was merely toying with them. The sadistic glee that painted her face easily told them that. What was her end game? Why

313

drag this fight out if she could just kill them at any moment? Something wasn't right about any of this. By all rights, they should have been dead the second the fight had begun. As he blocked and parried Yuuko's next vicious attack, Hideki realised something. She couldn't be omnipotent otherwise she would have ended the battle already. And if she wasn't all-powerful, then she could be defeated. There had to be a way.

Hideki tried to back away towards Rosalina but Yuuko merely vanished and sprang at him from a different angle. There was no let up. No chance to communicate with Rosalina. No time to come up with a plan.

And then Yuuko took to the air and began raining down spells of every description down upon them. It took everything Rosalina had to shield them both from the onslaught. Hideki tried to help but Rosalina merely yelled, "Focus on her. I've got this."

"*AVAVAGO VPAAH!*"

Hideki joined Yuuko in the air and sped towards her to stop the onslaught. Yuuko took one look at him racing towards her and her eyes lit up. She pointed one finger at Rosalina and grinned. The instant Rosalina's shield shattered because her mana was wearing thin, Yuuko fired a piercing ball of fire straight at her.

It all happened in slow-motion. The fireball left Yuuko's fingertip. Hideki flew desperately towards Rosalina to get her out of the way. Rosalina looked at the fireball in heartbroken resignation. It flew straight and true.

Time stopped.

"Healing… Circle…"

The green glow of healing mana surrounded Rosalina as she tightly clutched her stomach. She crumpled to the floor.

"ROSE!"

Hideki lost all concept of what had been going on around him. All he could focus on was her. He reached her seconds too late. "Rose, don't do this to me. Please don't do this. I can't win this fight without you. I need you, please."

Her lifeless body didn't respond.

"I'm so sorry, Rose. I'm so sorry…"

He felt a hand on his shoulder and as he looked up he saw Yuuko with that awful malicious smile, "It's too late, my dear sweet child. She's dead."

Chapter 39
The Sun Rises

Hideki felt numb. He could feel the tears streaming down his cheeks and he could see his hands trembling as they cradled Rosalina's body. He didn't care about that despicable hand resting gently on his shoulder. He didn't care about anything around him. She was dead. He had failed in his duty both as her one true love and her protector. What point was there in carrying on?

"Oh my dear sweet child, does it hurt? Is the pain too much to bear?" Yuuko's voice sent its sarcasm-laced tendrils into Hideki's consciousness.

Though he didn't respond, that melodious poison sparked the fury in his heart. He still had a job to do. Diana, David, Arthur and now his beloved Rosalina had not given their lives for him to just give up now. The tears stopped and he gently laid Rosalina's head on the cold stone floor. Shrugging off Yuuko's hand he slowly turned and rose to face her.

"Oh, what's this? There's still some fight left in you?"

With determination, Hideki responded with a curt, "You will pay for everything you've done, Yuuko. You've hurt so many people and caused so much pain and suffering. This cannot go on."

She laughed. "And you haven't?" She bent down slightly to stare him straight in the eyes. "Killing the gods of Ryushima? Stealing their precious princess away from them? Murdering so many hurting souls?"

Hideki paid little heed to her first questions, "What souls have I murdered?"

Yuuko stepped back and gestured at the crystalline chambers that surrounded them. "Where do you think the demons came from?" Her laugh became a cackle. "When man dies, their souls can become corrupted by their emotions. The seething anger, burning pride, the lascivious lust; in death, their corporeal forms change to reflect the darkness in their souls. All those monsters you've killed since you arrived – they were all once human. Your hands are not clean, Hideki. They never were."

It took Hideki a moment to take it all in. Those poor people. But then, they had ceased to be human and preyed upon the souls who had not been corrupted. Killing to save the lives of others was not an entirely immoral compromise. "Think of me what you will Yuuko. Every demon I've killed I have killed to protect the people of Helheim and Ryushima. And when you are gone, I won't have to fight anymore." He raised his sword toward her. "Let's finish this."

Yuuko licked her lips as though savouring the moment. "Indeed, let's!"

Their weapons collided in a flurry of vicious sparks. Blade and scythe clattered and clanged, limbs dipped and wove to dodge, eyes stared intently. There was no room left in Hideki's mind for sorrow, his every thought needed to be on this battle or he too would perish. Yuuko was there one moment and gone the next, appearing behind him so quickly that he barely had time to block her attacks. With one strike he managed to tear a hole in her sleeve and in another he managed to slice through the bottom of her gown but none of his attacks could truly land, she was just too fast.

Yuuko pulled away for a moment and snapped her fingers. The arena around him vanished into blackness. He couldn't see the crystalline chambers, he couldn't see the flames, he couldn't see Rosalina. A blood red moon appeared from the shadows as tiny stars pricked into life. He looked down at his feet and saw that he was now standing on a gigantic clock face. Beneath him he could see the crown city of Ryushima and then Yuuko launched herself towards him. Against all laws of gravity, they were fighting on the side of the clock tower.

"*IALPIRGAH!*"

The flames engulfed Yuuko but she just smashed through the other side and swung at him with her now red-hot scythe. He jumped out of the way and her scythe went straight into the clock-face. As she pulled it free, everything around them exploded. As everything was blown high into the sky Hideki jabbed his sword into the clock-face. It span through the air and it took everything Hideki had not to throw up. Then he spotted Yuuko running upside down towards him on a piece of debris high up in the air. They weren't affected by gravity in this place.

"*AVAVAGO!*"

The tremendous forks of lightning struck Yuuko and though they stunned her momentarily and Hideki was able to land a powerful slash across her stomach, she quickly recovered. With a swift kick she managed to send Hideki flying into a nearby chunk of debris. He fell down onto a much larger piece and after quickly casting some spells of strength he pushed down hard on the debris and used it to launch himself back toward Yuuko. They clashed in mid-air and the resulting collision sent them both surging backwards.

Yuuko's free hand shone crimson beneath the blood red moon. In an instant, a circle of twenty concentrated little infernos appeared above him and sped towards him in quick succession. He set off at a run and leapt from one piece of debris to another, each melting into the ether as he left it and the infernos struck. When all twenty infernos had failed to hit their mark, Yuuko prepared another spell in her hand but held onto it for the time being.

Hideki used this brief pause to yell, "*YOLCAM GIXYAX, MICAOLI VOVINA DS MACOM CAOSG, JÖRMUNGANDR!*"

The serpentine dragon burst forth from the ground sending forth huge boulders at Yuuko which, though they struck her, she just shrugged off. Jörmungandr flew past her and caught her with its tail, wrapping her up in snake-like coils, trying to squeeze her to death and devour her. Yuuko merely cackled from inside Jörmungandr's tightly wound prison. A bright white glow began to shine through before exploding. The serpentine dragon let out a roar of intense pain as its body dissolved into fragments of dirt that plummeted towards the ground.

Hideki cursed under his breath.

Yuuko snapped her fingers once more and everything returned to blackness.

Hideki could smell burning around him but couldn't see anything until suddenly the charred ruins of his childhood home stood before him. To his horror, he saw the hanging corpses of Diana, David, and Arthur swinging from the roof, suspended by thick black chains. He turned away and high up on a cross was Rosalina's corpse, with Hershel and Claire swinging from the roof on either side of her.

"It's just an illusion. It's not real. It is not real." Hideki said to himself. His grip tightened on his sword and as soon as Yuuko jumped down from a nearby roof, twirling her scythe like a madwoman, he lunged at her. They traded blows, Hideki receiving a nasty cut down his left arm and Yuuko taking a slice across her chest. "It doesn't matter what you show me, Yuuko; you will not reach the end of this day."

"That, my dear sweet child, is where you are so very wrong." Her hand glowed a malevolent green before she plunged it into the ground. Black thorny vines sprung up from the earth, aiming to grab hold of Hideki. He cut the tendrils off the vines wrapping themselves around his feet before running as fast as he could through the remains of his village. He launched fireballs whenever the vines got close, but they just kept coming. In the meantime, Yuuko just calmly followed behind, cackling all the way.

"*AVAVAGO VPAAH!*"

Hideki jumped into the air and landed on one of the sturdier roofs but the vines burst through the stone and started to surround him. "*YOLCAM CORAXO, ARPHE, TELOCVOVIM MJÖLNIR!*"

With the thunderous wings of Mjölnir, Hideki ran off the roof and landed on Mjölnir's back as the dragon swooped under him. "This fight seems particularly fraught, Master Hideki. Have you got a plan?"

"Not really, just climb and stop those vines if you could?" Hideki really didn't have a plan, everything was just happening so quickly that there was no time to plan. The one thing he knew was that he couldn't keep this all up for much longer. All that running, all that emotional turmoil, all that mana; he was getting exhausted. He need to end this fight and soon, but from everything he had seen so far, he was no match for Yuuko. She controlled space in this arena, she batted away his magic like it was inconsequential, and though he could clearly see that she had been bleeding from his direct hits, she didn't seem fazed by them at all. He needed more power, but he had nowhere to get it from.

"The souls… Use the souls…" He could hear Rosalina's voice on the wind, but it was clearly just in his head. Even from beyond Rosalina was still doing everything she could to help him though whatever she was saying didn't make much sense to him.

"Mjölnir, any idea how to use souls?" he asked.

"Unfortunately not, Master Hideki, I –"

Mjölnir never managed to finish his sentence. Yuuko had appeared in the air just in front of them. Mjölnir sent a lightning torrent from his great maw and beat his thunderous wings, combining them to call down the almightiest explosion of lightning. They hit their mark and Yuuko looked visibly shaken by the blow but not undeterred. She vanished and appeared right under them, stabbing her scythe into Mjölnir's underbelly and tearing straight through down the length of his body. He roared in unspeakable pain but was cut short as Yuuko floated before his jaws and let loose a monstrous beam of darkness that ripped through the dragon. His body dissolved into little crackles of electricity and Hideki began to plummet towards the village.

Yuuko snapped her fingers again and he stopped falling as the blackness surrounded him once more.

"You can do it Hideki, I believe in you." There was Rosalina's voice again, much closer than before.

Tiny stars whirled around him and he began to notice something enormous nearby. Thousands of millions of stars hung above him, bound together like the boughs of a tree, developing a great canopy that stretched as far as the eye could see. A tremendously thick pillar of light pulsed in front of him with roots weaving down into the blackness below. What was this place?

"The world tree, Yggdrasil…" Rosalina's voice spoke out in wonder.

As his mind struggled to comprehend the enormity and beauty of what he was seeing and his body refused to move from his exhaustion, Yuuko readied her final blow. She would strike Hideki down with every inch of her power. He would be obliterated from the face of the universe. Her hands glowed brighter and brighter and brighter until they could no longer be seen in the light and with a sadistic wink of glee she fired.

"O holy spirits, hear my plea, lend us your power, protect us with your mercy, and guide us with your wisdom; in the name of all that walks the earth, heal us with your salvation, RESTORATION!"

That was Rosalina, her voice wasn't in his head at all. Hideki snapped out of his exhaustion and looked around for her but couldn't see anything except the gigantic beam of light that was hurtling towards him. Rosalina had never used that spell in front of him before, ever, and that meant she must still be alive. He could still win this.

He readied his sword in the hope that he could cut straight through the beam and break it in two. But then the stars on the celestial Yggdrasil surged towards him, merging their mana with his. His sword began to sparkle and shimmer as the stars took hold and worked their way out and around him in a shield of starry light. The beam hit but could not penetrate the barrier.

In his heart, Hideki could feel the warmth of millions of people, all their hopes and dreams for the future of the worlds they loved so much. Wings of stardust sprouted from his back and he flew forth over the remnant of Yuuko's attack and soared high above her. She looked up and readied another attack.

Hideki's wings stopped beating and he plunged towards Yuuko, blade held down. Yuuko fired her attack once more and Hideki collided with it. Protected by his starry shield he sliced straight through and shattered the beam.

For a moment, everything seemed to stop. Hideki hung in the air as his shining sword was perilously close to Yuuko's head. She was looking at him with an indecipherable emotion.

Was it fury? Was it resignation? Was it triumph? Her cold, violent cackle rang out as the moment ended and Hideki's sword ran down through her skull.

The celestial Yggdrasil vanished. Everything went black. Everything was silent. The battle was over.

CHAPTER 40
APOTHEOSIS

The sun rose and with it came a moment of calm. Yuuko's body began to flake away in crystalline petals until nothing remained. The temple chamber reformed itself in front of Hideki's eyes and he sighed with relief. Standing a metre or so away, clutching her stomach but still very much alive, was Rosalina. "Couldn't be bothered to check for a pulse, eh? It's a good job I know how to work my way around a healing spell or I really would've been dead."

Hideki didn't care, he just ran up to her and embraced her tightly before kissing her lips. "Don't ever do that to me again Rose, I can't let you go, I won't."

She laughed gently. "Could you maybe let me go now? You're crushing me."

"Oh, sorry." He looked intently in her eyes, those little galaxies filled with such warmth and love.

Nearby, flowering shoots began to grow from the crystalline petals of Yuuko's remains, the vibrant reds and pinks and blues bursting with life as they sprouted up through the stone floor. A great swell of mana rushed up through the flowers before crashing down and sweeping across the ground, bringing with it a rush of vivid green grass and more blooms than could ever be asked for. The swell of mana kept moving through the temple, turning its lifeless stone husk into a magical homage to the beauty of nature. The mana rushed out through the mighty doors and across the cracked plains of Helheim. As the clouds parted, a clear blue sky appeared and the shining sun gave life to the fields and flowers that spread across the earth. Helheim had once been a paradise and now it could be a paradise once more.

But this miracle came at a cost. As the mana brought life to a lifeless world, it sapped that world of a memory; one life for another, a parting gift of the Fallen Goddess. No longer would the world remember the one who had killed a goddess. Just as the memory of Yuuko had been wiped from Hideki's mind when he reached Ryushima, the memory of Hideki vanished from the face of Helheim and as the mana continued to spread, it vanished from the face of Ryushima, it vanished from the face of the universe. He didn't know it yet, but despite his victory, no one would remember him.

"So, what do we do now?" he asked.

"Well, I suppose we find Diana, David, and Arthur and then we go home…"

They stood for a moment, both thinking that there was no way their friends had survived the battle but not allowing themselves to dwell on the prospect for too long. Nothing could change what had been, only the future mattered now whatever form that would take.

One by one the souls that had been trapped in those crystalline chambers on the walls began to fade out of existence; their life-force having been entirely spent in helping Hideki land the final blow, they looked forward to finally being able to rest in peace. Though most were too weak to do anything other than sleep, two spirits spoke clearly through the air. "Our darling Hideki, we're so very proud of you, we've loved you forever and always, goodbye our darling son."

Hideki looked around to see where the voices had come from but couldn't find them. He felt the tears rolling down his cheeks but he didn't care. "Goodbye, Mum, Dad."

Rosalina gently hugged him from behind and put her head on his shoulder. She didn't need to say anything, just being there was enough.

Everything they had ever done had brought them to this moment and now they stood alone in a great echoing hall now flourishing with life as the victims of Yuuko's plots went on to their final rest. There was silence and peace and, in many ways, it provided both Hideki and Rosalina with the beautiful moment of calm that they hadn't realised they had needed so much. It was nice to just be close to one another and not have to worry about imminent death. They could just stand, holding each other, breathing in and out, in and out, in and out.

But as Rosalina would tell the people of Ryushima so many years later, that beautiful moment did not last forever.

They began heading for the temple's exit, hand in hand and bursting with joy when the ground beneath their feet began to shake. Some of the stonework crumbled away to reveal an endless abyss below and they started to run as fast as they could. Rosalina was still limping and Hideki was exhausted but they made good progress, dodging their way around the deathly gaps that appeared and the rubble falling from above. They wouldn't let their victory be tarnished at the final hurdle, not when they were so close.

The great open doors of the temple stood before them, huge monoliths of mahogany wood through which they could see the otherworldly paradise that Helheim had been restored to. They were nearly there. Neither of them had enough mana left to hasten their feet, so all they could do was run. One foot after another, they bounded across the floor as quickly as they could. Then they were seconds away from the great doors and part of the stonework gave way under Hideki's foot. He nearly pulled Rosalina down with him as he felt himself falling but she yanked him forward with all of her might and was now powering across the threshold just ahead of him.

In a moment that would haunt Rosalina for the rest of her days, she felt Hideki's hand slip out from hers. Her heart skipped a beat as she turned to see him with his foot stuck in a hole that had appeared the moment he applied pressure to the crumbling stonework just shy of the great doors. She dropped her staff and ran back to get him. Then to her horror, she realised that the doors were sliding shut. "No, no, no. Not like this." She fumbled with his foot, trying to pull it from the hole, trying to get his boot off, just anything to get them both out of this alive. She couldn't let it end like this, she couldn't let him die on her watch, it just couldn't happen. That wasn't how their story ended. It couldn't be.

Hideki realised long before Rosalina did that this was it for him. There was no time left to free him. He was stuck fast and they had no energy or mana left to even try anything else. "Rose… You've got to let me go…" He could feel himself welling up. He'd never been scared of dying, but he couldn't bear the thought of leaving Rosalina all alone and certainly not leaving her like this. "I know I said I can't let you go again, but I can't let you die because of me. So please…" Rosalina wasn't paying any attention to him, so he had to grab her by the shoulders and force her to look at him. "Rose, you need to go. Now."

Rosalina was crying and so was he. "But I can't leave you, Hideki, it can't end like this, it can't…"

"Rose, I made a promise to your father and your mother, and Granny Bea that I'd get you back home safely. Let me keep that promise." He tried for one last time to lift his foot up but even as it snagged he knew it was in vain. "You've done so much for me Rose. You saved me when I arrived in Ryushima and many countless times after that, you gave me a home, you gave me a family, you gave me your heart. We came

330

on this journey to make sure everyone could live happily, please make sure that at least one of us sees the fruits of our labour."

Every inch of Rosalina's being screamed out. No, no, no, no, no, no, no, no, no, no.

"Please do this for me, Rose. Live for me and one day we'll see each other again. You're going to be an amazing queen and the people of Ryushima need you, they always have and they always will. Now go, Rose, there's not much time left."

The doors were mere inches away from closing now and Rosalina had to stand and clutch onto Hideki's hand. "I love you, Hideki."

"I love you too, Rose. Always."

And then he was gone. Their hands parted and the doors shut tightly together, never to be opened again. Rosalina hit the wood with her fist and screamed, letting out all of her hurt and pain and anguish. She kept hitting it until she had no more strength to move. She placed her back against the door and slid down to the floor. It couldn't have ended like this, not when they were so close. There was no need for life to be so cruel. That wasn't how the stories ended. The hero was victorious and returned home to his family and friends and everyone celebrated. That was what was meant to happen. Not this. Anything but this. And as Rosalina looked up at the clear blue sky and the beautiful world around her, she felt numb. With Hideki gone, part of her had died with him.

EPILOGUE
ALWAYS

Rosalina looked down at her people and openly wept. She had clung on to that moment for so long, kept it locked away in her heart so tightly, that to let others know of it was the greatest relief she had ever known.

A woman from the queen's retinue, only slightly older than Rosalina herself, stepped forward and held the queen in her arms. There were tears forming on her cheeks too but she maintained her composure. "I am so sorry, Rosalina."

Rosalina looked up at the woman, "It's not your fault, Diana." It may have been five years since that journey through Helheim, but Diana hardly looked a day older bar an increasingly furrowed brow.

Diana glanced over at the amber-eyed duo looking after her two-year-old son while she did the hard work, as usual. David was still his frustratingly charming self, but he had begun to go prematurely grey in his late twenties, the little silver streaks flecking his once dark black hair. Arthur meanwhile had grown up quite a lot. Gone was the long hair he used to hide behind, his shoulders were much broader now too and he held himself with a confidence that said, yes, I do deserve to be here.

None of them could explain how they'd survived the battle in Helheim. One moment they were as good as dead, the next they woke up in Hershel and Claire's home to find the world bursting with colour. The old couple had explained that once the dust had settled they had opened their door to find the wolf, Yggdrasil, standing there with the four of them floating around him. The wolf had merely said that they would recover in a few days' time before it vanished into the distance and so they did. When they awoke, Rosalina wouldn't say a word. It took them until they'd reached the gateway home for her to say that the Fallen Goddess was dead but she wouldn't say any more than that. When they'd gotten home, they were welcomed like heroes even as the crystalline tree, Yggdrasil shattered into nothingness.

With a melancholy smile, Rosalina continued her speech to her people. "It took me a few days after getting home to realise that nobody remembered Hideki. At first, I couldn't think about anything and so didn't notice that no one had asked about him, not even Diana, David, or Arthur. But whenever I tried to broach the subject with anyone I just broke down. Not only had I lost him, I'd also lost any hope I had of keeping his memory alive." Her tears slowly dried as she found herself at peace for the first time in five years. "But now, even if you don't remember, you know the truth and that means he'll be in your hearts just as he is in mine."

The Great Sakura Tree rustled in the wind as the people thought deeply. King Lee and Queen Sakura had passed away a year ago, and the cherry blossom had been planted in their honour and brought to its current form through magic. The people knew that their death had affected Queen Rosalina deeply, but now they understood why she had withdrawn even further into herself after her coronation. Sniffles and sobs could be heard around the courtyard as they took it all in.

"Thank you all for taking the time to listen to me." She brushed a stray hair out of her eyes and noticed an orange glow on the horizon. Had she really spoken all night? "Now, it's time to go to bed I think. I'm sorry to have kept you all up for so long, I guess once I started it just all had to come spewing out. I can't thank you all enough for everything you've all done for me and I promise that from now on things will get better. I will be better." She stared wistfully at the sky, thinking. *Are you watching me, Hideki? I've done it. I've told your story, and mine. I'm sorry I took so long, my love. I know I'll see you again someday, so just wait for me, ok?*

The great crowd slowly began to disperse. They were all completely knackered after such a long night, but it had all been worth it to see the queen finally come to terms with her grief. Some wondered if any of it were real since they did not remember it, but something in their guts told them the queen spoke truly. After a good long sleep the real party would begin and this was going to be the best yet, they could all feel it.

On the balcony, Rosalina bent down to pat little Owain on the head. "Hello little man, I hope you slept through at least some of that or Auntie Rose is going to be very grumpy with you."

David lifted the little tyke onto his shoulders and it was clear to see that though Owain had inherited his mother's blonde hair, he was the spitting image of his father. "He closed his eyes and pretended to sleep whenever you got to the kissing. He might look like me but he's not going to be the love god his father is."

"And thank goodness for that," Diana joked, tousling her son's hair.

Arthur laughed, "Too right." He put his arm round Rosalina's shoulders as she began to shake a little from a brief welling of emotion. "Sounds like Hideki and I were quite good mates. But he'd be proud of you, Rosalina, he'd be so proud of everything you've achieved. I know we were all really worried about you, especially after King Lee and Queen Sakura and Granny Bea, but you know what? You're going to be fine. It's good to see you smile again."

She laughed too as she wiped a tear from her eye, "No thanks to you, you ignoramus."

"What can I say? I'm about as emotionally intelligent as a rock. Though, you didn't have to tell my bits of the story so well you know! I thought I'd finally gotten people to forget how much of a fool I was back then." He clapped her slightly on the back and she whacked him in return.

"Well, I had to tell the truth now, didn't I?"

Together Rosalina and her retinue descended the staircase into the emptying courtyard and while most of the retinue returned to the palace, Rosalina, Diana, David, and Arthur remained to watch the sunrise.

"You know, Hideki never actually died in the story as you told it, he merely got trapped. Did you ever think there might be a way of rescuing him?" David suggested as they sat down on a blanket nearby to the Great Sakura Tree.

Rosalina was well within her right to snap at David but she didn't, she just answered him with that melancholy smile, "Of course I thought about it, David. I thought about it every single day but nobody knows any spells that can bring people back from death other than Resurrection and nobody has ever managed to figure out how it works or how to use it."

Little Owain giggled and jumped into his mother's arms while she looked at Rosalina deep in thought. "You never stopped loving him, did you?" Diana said.

Rosalina shook her head, "Never."

Diana carefully chose her words when she next spoke. "He might have very well died in the time since then, but surely it is worth a shot. All it would take is the right words, the right intent, and the right amount of mana. Perhaps we even misunderstood what the mythical spell was capable of. We always thought it could bring back the dead, but what if it could only bring people back *from* death or from the brink of death. If Hideki never died, then there's a chance, a small one I'll admit, but a chance nevertheless that Resurrection could return him to us."

"Sounds like a long-shot," Arthur said, "But I'm up for giving it a go."

Rosalina stared at her friends in disbelief, "But it's impossible."

Arthur grinned cheekily, "But wasn't Hideki arriving here impossible? Wasn't the death of the Almighty Dragons impossible? Wasn't our journey into Helheim impossible? Wasn't beating the Fallen Goddess impossible? Wasn't our survival impossible? Impossible is our middle name."

"But –"

A velvety voice floated on the wind to Rosalina's ears, it sounded familiar but she couldn't quite place it. All she knew was that she hadn't heard that voice for a very long time. She repeated its words to herself until she realised what it was saying. A seed of hope was planted in her mind. She stood up with her staff in hand and gave herself some room. Magnificent golden mana swirled in the crystal orb as she twirled it through the air, creating a spiral of stardust around her. She spoke with confidence and clarity, "*Holy spirits hear my plea, rescue his soul from purgatory, return him to those that love him, please listen to this sacred hymn, Resurrection!*"

The mana bubbled and morphed in the most unusual ways, at once exploding and imploding, as though struggling to do what was asked of it. But Rosalina only closed her eyes and focused. She repeated her words pouring every ounce of her being into the spell. The mana solidified and shot high into the air, swirling in a stream of life given form, before slamming into the earth beneath the Great Sakura Tree. Rosalina stopped and stared at the tree. What was the spell doing? It couldn't work, surely? Why did it go to the roots of the Great Sakura Tree? Something was certainly happening. That seed of hope began to sprout forth.

Before their very eyes the tree turned to crystal and chimed in much the same way Yggdrasil had done all those years ago. A crack formed in its trunk before the tree cleaved itself in two.

"Hideki?"

Inside the tree was a man she recognised. That brown messy hair, those big brown eyes, that soft and gentle smile... He looked older, his brow was more furrowed and a scar cut through under his chin, but it was him. It was definitely him.

She ran to the tree screaming his name, "Hideki?! Hideki!"

He looked carefully at her as he stumbled his way down from the tree's cloven trunk. He'd not seen that sweet face for so long but he'd never stopped loving it. "Rose?"

She ran straight into his arms before he'd even had the chance to settle on the ground. "It's you. It's really you."

"I'm pretty sure it's me, yes."

Rosalina glowered up at him, "Oh don't ruin the moment by being sarcastic."

"Yeah, that's my job," quipped David.

She stared down David and as he sheepishly backed away she said, "Not helping, David, not helping." She turned her attention back to Hideki and still couldn't quite believe what she was seeing. "I thought I'd lost you forever... What happened to you after..." She couldn't quite finish her question, as after all, did it really matter?

"I'm not really sure. The ground gave way beneath me and I fell into a glade beneath the temple. There was an enormous labyrinth that surrounded it and though I searched for a way out, I was never able to find one. Either way, the glade and labyrinth were filled with everything you could hope for to survive. I guess you'd expect it of a place called the Temple of Creation, right? I was pretty sure I was going to trapped there for all eternity, but looks like I needn't have worried, eh? What took you so long anyway?" There was a mischievous fire in his eyes and as Rosalina looked at him she couldn't help grinning from ear to ear as she hit him hard in the chest. "Hey, I was just kidding!"

"I know you were... I missed you so much, Hideki."

"I missed you too, Rose."

They kissed and everything felt right with the world once again.

"I guess we've got a lot to talk about, haven't we?"

"We do."

The morning sun sent its rays across the sky as the two drew into a close embrace and stared into each other's eyes as their tears fell and their smiles beamed.

With that sunrise, they were finally together again and this time, nothing was going to separate them ever again.

"I love you, Rose."

"I love you too, Hideki. Always."

Glossary
Spells and Phrases

ARPHE MICAOLI VOVIN, EF OD PASDAES VANGEM
Descend Mighty Dragons, visit us and profess the truth of the will of the heavens!

AVAVAGO
Thunders

AVAVAGO VPAAH
Thunderous Wings

BALIT BRANSG EGO DAXZUM LAP ASPAH
The just guard the holy seed for the infinity within

BALZIZRAS
The Judgement

BRGDA
Sleep

BRGDA NOTHOA PERIPSOL DOH
Rest in the midst of the heavens' holy fire

CAOSG
Earth

CAOSGON
To the Earth

CHRISTEOS MOZ
Let there be joy

CORAXO
Thunders

DODS IALPIRGAH
Vexing God Flames

DOOIAP PIR
In the name of the holy ones

DOOIAP EGO OLPIRT, PHAMAH TOLTORG LN VBRAH
In the name of the holy light, give the creatures of the earth the guardian star

EGO ZUMVI
The Holy Seas

FABOAN GIXYAX
Poison Earthquakes

GEMPH PAMBT OD OM TELOCH OLNA DOX
Yield unto me and understand Death created within the Sacrificial Fire

GIXYAX
Earthquakes

GRAM ZUMVI
Lunar Seas

IALPIRGAH
God-Flames

IALPIRGAH OIAD
God-Flames of the Just

IALPON
Burn

MALPRG
Fiery Darts

MANO I AXOL
The Soul of Humanity is the Glory of God's Creation

NAPEAI VEH AVAVAGO
O Ye Swords Create Thunders

ODO OD OM OHIO
Open and Know Woe

OIT IANA. IXOMAXIP TA FAXIMAL AAO IHEHUDZ.
This is the Daughter of Light. Let her be known as one with the infinite among the children of the light.

OZONGON
Manifold Winds

PIADPH ORS
In the depths of my jaws of darkness

TELOCH
Death

TELOCH PIADPH ORS
Death in the depths of my jaws of darkness

VPAAH
Wings

YOLCAM LAS IALPRG, VEH DONASDOGAMA TASTOS
Bring forth the Rich Burning Flame, Create Hellfire

ZLIDA
Water

ZUMVI
Seas

Vardr Summoning Spells

ARP LN AMMA A-C-LONDOH, NAT OD BNG CAOSGO, BRAN!
Conquer the cursed in thy kingdom, the Lord and Guardian of the earth, Bran!

ARPHE MOMAR BASGIM, ILMO, HELIOS
Descend to crown the day, Essence of the Sun, Helios!

ARPHE PERIPSOL, VPAAH ZONG, ZIZ
Descend in the brightness of the heavens, the Wings of the Winds, Ziz!

CACACOM OD FIFALZ QTING, EXENTASER TOHCOTH, GLORIANA
Flourish and weed out the rotten, Mother of all Faeries, Gloriana!

CORONZON CAOSGO, TORZU, BEHEMOTH
Demon of the Earth, Arise, Behemoth!

DOOIAP PIR, ADRPAN TOL HAMI DODSIH, ENAY DE EGO ZUMVI, SUSANOO
In the name of the holy ones and justice, cast down all creatures of vexation, the Lord of the Holy Seas, Susanoo!

DOOIAP PIR, ODO MADRIAX OD TORZU, NE EXENTASER, AMATERASU
In the name of the holy ones, open the heavens and arise, Holy Mother of All, Amaterasu!

PAMPHICA, A GRAA ORS, YOLCAM VANGEM, SELENE

Infernal Mother, the Moon of Darkness, bring forth the will of heaven, Selene!

YOLCAM CORAXO, ARPHE, TELOCVOVIM MJÖLNIR

Bring forth the thunders of wrath and judgement, descend, Death Dragon, Mjölnir!

YOLCAM GIXYAX, MICAOLI VOVINA DS MACOM CAOSG, JÖRMUNGANDR

Bring forth earthquakes, mighty dragon that encompasses the Earth, Jörmungandr!

ACKNOWLEDGEMENTS

The Burning Ash has been a labour of love for me for over a decade. It would not exist without the help of my amazing Dad, one for passing on his love of literature to me, but also for being my test reader and editor all the way along. I cannot thank him enough for all the hours he's spent helping me make this dream become a reality.

Thank you to the rest of my wonderful family for always letting me be me, quirks and all, and having faith in me throughout the years.

Thank you to all of those that have read parts of and given feedback on The Burning Ash in its different iterations over the years, Sarah Brennan, Diarmuid Maguire, Tony Leech, Robyn Summers, Milena Messner, and Tom Bell. Every bit of feedback big and small was a great help.

And thank you to you, the person reading this book. It has been a dream of mine for so long to write a story and share it with the world. Thank you for making that dream a reality and I hope you had as good a time reading it as I had writing it.

Richard Kish is Nottingham born and bred. His love of literature led to a BA in English from the University of Cambridge and his writing skills and creativity have led to communications jobs in theatre and local government.

Inspired by modern writers like Patrick Ness, Terry Pratchett, Phillip Pullman, Christopher Paolini, Garth Nix, and more historical writers like Chrétien de Troyes, Marie de France, F. Scott Fitzgerald, H.G. Wells and John Milton; Richard has always wanted to write.

A life-long fan of video games, film, theatre, and literature; Richard is always trying to find new ways to integrate his hobbies into his writing allowing him to explore connections across mediums and genres.

Follow Richard on Facebook, Twitter and Instagram @RichardAKish

Stay up to date with the latest news and information www.richardkish.co.uk

Printed in Poland
by Amazon Fulfillment
Poland Sp. z o.o., Wrocław

53845573R00209